BIG BADD WOLF

A BADD BROTHERS NOVEL

Jasinda Wilder

Copyright © 2018 by Jasinda Wilder

BIG BADD WOLF: A BADD BROTHERS NOVEL

ISBN: 978-1-948445-03-0

Cover art by Sarah Hansen of Okay Creations.
Cover art copyright © 2018 Sarah Hansen.

Formatting: Champagne Book Design

BIG BADD
WOLF

ONE

Lucian

MY TEETH WERE CHATTERING, MY BONES WERE shaking, and I was shivering uncontrollably. Jumping into frigid water in the middle of winter will do that to you. On top of it all, I was fighting an erection the size of Montana. The girl I had just rescued was seriously gorgeous and completely naked under the blanket I'd wrapped around her as soon as I'd gotten her to the bar and out of her wet clothes. I'd done my best to keep my gaze on hers while undressing her, but it had taken all of my not-inconsiderable willpower to do so—I'm a red-blooded, heterosexual male in the middle of a dry spell that's lasted over a year, and she's a woman with the body of a siren.

Still, despite keeping my eyes on hers, I couldn't help seeing her body…and *god* in heaven, what a body.

Medium height—maybe five-five or six. Skin the color of rich, dark caramel, exotic and flawless. Black hair dreadlocked into dozens of dreads about the thickness of my thumb, the tips hanging to just above her waist. Eyes somewhere between tan and hazel, so light brown they appeared to be nearly golden—the eyes of a lioness. Those thighs? Those hips? Those breasts? Jesus. Perfect. I've never met a woman I'd describe as perfect looking, until now. And that's really the only word that comes to mind as an apt descriptor for Joss Mackenzie. Beautiful, yes. Lovely, yes. Sexy, hell yes. Curvy, absolutely. Exotic, for sure.

Okay, enough gushing.

Looks aside, I had questions for her, or rather, about her, which I won't ask right now. Such as:

How did she end up in the water?

Why was she wandering the Ketchikan docks in the middle of a blizzard?

Why were her clothes so…baggy?

I mean, I'm not one to judge someone based on their clothes, but this girl, Joss, had been wearing faded, tattered gray sweatpants underneath loose blue jeans clearly cut for a male, several sizes too big, with giant holes in the knees. Her coat, hat, and mittens looked brand new, but underneath the coat she'd been wearing a thin, aged red fleece jacket, and underneath that a voluminous NYU hoodie, and underneath *that*, several layers of shirts—a long sleeve thermal, what looked like a shirt from a long-johns set, and three more baggy T-shirts. Her hiking boots had holes in the toes and the soles were coming loose on both heels, and she was wearing three pairs of wool socks, all of which were old and well worn. Her undergarments were in no better shape—white cotton granny panties with holes in them, and a white bra with the underwire poking out in places.

I can put two and two together, and the story behind the multiple layers of clothing, and the condition of them is…sketchy.

But that was none of my business.

What was my business was keeping my front facing away from her until I could get my erection to subside.

When I managed to get myself under control and turned back around to face her, still wearing my soaking wet jeans, I said, "I have to change. I'll grab you something to wear, too."

She stared up at me with those golden-brown eyes. "Just throw mine in the dryer for a few minutes. I'll put them on as soon as possible and get out of your way."

I snorted. "Not likely."

She frowned. "What do you mean?"

"This blizzard isn't going to let up anytime soon, which means you're stuck here with us for the time being. So you might as well take a long hot shower and put on clean, dry clothes."

"I don't have any clean or dry clothes." She gestured at the backpack on the floor nearby. "That's got all my clothing in it, and it went swimming with me."

"Lucky for you my sister-in-law lives here, and she's close enough to your size that she'll have something you can wear."

She sighed. "Okay. But as soon as the snow lets up, I'll leave you alone."

"You're fine. No worries." I twisted the doorknob and exited the room on shaky knees.

I was playing tough for the sake of appearances in front of Joss, but I was feeling the effects of the icy water myself. Once out of the room, I let myself slump back against the wall, tugging my hair out of the ponytail holder.

Bast and Dru were in the kitchen, anxious to hear my side of the story.

"What the fuck happened, Luce?" Bast asked. "Who's the girl and why are you both wet?"

"I need a change of clothes," I said, rather than answering his question. "For myself and for her. No way in hell I'm going to my place now—I barely made it here."

Dru went into their room and emerged a minute later with two stacks of their clothes—yoga pants and a hoodie for Joss, and a pair of drawstring track pants and a hoodie for me.

"Thanks," I said. "I'm gonna get her in the shower. Can you make some coffee?"

Dru just nodded, and Bast stood with his arms crossed over his powerful chest.

I stepped into the bathroom, flicked on the hot water, and stripped out of my wet jeans and underwear. I rinsed the cold water out of my hair and off my body, and then got out much sooner than I'd have liked. I toweled off, wrung my hair out and left it loose—a rarity for me—and then donned the clothes borrowed from my oldest brother. They were huge on me as Bast is a couple inches taller than me and at least fifty pounds heavier, but they were warm and dry, and the drawstring let me keep the pants from falling off. I left the hot water running, put the clean clothes on the closed toilet seat lid, and returned to see Joss.

She was sitting where I left her, wrapped in the blanket, shivering, teeth clenched together, looking wet and miserable and uncomfortable, and beautiful as hell despite it all.

"I've got clean clothes in the bathroom for you, and the hot water is running." I held out my hand to her. "Here, let me help you up."

She ignored my hand and stood up on her own, but it was obvious she was weak still, and shaky. "Just show me the bathroom."

I frowned at her sharp response, but shrugged it off. "Okay."

She held the blanket tight around her, and seemed to be trying to shrink as small as she could, especially when I entered the bathroom behind her. She shrank away from me, her fists clenched into the fleece of the blanket, huddling against the bathroom wall, as far away from me as she could get.

"I know how a shower works," she snapped. "I don't need help."

I blinked, surprised. "I was just—you almost died. I don't want you to pass out in the shower, or fall and hurt yourself."

Dismissively, she said, "I can manage. I'll be fine, thank you."

I held up both hands palms out. "Okay, then. Take as long as you want."

"I will, once you leave the room."

Wow, okay. Better add snarky and ungrateful to the list of descriptors.

I backed out, closed the door behind me, and went into the kitchen. The scent of brewing coffee filled my nostrils, and I inhaled deeply as I slumped exhaustedly into a chair at the breakfast table. Dru was at the stove, cracking eggs into a blue ceramic bowl two at a time. Bast reached into a cupboard and snagged a chipped white mug with the logo of an alcohol distributor on it, poured coffee into it, and handed the mug to me; the coffeemaker gurgled and hissed as it resumed brewing.

Sitting kitty-corner to me, Bast rested his thick, tattooed forearms on the edge of the table.

"So, why'd you go swimming in the Passage in the middle of a blizzard in December?" he asked.

I sighed. "We're out of real food over at the other apartment, so I was heading over here to make something for lunch. I heard a splash." I sipped the hot, bitter coffee; Dru makes coffee the way our family likes it best—strong enough to float horseshoes in it. "I went to see what the splash was, figuring in this weather, at this time of year, since a splash that loud probably meant trouble."

Bast glanced past me at the bathroom, where the shower could be heard running, along with the faint hint of a female voice singing something. "The splash was her, I take it?"

I nodded. "Yeah. I jogged across the street to the docks, and saw her in the water."

"And jumped in after her," Bast filled in.

"Well...yeah. I mean, she'd have died in that

water. It's cold, man." I shrugged. "She's…prickly, so I don't really know much."

A few minutes later, I heard the bathroom door open, turned around in my chair to watch steam billow out of the doorway, and then Joss emerged, wearing Dru's yoga pants and hoodie. Dru was a couple inches taller than Joss, and slightly more slender, so the pants were tighter on Joss than they would have been on Dru, which meant they were *tight*. The hoodie was an old one of Dru's, a faded gray with "Seattle Police Department" emblazoned across the chest. It fit Joss like a glove—maybe a little *too* well, especially for my libido, which had once again sat up and taken notice of this girl. She wasn't wearing a bra, obviously, and when she walked out of the bathroom and down the hall toward the kitchen, her lack of…erm, support… was evident in the way her breasts swayed under the soft, thin, faded cotton. She had a towel in her hands and was squeezing it around her dreads to dry them as she entered the kitchen.

Bast gestured at an open seat on the other side of me. "Have a seat. Dru's got some eggs and bacon finishing up. Hungry?"

She took the offered seat hesitantly, still sponging at her dreadlocks. "I—no, thanks. I'm fine."

Her stomach growled volubly at that moment, though, putting a lie to her demurral.

Dru laughed again, plated a few strips of bacon and a heaping pile of eggs, and set it in front of Joss. "Hope you're not a vegan." She then divided the rest between the three of us.

Joss snorted. "Umm, no." She sucked in a deep breath, held it, and let it out slowly. "I guess I am a little hungry. Thank you very much." She picked up the fork and stabbed some scrambled eggs. "I've never had eggs and bacon in the middle of the afternoon before."

"We like to eat what we want, when we want around here, and eggs and bacon is good anytime." Bast tipped backward in his chair, tugged open the fridge, reached in, and pulled out a bottle of hot sauce, a jar of salsa, and a container of sour cream, and piled the lot in front of Joss. "Dig in."

Joss stared at the array of condiments and then, hesitantly, reached for the salsa and sour cream. She glanced around as she took a dainty spoonful of sour cream, as if wondering if it was even okay to do so.

Bast cleared his throat. "Don't know how you do it where you're from, but around here, we don't skimp. So pile that shit on, babe."

Joss eyed him, hesitated again, and then dug a larger glop of sour cream and piled it on. "Better?" she asked, eyebrow lifted.

Bast laughed. "Hey, I just meant to not be shy about it. We won't bite." He paused, and then jerked a thumb at me. "Well, Luce here is kind of a wild card, so you never know about him."

I glared at him. "Really, Bast?"

Bast chortled. "I'm just fuckin' with you. Luce don't bite."

I glanced at Joss. "Don't mind him. He's just an idiot who doesn't know when to stop."

Joss paused in the act of spooning salsa onto her eggs, glancing between Bast and me. "Bast? His name—your name is Bast?" She stirred her eggs with her fork. "Like…Bast, daughter of Ra, Egyptian goddess of cats?"

Bast frowned. "Wait, what?"

Joss shrugged. "That's who Bast is, in Egyptian mythology. Depicted as a woman with the head of a lioness."

"Well, I don't know shit about Egyptian mythology," Bast said. "My name's Sebastian, but everyone calls me Bast."

"Oh. Well…that's marginally less interesting." Joss blinked, as if realizing what she'd just said. "I—I mean, um. Shit."

Bast was belly laughing. "No, no, don't apologize, that was funny." He glanced at me. "You fished yourself a winner out of the Passage, Luce. Damn."

"Passage?" Joss asked.

"The Inside Passage," I answered, pouring coffee

for everyone else and setting it to brew another pot. "Don't know how much you know about the local geography—"

"Pretty much zero," Joss cut in.

"Well, Ketchikan is located on what's called the Inside Passage, a coastal route through all the little islands around here."

"Oh."

Bast eyed Joss as he added hot sauce and sour cream to his eggs. "So. Who're you?"

"Joss Mackenzie," she answered, after swallowing her bite.

"Well, Luce you know, I'm Bast, and this is my wife Dru. There are a bunch more of us around, you'll probably meet the rest of them later, though."

"More?" Joss sounded a little alarmed by this. "There are *more* of you?"

I snickered. "I'm the second youngest of eight brothers."

She blinked at me, absorbing this. "Eight—you have...*seven* brothers?"

"Yep."

"And...they all live here?" She turned to glance at the hallway, trying to figure out the room math.

Bast cackled. "Oh, *hell* no. There's another apartment down the street, and several of our brothers live close by with their wives or girlfriends. Can you imagine all eight of us plus women in this little apartment? Jesus."

"Wait—eight brothers *plus* wives and girlfriends... how many of you *are* there?"

"Umm..." I counted on my fingers as I listed everyone. "Bast and Dru, Zane and Mara—plus Jax, Brock and Claire, Bax and Eva, Cane and Aerie, Cor and Tate, me, and Xavier, so...fifteen?"

Joss chewed, swallowed, and blinked, looking overwhelmed. "Wow. That's...that's a lot of people."

"Only child?" I asked.

"Uh...something like that," she answered.

Dru, now seated with her own food and coffee, wiggled her fork at Joss. "Oh, she's totally an only child."

Joss frowned. "How do you know?"

"I recognize that look on your face," Dru said. "I'm an only child too. I was the first woman to snag a Badd brother, and let me tell you, trying to civilize this pack of wolves has been...amusing, shall we say."

"How bad can they really be? Lucian seems okay, so far." Joss allowed the tiniest hint of a smirk to touch the corners of her mouth, the first sign of amusement or humor I'd seen from her.

Dru burst out laughing, and had to cover her mouth with her hand, as she had a mouthful of food. "Oh, honey. No—the brothers, their last name is Badd,

B-A-D-D." She grinned at Joss. "And, as the first Badd *girl*, I can testify that they can be all kinds of *bad*." She punctuated this with a suggestive wiggle of her eyebrows.

Joss colored. "I didn't mean—" She seemed unable to explain what she meant, and didn't finish her statement.

"Don't scandalize the poor girl, Dru. Jesus." Bast managed to say this with a straight face. "Can't you see she doesn't find your crude humor entertaining?"

"*My* crude humor?" Dru protested. "You're the one who thinks it's funny to smack my ass in public."

"You're my wife. I'm allowed."

"Yeah, but not in front other people, you goddamned orc."

Joss spluttered at this, and tried to cover it with a cough.

Bast winked at her. "It's okay to laugh, Joss. You landed smack dab in the middle of a bunch of real comedians."

"So I'm finding out." Joss had cleared her plate already, and I'd only gotten started. "That was delicious, Dru. Thank you."

Dru eyed the plate in surprise. "Damn, girl." She set her fork down. "Still hungry? I can whip up some more real quick."

Joss looked almost a little frightened. "Oh, no.

No, thank you. I'm fine."

Dru narrowed her eyes. "Sure? It's no trouble. How about some toast?"

Joss shook her head. "Oh, no. Really. I wouldn't want to...I mean, I don't want to be an inconvenience." She looked at me. "I can't thank you enough for rescuing me, Lucian, but I really should be going."

"This blizzard is gonna blow for a few days yet," I said. "I live here and I barely made it a quarter of a block from my apartment to here. You really should just hang out until it blows over."

"Ain't an inconvenience if we're offering," Bast said.

"I just—" Joss shifted on her chair, toying with the fork. "If you're sure it's not a problem, I could probably eat a piece of toast or something. And then I really will go. I'll find a hotel or something."

I snorted. "Not much to choose from, and they're all full."

Joss shook her head. "I'll figure something out. I just met you. Lucian already jumped into the bay—the Passage, I mean—saving me. You've made me food, given me clothes. I can't—I couldn't impose on you any more than I already have."

I twisted in my chair to face her more directly. "Joss, it's fine. Really."

"Shit, babe, you heard the count," Bast said.

"Fifteen of us. You think one more person is gonna, what, put us out of business?"

"Out of business?" Joss asked. "What business?"

"Well, it was a figure of speech, but we own a bar. It's downstairs."

Joss wrapped a finger around a dreadlock, while Dru popped bread into the toaster. "Let me get this straight. There are eight brothers, your last name is Badd, and you own a bar in Alaska?"

Dru nodded seriously. "*And* the other brothers are all just as sexy as these two. Legit."

Joss blushed again. "I hadn't noticed," she said, glancing down.

Dru blew a raspberry. "Oh bullshit you haven't noticed. You wouldn't be blushing if you hadn't noticed that Lucian here isn't exactly hard on the eyes." She bumped her hip against Bast's arm as she walked past him. "And my macho fuckstick orc of a husband is pretty nice to look at, too."

At that moment, Xavier, Brock, Claire, Bax, Eva, Zane, Mara, and little baby Jax all trooped in; everyone except Xavier was coated with snow, which meant the others had just arrived from their respective homes while Xavier had been downstairs doing who knew what. The noise level increased, well…nine-fold, at least, as they all tromped in, half a dozen different conversations going on at once.

Joss froze, and the knuckles of the hand gripping the fork went white. "Holy shit," she muttered under her breath. "More people. Great."

"Not a fan of people?" I asked.

She blushed yet again, not looking at me. "No, I like people okay, I'm just—it's just—" she shook her head. "It's fine. I'm fine. Forget I said anything."

"They're all cool. Just relax."

"Easy for you to say." This was more to herself than to me, though, and she took a deep breath and straightened her spine.

"Let me see my nephew," Bast said, in his loud, booming bartender voice, cutting in over the chatter. Mara handed Jax to Bast, who immediately softened, taking the six-month-old baby in his arms and muttering at him, his gruff, growling voice gone tender. "Hey there, little man. How ya doin', champ? Oh man, look at that grip—you're a monster! Oh yeah, get it, boy. Grab it! There ya go…"

Joss stared at Bast, as amused as everyone else as the big, burly, tattooed Bast went all Papa Bear with Jax.

"It's like watching a pit bull play with a kitten," she said to me.

"It kind of is, isn't it?" I said, chuckling.

Joss was breathing slowly and evenly, as if trying to regulate her breathing to prevent a panic attack. "So many people."

They were all clustered in the kitchen—Zane was pouring coffee, Claire was buttering toast, Mara was rummaging in the fridge, Brock and Xavier were raiding the snack cupboard, and Bax and Eva were twisting the tops off of beers. The previously quiet four-way conversation around the kitchen table had turned into 11/15 of the full Badd family experience. All we needed now was—

Corin, Canaan, Tate, and Aerie.

And about ten seconds later the four of them, involved in a loud four-way argument about the merits of a certain band's early work versus their newer material, came in through the doorway which led up from the bar.

"Fuck me running," Joss muttered.

I laughed, then. "That's everyone."

Joss was losing the battle against hyperventilation. "This is…a lot."

I eyed her—she was pale, and her hands were trembling. "Too much?"

She nodded. "Yeah." She backed her chair out and stood up. "I'm gonna…I'm gonna go. Thanks. I just—I have to go."

I stood up with her and caught her arm; I didn't miss the way she tensed at my touch. "Hey, I know there's a lot of us, but—"

"Lucian, I really, *really* appreciate you saving me. I'll never be able to repay you for that. But this is just…I need to go."

"Where are you going to go? I'm not trying to, like, trap you here, but this blizzard is no joke—I'm not even sure how the ferry made it in."

Zane sidled up, mug of coffee in hand. "Luce. Who's your friend, bro?"

"This is Joss Mackenzie. Joss, this my second oldest brother, Zane."

Joss and Zane shook hands, and Zane eyed Joss. "Heard you talking about leaving, and I gotta say that's a bad plan. I grew up here, and we only live a couple blocks away, and the trip here was harrowing as fuck. I didn't realize how bad it was myself until we were halfway there; if I had known, we wouldn't be here in the first place. If you don't *have* to be anywhere, stay."

Zane's attention on Joss brought everyone's attention to her, and soon she was inundated with questions, introductions, handshakes, and a gentle hug from Eva.

Seeing that Joss was seriously struggling, I knew I had to do something to ease her tension. I put my fingers to my lips and blew a piercing whistle, which silenced conversation. "This is a hell of a lot of people in a very small space," I said. "Why don't we move this party downstairs to the bar? With the weather being the way it is, I say we keep the bar closed and just have a family day."

Bast groaned. "Well, there goes my overhead for the month."

Xavier, a jar of peanuts in hand, spoke up. "Actually, speaking as the one who does the books, we made enough just on the day before Thanksgiving to cover our overhead for December." He popped a handful of peanuts into his mouth. "So, you know… we're good."

Somehow or another, everyone ended up downstairs. Several tables were shoved together to make room for everyone, and Bast and Zane headed behind the bar to pour a few pitchers of beer.

Xavier wandered toward the kitchen, stopping to tap me on the shoulder on the way past. "Help me in the kitchen, Luce? I'm gonna fry up some snacks."

I stood up. "Sounds good."

Joss was standing in the middle of the bar, several feet away from everyone, shoulders hunched, just watching as my family settled in, tossing jokes and insults back and forth, telling stories, doing what we do.

I'd never met anyone so socially uncomfortable and standoffish my life, and I wondered, not for the first time since pulling Joss out of the water, what her story was.

TWO

Joss

I'D NEVER SEEN SO MANY BEAUTIFUL PEOPLE IN ONE PLACE in my entire life. Literally, not one of them was anything less than stunning looking, but each in their own way.

The Badd brothers were, easily, eight of the sexiest men I'd ever seen in one place. All the men were easily identified as brothers with their rich, thick, deep brown hair and, except for Xavier, they all had expressive mocha brown eyes. What a gene pool.

Luce, though… was the only one who made my heart pound. There was …something about him. I couldn't identify it or place it, beyond raw physical attraction to a gorgeous man. Which in itself was unusual for me, as my life had not, over the past few years, lent itself to idle nonsense like crushes on guys. I'd been too wrapped up in survival to be bothered with guys. But Lucian? It was impossible not to be attracted to him. He gave off a quiet, mysterious, calm confidence. His eyes, whenever they landed on me, seemed to see into me, into my soul. I'd exchanged a handful of words with him, and knew literally nothing about him nor he about me, but I...

I felt like I *knew* him, somehow.

But this didn't explain why I was in an industrial kitchen, standing at a massive grill, helping Lucian flip two dozen burger patties. Nor why I kept forgetting to breathe whenever Lucian got too close to me, when his thigh nudged mine, or his hip bumped mine, or his elbow brushed mine. Nor did it explain why I was so reluctant to leave, so eager to stay here in this bar and have this meal with this enormous gathering of people—these perfect strangers.

Lucian prodded a few of the patties with his spatula, and then glanced at me. "So. How'd you end up in the Passage?"

"I fell in. Didn't see the edge."

He frowned. "Right, but what were you doing on the docks in the first place?"

"Walking."

Lucian laughed. "I thought *I* was terse, but wow."

He bumped me with his hip. "You're taking uncom-municative to a new level."

"I'm uncomfortable with personal questions." I poked a patty with the tip of my spatula. "I have no idea how to tell whether these are done."

Lucian's eyebrow quirked up. "You've never made hamburgers before?"

How to admit to that without answering a lot of personal questions? I didn't want him to see me as... well, as what I was—a homeless orphan.

I just shrugged. "I don't cook a lot."

He nodded. "Fair enough, I suppose. Well, we're going for a nice medium. Take your flipper and poke a little hole in the burger with the corner of it, pry the hole open, and see what color it is in the middle."

I frowned at him. "Flipper?"

He lifted his...what I'd been thinking of as a spat-ula. "This. It's a flipper."

"I thought it was a spatula."

Xavier, at the deep fryers, reached over to an open-sided metal shelving unit, grabbed and held up three different utensils. "The word 'spatula' is, in fact, an umbrella category for a whole wide array of kitch-en utensils. It is not incorrect to call that device you're holding a spatula, but it is, more accurately, a flipper or turner." He held up the thing you'd use to scrape the last of the pancake batter out of a bowl. "This is

also a spatula, but it is correctly termed a scraper."
He held up a slotted, wide-bladed…um, thing. "This
is also spatula. But they each have different specific
names and uses."

That eyebrow of Lucian's arched yet again—I
was noticing he could communicate a wide variety
of emotions with just that one eyebrow. "Thank you,
Xavier, for that highly informative breakdown on
spatulas."

"You're welcome." Xavier seemed to have completely missed his brother's searing sarcasm.

I gripped my…utensil, and followed Lucian's in-
structions. "So. I've used my spatula flipper mc-deal
thingy to poke a hole. What color is it supposed to
be inside?"

"A nice pink. Not too red, like raw, but not brown
all the way through either."

I peeked inside the patty. "Well, this one looks
kind of like that."

Lucian looked too. "Yeah, that one's done." He
gestured to the patties on the grill, in rows of four
burgers across. "I put these on here back to front, so
the burgers closer to the back will be done before the
ones in front. So we can probably start taking the
ones farther back off the grill."

We stacked the burgers on a giant platter, and
then Xavier took the platter, along with a giant bowl

full of French fries, and another full of chicken tenders, out to the table.

"So," I said. "We're done cooking burgers?"

Lucian laughed as he opened a refrigerator unit
nearby and pulled out a tray of patties. "Hardly. That's
only twenty-four burgers."

I stared at him. "*Only* twenty-four?"

"Have you *seen* my brothers?" He gestured
through the open doorway, to where Bast, Bax,
Brock, and Zane were standing in a line abreast, each
of them holding a pitcher of beer in one hand. "That
plate will be empty in five minutes."

"Are they…are they competing to see who can
drink an entire pitcher of beer the fastest?" I asked.

Lucian leaned backward and watched through
the doorway for a moment, and then nodded. "Looks
like it."

"It's two in the afternoon. On a Wednesday."

"We own the bar, and the bar's closed for the
day." Lucian shrugged. "That's my brothers for you."

"Who will win, do you think?" I asked.

Lucian snorted as he laid patties on the grill.
"Bax, by a lot. Zane won't be far behind, Bast will be
third, and Brock last."

I watched the contest: When one of the twins—I
wasn't sure which was which—said "Go!" all four
men lifted the pitchers to their mouths and began

chugging. Sure enough, it was clear within seconds that Bax was going to win. He finished the pitcher faster than I'd have believed possible, and Zane was only a few seconds slower. There was a lot of cheering as Bax finished, each of the women howling for her man. It was a loud, boisterous event, this chugging competition. And then, to cap it all off, Bax held up a finger, quieting everyone, and then let loose a belch so loud I think the glass of the windows rattled.

I shook my head at the spectacle. "That's disgusting."

"The burp or the chugging?"

"Yes."

"Oh, come on." He rolled his eyes at me. "Like you've never chugged beer before?"

And here we were again, at an awkward question. "No. I don't *chug*. Beer or anything else."

Lucian made a sarcastic face. "Well pardon me, m'lady. Sorry my family offends your delicate sensibilities."

I stepped away from him, one hand on my hip. "Fuck off." I flipped him the bird. "I said nothing about you or your brothers, just that *I* don't chug."

"Have you ever tried it? It's fun."

I rolled a shoulder, discomfort rifling through me. "I'm...not twenty-one yet."

"Neither am I." He just waved a hand. "It's a

family party, so it's not like anyone's going to report us. No big deal."

"Not interested."

He sighed. "Suit yourself." He flipped burgers, each motion neat and smooth and economical.

"I feel like you're judging me." I helped him flip, but made sure to stand far enough away that he couldn't make contact with me again.

"I could say the same."

"I just...drinking like that isn't my thing."

"Look, I'm just trying to make you feel at home, okay?" Lucian met my eyes. "I know we can be loud and crude and vulgar, but we're good people."

"I don't doubt that. I'm just...I'm used to being on my own."

"Yeah, I can tell."

I whirled to face him. "What's *that* supposed to mean?"

His gaze on mine was even and unruffled. "You don't answer the smallest, most innocuous question." He shrugged and turned his eyes to the grill. "You're prickly."

"Well what, you want my life story within ten minutes of meeting me?"

"No, but you could pretend to be interested in, oh, I don't know...basic conversation?"

"I don't know you. I don't know them. I'm new

to Ketchikan." I threw both hands in the air in an I-give-up gesture. "This whole day has been kinda overwhelming for me."

He did the eyebrow again. "The whole day? It's not even three o'clock in the afternoon."

I sighed, and set down the spatula...flipper... whatever. "Look, it's just been a very, very, *very* long day for me. Falling into the water was just the cherry on top. And then you saved me, and then you have a million brothers and sisters-in-law and whatever, and now there's a chugging contest, and I'm just...it's a fucking lot to take in, okay?"

With a nod, Lucian seemed content to let it go, and we finished cooking the burgers in silence. When they were done, Lucian stacked the finished burgers onto another platter. "Come on. Come sit and eat."

"We just had eggs and bacon."

"And now we're having burgers and fries." He led the way to the table, where two spaces had been saved for us, sandwiched between the two sets of twins who seemed to be married to each other, or something. "If you're not hungry, don't eat. If you're hungry, eat."

"Oh is *that* how it works?" I asked sarcastically. "I had no idea how appetites function."

Lucian hadn't been kidding when he said the first platter would be gone in minutes; by the time we sat down, the platter was totally empty, and Bax reached for another burger even as Lucian set the platter down.

Bast eyed me as I sat, spine straight, hands on my lap. "Want a beer, Joss?"

"I'm not—I'm not twenty-one."

Bast waved a hand dismissively. "Meh, it's just a beer, it's not a big deal. Besides, you're about the same age as Luce, which makes you close, right? I wouldn't serve you if we had customers around, but this is family. It's cool."

Not wanting to appear ungrateful or rude, I shrugged. "I guess I'll have one. Thank you."

There were at least half a dozen pitchers of beer on the table, not counting the four empty ones the brothers had chugged from.

Bast poured beer into a clean glass and slid it across the table to me with the practiced ease of a bartender. "Bottoms up, sweetheart."

"Wait, hold up!" Bax, sitting across the table from me, interrupted. "Don't drink yet—everyone, glasses up. We're doing a toast!"

"What are we toasting to?" asked one of the female twins—she was the only person at the table aside from Jax who wasn't drinking a beer, now that I had one, and I noticed her T-shirt was a little tight around the belly, likely making her a few months pregnant.

"To Joss," Bax suggested, lifting his beer high.

"For falling into the Passage, and into our lives."

"To Joss!" was echoed by more than a dozen voices all at once.

"Um. Thanks?" I managed to speak in something louder than a whisper, somehow.

My cheeks burned. I don't think I'd ever felt so awkward or on the spot in my life, even though no one seemed to expect anything of me. Everyone lifted their glasses and held them toward the center of the table—there were far too many people for everyone to clink, but everyone made the gesture, at least.

I wondered, though—how had I fallen into their lives? I was spending the afternoon with them, not staying forever.

After everyone had toasted and taken a drink, a dozen different conversations erupted, and the focus was no longer on me.

Bax, now on his third—or was it fourth?—burger, winked at me. "Welcome to the fam, babe. We just made your life a *whole* lot more interesting."

I blinked at him. "All I did was fall into the water."

Bax grinned and wiggled his eyebrows. "Yeah, well, you clearly don't know how things work in this family."

Eva, a stunning woman with jet-black hair and a perfect hourglass figure, giggled. "Don't scare the poor thing, Baxter. She's new and you people are a lot to take in." She addressed me, then. "The Badd brothers kind of have their own gravitational pull. Once you're in their orbit, it's hard to escape."

The woman next to Eva was a small, delicate, loud woman, with blonde hair cut at her chin. Clea? Claire? Something like that. "What Eva means is that these boys have a way of pulling you in and making you never want to get away. It's not that you *can't* escape their orbit, it's that they have a way of making you not *want* to, even the ones you're not actually with."

"What can I say—" one of the Badd brother twins said.

"We're just that lovable," the other finished.

What made their ability to finish each other's sentences impressive was that they had the girl twins, Lucian, and me in between them.

I glanced at Lucian, who was watching all this conversation without comment; he seemed happy to let the conversation flow around him. "Do they do that a lot?" I asked him. "Talk in synch like that?"

"You're new, so they're showing off," he said.

Again, calling me new, as if by falling into the water and being rescued by Lucian, I had somehow opted into a Badd Family adoption without knowing it.

One of the male twins, with long, loose brown hair and a piercing through the center of his lower lip, leaned forward to catch my attention. "So, Joss. What's your story?"

I froze. "Um. My story?" I had both hands around my burger, but I suddenly had no appetite. "You know. Nothing special."

"Oh, come on. Everyone is special. Everyone has a story." The twin snagged a pitcher as he spoke and refilled his pint glass. "I'm not asking for your deepest darkest secrets here. Where are you from? That's easy enough, right?"

You'd think.

"Um, I'm from upstate New York, originally." A true answer, at least. "A little town outside Buffalo called East Aurora."

"Nice." He spoke around a mouthful of French fry. "And what brings you Ketchikan?"

I shifted on the chair. "I, um. I just kind of ended up here."

The other twin, the one with an undercut, guffawed as if I'd said something hilarious. "Yeah, okay. Like what, you went 'whoops, let me just *accidentally* end up in a remote Alaskan city accessible only by sea or air.'"

"I mean, yeah, sort of." I gestured at the first twin who had spoken, and then the second. "Which one of you is which?"

The first twin, with the long loose hair, lifted his

hand. "I'm Canaan. My wife is Aerie."

The other lifted his hand, then, in a mirrored gesture of his brother's. "I'm Corin, and this is Tate."

"So, you accidentally ended up here?" Bax asked. "The real question, then, is what you're running from."

I swallowed hard, tracing patterns in the sweat on the outside of my pint glass. "Um. I'm not running from anything."

Bax did the eyebrow thing, now—the expressive eyebrow quirk seemed to be another trait all the brothers shared. "And I'm Abraham Lincoln." He winked at me. "'Then you shall know the truth, and the truth shall set you free.'"

"I...um—"

Zane, the scary one, threw a French fry at Bax, interrupting my attempt to come up with an answer. "You did *not* just quote the Bible at her."

"I thought we've established that I *can* actually read," Bax said, "all appearances to the contrary notwithstanding."

"Quit trying to talk like Xavier," Zane said, and threw another fry, bouncing it off Bax's head. "Next thing you know, you'll be quoting Shakespeare or something."

I watched this exchange, waiting for someone to get angry.

"I can quote Shakespeare, I just choose not to." Bax drained his beer, poured another, and polished off the last of his burger. "I'm not into sounding like a pretentious douche. I think Xavier is the only person on the planet who can non-ironically quote poetry without sounding like a total asshat."

Zane reached for another burger, adding ketchup and mayo as he responded to Bax. "You can quote Shakespeare from memory?"

Bax shrugged. "Sure."

"I call bullshit."

"'These violent delights have violent ends. And in their triumph die, like fire and powder. Which, as they kiss, consume.'"

Zane laughed. "You only know that quote because you watch *Westworld*."

"Romeo and Juliet. Friar Lawrence in Act two, scene six." Bax gave his brother the double middle finger. "Bet you didn't know I played Friar Lawrence in college."

Eva twisted away from a conversation with Dru—Bast's wife, a curvy, gorgeous redhead—to stare at Bax. "You were in a play? You never told me this."

Bax shrugged, suddenly uncomfortable. "It was…ah…well—um."

Brock chortled. "It was to impress a girl, wasn't it?"

Bax blew a raspberry. "I didn't need to join a stupid play to get chicks, bro. Believe that shit." He sighed. "I lost a bet with a couple guys from the D-line."

Eva eyed him warily. "What was the bet? Or do I not want to know?"

Bax's grin was embarrassed. "Ah, you may be better off not knowing."

Bax only laughed all the harder. "Well, we were drunk and talking shit, and so of course the bets got crazy. None of us had a lot of money, so we were trying to come up with stakes that didn't involve money. Well, one of Bobby's best friends was the director of the drama team's play, and they still needed a Friar Lawrence, to the point that they were desperate. Apparently the guy they originally cast had come down with mono or something horrible, and had to pull out. Like, the play was literally in two weeks, and they had no Friar Lawrence, and nobody was stepping up. So the bet was if I failed to score with three girls at once I had to audition for the part, and if I did score, Bobby had to wear a dress to school every day for a month."

Eva laughed, now. "And you couldn't score?"

Bax faked outrage. "Of course I scored! Jesus, what kind of a loser do you take me for? I got four girls to agree to go to my dorm with me. But by the time we got back there, two of them were a fucking disaster, like couldn't walk on their own. So me and the other two got their friends to their rooms, and I ended up with those two girls in *their* room, just because it was closer."

Eva shook her head. "You're ridiculous."

"I was a player, babe, what can I say?" He grinned and winked at her. "So the next morning I got dressed and left their room, because I'd never actually gone to bed—ahhh…*any*way, I met Bobby, Mac and Deon for breakfast, and was all like, I won the bet! Better start picking out dresses, yada yada yada."

"But the bet was for three girls, not two," Bast said. "So you lost."

Bax nodded. "Exactly. But I'm a man of my word, so I tried out for the part, and I got it. But I did score, technically, meaning I didn't *totally* lose the bet, so Bobby had to wear a dress to school for a week instead of a month."

"And were you any good as Friar Lawrence?" I asked.

Bax cackled with laughter. "Hell no! I was terrible! I forgot half my lines, and the ones I did remember, I sounded like I was reading from a cue card, like a fucking robot or some shit." He shrugged. "But I still remember that speech."

He took a deep breath, staring at the ceiling as he

recalled the words, and then quoted:

"These violent delights have violent ends

And in their triumph die, like fire and powder,

Which, as they kiss, consume. The sweetest honey

Is loathsome in his own deliciousness

And in the taste confounds the appetite.

Therefore love moderately. Long love doth so.

Too swift arrives as tardy as too slow.

Here comes the lady. Oh, so light a foot

Will ne'er wear out the everlasting flint.

A lover may bestride the gossamers

That idles in the wanton summer air,

And yet not fall. So light is vanity."

Xavier clapped. "You are full of surprises, Baxter."

Bax bowed, laughing. "And that's the story of how I acted in a play with the Penn State drama team."

I leaned close to Lucian. "How much of that story is true, do you think?"

He grinned at me. "All of it, knowing Bax."

"And his wife is okay with that?"

A shrug. "I mean, it's not like he does that kind of thing now that he's married, so how can she be genuinely pissed at him for something he did when they didn't even know each other?"

"But I mean, the thing with the three girls or two girls or whatever? It's kind of gross." I shuddered.

Lucian just laughed again. "I told you, my older brothers are animals. They're settled down now, but in their wild days, they drank like fish and fucked anything that moved."

Baxter clearly overheard us, because he pointed at Lucian. "Hey now, I had standards! I didn't fuck ugly, and I didn't fuck desperate, because desperate means clingy, and clingy means I'd just break their heart when I left the next morning, and I'm not into breaking hearts."

Lucian held up both hands palms out. "I stand corrected." He addressed me. "My bad—what I meant to say was that Baxter was a connoisseur of hot but easy women."

Bax nodded sagely. "That's better. Although I take exception to the word 'easy.' Just because a girl likes a good time and isn't looking for commitment doesn't make her easy."

The petite blonde woman, who was with Brock— the brother who looked like a Greek god—raised her beer over her head. "Amen to that!"

Dru threw a packet of mayo at Claire. "What are you talking about? You've said yourself you used to be the world's biggest slut."

Claire just nodded. "But like Bax said, I had *standards* in my sluttiness, and I'm not about to apologize for liking dick."

Mara, a woman about my height with long blonde hair in a braid, howled in laughter. "Liking dick? You were a cock expert. You rode so much dick before you met Brock it's a wonder your vagina isn't a blown-out cavern."

Claire tilted her nose up in the air. "My pussy is tighter than a drum, thank you very much." She glanced at Brock. "Right, babe?"

Brock, tilted back on the hind legs of his chair, nodded. "Like a fuckin' vise, hon."

Claire pointed at Mara. "Unlike yours. Now that you've had a baby, I'm guessing you've got a nice case of beef curtains going on."

I about spit out the mouthful of beer. "Ohmygod!" I sputtered, coughing. "What the *fuck* is wrong with you people?"

Mara just laughed along with everyone else. "I did so many Kegels while I was pregnant, if you could see my P-C muscle, it'd look like Bax's bicep. My shit is just as tight as it was before I had Jax, thank you very much."

I wiped beer off my chin with a napkin. "This is the weirdest, grossest conversation I've ever heard."

Bax picked a French fry off of his wife's plate and threw it at me, and it smacked into my forehead before falling to my plate. "Like I said, welcome to the family, Joss."

"Seems like a dubious honor," I said, before I could think better of it.

"Ohhh! Burn!" Bax shouted, cackling. "Yeah, you fit right in, sweet thing."

I looked at Lucian. "Is it always like this?"

He nodded and shrugged a shoulder. "Pretty much, yeah."

I sank lower in my seat. "God, I need this blizzard to be over."

"Why? So you can keep running away from whatever it is you're running from?" Bax asked. "I mean, come on, quit acting hard and relax. You know you're having fun."

I stood up abruptly, knocking my chair over backward. "You don't know the first fucking thing about me!" I snapped.

Blood racing, pulse thundering in my ears, defensive anger raging through me, I whirled on my heel and stomped toward the stairs leading to the apartment. Within seconds, I had on my still-wet coat, hat, gloves, and backpack and all but ran down the stairs and to the door of the bar.

"You can all fuck off. You don't know me, or what I've been through." I shoved at the door, but it was locked, frustrating my attempt to make a dramatic exit. "Goddammit! How do I unlock this fucking door?"

"Good job, Bax," I heard Lucian say. "Way to push too far."

I found the knob to unlock the door and twisted it, shoved the door open and took three running steps outside, turning right as I exited. Of course, within three steps, I knew I'd made a mistake. What had been merely a very bad snowstorm when I arrived had worsened into a total whiteout blizzard, snow flying so thickly that I couldn't see a single foot in front of me. I stopped dead in my tracks, fighting tears. I had to go back. It was bitterly cold, the wind slicing through me like a razor sharp knife; the fact that my coat, hat, and gloves were still wet only made it worse. In the seconds I'd been standing here, I was already covered with snow. I had no idea where I was and I was low on money.

Helpless.

Alone.

Goddammit.

THREE

Lucian

WHEN SHE GOT UP, I FIGURED SHE WOULD GO upstairs and try to catch her breath, so to speak. Just sort of calm down. But then she had her backpack and coat, and was at the front door and telling us all to fuck off on the way out. It all happened so fast that she was gone before I realized she was serious about leaving.

I stood up. "Good job, Bax," I said. "Way to push too far."

He held up his hands. "Well shit, I didn't think she'd react like that. Jesus."

"We literally just met her," I said. "Tactful you are not."

Bax sighed. "I'm sorry. That was a dick move."

Dru gestured at the door, giving me a meaningful look. "Well? You'd better go after her."

"Don't be sorry to me you asshole, be sorry to her," I said to Bax. "Assuming I can get her to come back."

I didn't bother with a coat, knowing time was of the essence if I was going to catch her in this blizzard. I left the bar, tugging my hoodie up over my head and stuffing my hands into the front pocket. I stood outside the door and looked left and right, but the snow was so thick I could barely see the sidewalk in front of me.

How far could she have gotten? This was bad. If she got lost in this, she could freeze to death a lot faster than she would realize.

"Joss!" I called. "Come back!"

"Fuck you." I heard her voice not far away. "Just tell me where the nearest motel is."

"You'll never make it in this snow, for one thing," I said, moving toward her voice. "And it's booked solid, for another. I heard some customers talking yesterday about how all the hotels were sold out this weekend."

"I'll be fine." Her voice was a murmur, depressed, flat. "Just leave me alone."

I found her, then. Snow lay in a thick blanket

over her shoulders and head, and was sticking to her dreads. She'd gone about three steps and then stopped, probably realizing her own danger.

"Joss, please." I put my hand on her arm, standing in front of her. "Come back."

Her eyes were hard and flat and emotionless. "Why should I?"

"Because you'll literally freeze to death out here, if nothing else. Your coat is still wet, which will freeze around you and trap the cold in. It's actually doing more harm than good."

"So you just don't want my death on your conscience?"

I couldn't help a laugh. "Yeah, that's it. That's my only reason."

She couldn't stop a slight quirk of her lips as she attempted to suppress a smile. "How chivalrous of you."

I let out a breath. "Joss, come on. For real, I want you to come back. We all do."

"Your brother is an asshole."

I nodded. "I know."

"Your sisters-in-law are all intimidatingly beautiful and funny and cool."

I nodded again. "I know that too."

"Your family is overwhelming as fuck."

"Also true." I let my hand slide down to hers, and

wrapped her fingers in my hand. "But we mean well, and we're loyal, and we'd all give you the shirt off our backs."

"Well, I *am* wearing Dru's clothing."

Her teeth were chattering, now, and she was shivering. I tugged her back toward the bar. "Come on, Joss. Just come back with me."

"No more inquisitions."

"Not a single question."

"I'm not running from anything." She stopped and glared up at me, making sure I saw how serious she was. "And I don't like answering personal questions from people I don't know. I'm very private."

I led her back into the bar and relocked the door. "I understand completely. I'm pretty private myself."

"How's that work, in a family of fifteen people?"

I laughed. "It's tricky."

When Joss approached the table, Bax stood up and moved around to stand in front of her. "I apologize for being a dick," he said, shooting her his trademark sassy, naughty, charming grin. "Sometimes my mouth runs away from my brain."

"My dear, sweet husband has a chronic case of verbal diarrhea," Eva put in. "But he doesn't mean anything by it."

Joss was frozen again, tensed, as if all the eyes and attention on her had a physically paralytic effect.

"I—it's fine. No big deal."

Bax batted his eyelashes and did an impression of a sad puppy. "So you forgive me?"

Even Joss couldn't help laughing at that. "Yes, Bax, I forgive you."

Bax moved in, big burly arms held out wide. "Can I get a hug?"

If Joss was paralyzed by tense discomfort before, the prospect of hugging Baxter seemed to freeze her even further, to the point that she held her arms at her sides, hands fisted, shoulders turtled up, agonized awkwardness in every line and curve of her body.

"Ummm…"

I stepped up beside her and batted at Bax's arms. "I don't think she's ready for the full Baxter hug experience."

"I'm…not much of a hugger," Joss said.

Bax just shrugged. "I'll get you one day. You'll hug me and you'll love it. I'm a great hugger. World class."

"Is that what the kids are calling it these days? *Hugging?*" Corin quipped, snorting.

Bax was close enough to Corin that he reached out without looking and slugged him in the chest. "I meant a totally normal, platonic, innocent *hug*, you filthy pervert."

At that moment, Jax started crying, and despite

Zane's best efforts, he wouldn't calm down. Eventually Mara took him and headed for the stairs.

"I think this little Badd boy is ready for a nap," Mara said. "Which means this party has to quiet down."

"Hey, Zane, wanna get a few sets in while your woman puts your spawn down for a nap?" Bax asked.

Zane nodded. "Sounds good. You cool with that, babe?"

Mara waved a hand. "Go for it. He had me up a lot last night anyway, so I'm gonna take a nap with him."

Claire stood up and hauled at Brock's arm. "Come on, babe. All that talk about dick made me horny. Take me home and fuck me."

Joss choked on suppressed laughter, which made Claire cackle all the more loudly. "I think we're scandalizing poor Joss, baby."

Brock followed Claire, and then picked her up and pinned her against the wall with his hips, before turning his head to give Joss a playful wink. "Better avert your eyes, kiddo, this is about to get dirty."

Joss looked at me, and then back at Claire and Brock, who were doing a pretty convincing job at pretending to fuck right there against the wall, with lots of exaggerated grunts and moans.

"Oh my god," Joss breathed. "They're crazy.

You're all crazy!"

"They're just fucking with you." I shouted at Brock and Claire, then: "Get a room!"

"It's too far to make it home in this snow," Brock said, his mouth nipping at Claire's throat. "Can we borrow a room here?"

Bast waved a hand. "Zane's old room is still empty. Go for it. Just wash the sheets when you're done."

Claire slid down, wiggled out from between Brock and the wall, and hauled him toward the stairs. "Come on, Brock! I need your cock." She giggled. "That rhymes. Brock, Brock, give me your cock! Hickory dickory dock, I'm about to ride your cock."

"CLAIRE!" Mara shouted. "Keep your perverted poetry to yourself! None of us need to hear that shit, you slut!"

Brock picked Claire up, tossed her over his shoulder, and carried her up the stairs, spanking her at every step...and not gently. Which only made her squeal in what sounded like equal parts outrage, pain, and pleasure.

"Are they really going to go have sex right now? Like they literally announced it to the whole group?" Joss asked me.

I nodded. "Yep. That's Claire. She, ahh...her engine revs rather high, it seems."

Joss just shook her head, and then rubbed her

temples with her fingertips. "I was going to ask if I could go up there and be somewhere quiet, but now that they're up there fucking..." she groaned, tipping her head back. "I really need to just sit and be somewhere quiet. I'm exhausted."

I felt like an ass. She'd already said her day had been crazy long and hard, and she *had* already fallen into ice-cold water, and now she was struggling to deal with my crazy brothers.

"If you can brave the outside for another few seconds, we can go to the other apartment." I addressed the rest of the group. "Joss *did* just fall into the Passage, guys. I'm gonna run down the street with her where it's quieter."

"Keep one hand on the wall," Bast said. "Super easy to get turned around in shit that thick."

"We'll clean up here," Xavier said. "You guys go. She's probably crashing after the adrenaline rush of falling in. That can make you even more tired than the shock to the system itself."

Bax grabbed his coat off the back of his chair and held it out. "You want this?"

I shook my head. "Nah. It's not that far. Thanks though."

I led her back outside. "It's literally two doors down," I told her. "So we'll just follow the wall and jog. Ready?"

She nodded. I put her against the wall, and we trotted down the street. The wind blew the snow in swirling, sideways drifts, turning the snowflakes into a battering ram of icy razor blades, obscuring everything in a wall of white. I felt the brick transition as we passed the travel agency that was sandwiched between Badd's and the studio, and then I felt the next transition, and then the front door of the studio was right there. I shoved the door open, keeping a tight grip on the doorknob as the wind tried to snatch the door away from me. We stumbled inside, mounds of snow drifting in after us, and then I put my shoulder to the door and shoved it closed, falling back against it, out of breath from the effort and the cold.

"Holy shit," I panted. "Never seen a blizzard this bad in my life."

"I heard it was supposed to be pretty temperate here," Joss said, shaking snow off her head, her dreadlocks wiggling and dancing.

"It is, usually. But when people think of Alaska, they think it's like this all the time, but it's really not. I mean, unless you go up near the Arctic Circle, like in Barrow or somewhere way north. But down here? It snows, but not usually like this."

I found the light switch and flipped it on, revealing the twins' studio—racks of guitars, a stand holding several ukuleles, a banjo, and a mandolin, a drum set, several different types and sizes of hand drums like bongos and cajones and such, a sectioned off, soundproofed isolated recording booth, a high-end mix board, speakers, amps, microphones, a snake pit of cords and wires, concert posters on the walls from Canaan and Corin's stint as Bishop's Pawn as well as newer posters billing Canaan and Aerie as Canary, and a small desk with a pair of mammoth iMacs side by side.

Joss stared around at all the equipment. "Geez. Somebody must be hardcore into music."

"The twins," I answered. "They used to be Bishop's Pawn. Now they own their own record label, and Canaan and Aerie tour as Canary."

Joss snapped her fingers. "That's why they look so familiar! I was sleeping at a bus station a week or so ago, and they had MTV on the TVs for some reason. They were playing a live recording of a Bishop's Pawn concert from like two years ago or something."

I nodded. "Yeah, they recorded a live concert special from…Atlanta, I think it was? Pretty big deal. Scored them their world tour with Rev Theory." Something she said had me frowning at her. "Wait. Did you say you were sleeping at a bus station?"

She hung her head. "Shit. Forget I said that?"

I sighed. "Sure. I did promise no questions." I jerked a thumb at the door behind where there were stairs leading up to the apartment above. "Let's go upstairs. You can crash on my bed if you want."

I preceded her up the stairs, but the silence between us was thick with the questions I wasn't asking. That slip, added to the way she was dressed when I rescued her from the water, made me think she didn't have a permanent housing situation.

I showed her my room—it's small, but it's mine. Most of the wall space is covered in bookshelves, stuffed and overstuffed with paperbacks and hardcovers, all well worn and dog-eared. My bed was underneath the window, the headboard something I made myself out of a set of bookcases, two on either side of the mattress and a third set on end horizontally across the top of them, with the books stacked vertically between the shelves in neat rows. The frame of the bed, underneath the mattress, was a bureau, essentially, with three large drawers on each side and two more at the foot, creating enough storage for all my clothes.

The only decoration in the room aside from the books was a large corkboard nailed to the backside of the door, on which are postcards and photographs from all the places I've been—Hawaii, Thailand, Burma, Laos, the Philippines, Taiwan, and most of the Indonesian islands.

Joss examined my room—it's a queerly

vulnerable feeling, showing someone my bedroom. This is my space, my private haven. It's where I go to be alone—alone time is something I crave, and it is hard to come by with eight brothers and six sisters-in-law, plus a nephew, and my ever-increasing responsibilities at the bar.

As my brothers settle into life in Ketchikan for what has been just over a year now, several of them have found work outside the bar. Bax has the gym and his growing list of clients, Brock has his air service, flying tourists around the local area and points abroad, the twins have their music, so it's really just Bast, Zane, Xavier, and me running the bar fulltime.

She shot me a look. "You read a lot, huh?"

I shrugged. "Yeah, it's my only real hobby. I don't get a lot of downtime from the bar, and what I do get, I spend in here reading."

"That bar, where we were all eating—you own that?"

I shook my head. "I don't—*we* do. My brothers and I. Our grandfather started it, our dad ran it, and then Dad passed a little over a year ago and now we run it."

She perused the titles of the books—my tastes are broad, ranging from sci-fi to historical fiction to biography and science and mathematics.

"Little bit of everything, huh?" She plucked

one of my favorite biographies on Teddy Roosevelt and thumbed through it. "He was a fascinating guy, Teddy."

I nodded. "Sure was."

She put the book back where I had it, and continued her examination. I hadn't closed the door behind us, not wanting her to feel trapped or enclosed or awkward, but she caught a glimpse of the corkboard on the back of the door, and she closed the door to look at it.

Her breath caught when she saw the huge collage of photos and postcards. "Wow. I mean—*wow*. You've been to all these places?"

I nodded. "I started working on a fishing boat when I was...thirteen? The owner, Clint Mackey, was a friend of my dad's, and I was obsessed with his boat from when I was a kid. I'd beg to go play on Captain Mackey's boat whenever he was docked, and eventually he just told me if I'd come help him on the boat after school every day, he'd pay me. So I started cleaning and repairing nets after school, and he paid really well. I worked for Clint for years. I was never a very good student, not because I'm not smart, I was just...I was restless, you know? I wanted to be on the boat. Out on the water. I wanted to fish, not take stupid tests and do homework. I didn't see the point. I'd have just dropped out and worked on the boat full-time, but my dad wouldn't let me. So he made me a deal—if I got my GED, I could drop out of school and work with Clint full time. So I busted my ass, got my GED in a matter of months, and worked for Clint full-time until I was eighteen. The day I turned eighteen, I took a berth on a deep-sea fishing boat and sailed away. Never looked back, either, not till I got the email last year about Dad passing."

"Sorry to hear about your father."

I let out a breath. "Yeah, it was…I don't know. Unexpected and not, at the same time. He wasn't in good health during most of my life."

She looked at me with compassion. "He was sick?"

I sat on my bed and wondered how much I should tell her. "Um, not sick, exactly." I let out another slow breath. "My mom passed away when I was nine, and Dad was never the same after that. Drank a lot, worked open to close all day every day, and then passed out as soon he closed the bar. After Mom died, my only memories of Dad are of him behind the bar, a drink in hand, watching ESPN, or serving customers. Bast raised the rest of us, essentially. My dad just kind of…checked out. Mom was his whole world, I guess, and without her, he just couldn't cope."

Joss plopped down on the bed next to me, close but not touching. "So you're an orphan."

I nodded. "I guess so. Never really thought of it like that."

Silence settled between us.

Joss sighed, flipping one end of a dreadlock between her fingers. "I guess we have those two things in common, at least."

I eye her sideways. "That being what?"

"No parents and a penchant for travel."

"I see." I didn't know what else to say.

She dug in her backpack and pulled out a pink pocket folder full of postcards and travel brochures—I noticed all the locations in her collection were Canadian. She opened the folder carefully—it was soaked from her fall, and everything in it was soft and wet, easily ripped.

"Dammit," Joss whispered. "It's all ruined."

I know exactly how important a collection like that can be to someone for whom travel is a way of life. "Not necessarily," I said. "We can salvage most of it." I reached out a hand for the binder. "May I?"

She met my gaze warily. "What are you gonna do with it?"

"Blow-dry it."

She smiled hesitantly. "I guess that could work."

"I dropped a backpack full of books into the ocean once. I jumped in after it, swam down almost ninety feet before I caught it. I spent hours blow-drying those books to save them."

I grinned at her, and then carefully removed each item from the binder and spread them out on the floor. I grabbed the hair dryer from the bathroom and brought it into my bedroom, plugged it in, and turned it on. Joss just sat and watched; hope blossomed in her eyes, as I spent the next hour saving her postcards and brochures.

We chatted as I dried her collection, talking about the places we've been. I told her about adventures from my travels, getting lost on a trip to a temple in Burma, almost getting shanghaied by pirates in Taiwan, weathering a typhoon off the coast of Java. In turn, she told me about walking across all of Canada by herself, and the people she met—long-haul truckers, farmers in their beat up old pickups, kind old ladies who insisted on putting her up the for the night, dodging local police as she tried to find somewhere to sleep. I still didn't know exactly how she lost her parents, or how she ended up walking across Canada or why, and I didn't ask.

When everything was mostly dry, we sat on the floor and just talked. I think I talked more to Joss in those hours than I have to anyone in my whole life. There's just something about her that drew me in, made me want to hear what she had to say, made me want to share my own stories. Time vanished—we just talked. We talked music, politics, books, movies, our childhoods. The sky outside the window grew dark.

At some point during the course of the conversation, we ended up side by side on my bed, backs to the headboard, shoulders brushing. Gradually, we sank lower and lower, until somehow we were both lying down. It was comfortable, easy. We just lay there, and we talked to each other. Full night dropped in around us, and my eyes burned with fatigue, and Joss was clearly fading herself.

There was a pause in the conversation and, for the first time in hours, there was silence between us. It was utterly dark in my room—we never turned the light on, so we'd been talking in the darkness for a while now. I heard her breathing slow down and even out. I felt her twitch a little, toes curling in and relaxing, her thigh muscles where they brushed against mine tensing and relaxing.

I was utterly comfortable. Relaxed, more at ease at this moment, with this near-total stranger in my bed beside me, than I maybe have ever been.

The thought made my heart pound.

Deciding to give her space to sleep so she didn't wake up disoriented and in a strange bed with a strange man, I sat up and twisted my legs off the bed. I felt her hand latch onto my wrist.

"Stay." Her voice wasn't even a whisper, just a sound so quiet, so sleepy, that if the room hadn't been dead silent I would have missed it.

"You're sure?"

She let go of my wrist. "Just don't try anything."

I lay back down, gingerly. Now that I'd decided to get up, my comfort and ease vanished. I was tense, hyperaware of her presence.

It took a long time, but I eventually fell asleep.

FOUR

Joss

I WOKE UP DISORIENTED. WHERE WAS I? HOW HAD I gotten here?

Sleeping on park benches and in bus stations, you never really truly fall asleep, never totally relax your guard, so there's no chance of falling so deeply asleep that you risk waking up disoriented. When was the last time I slept in a real bed? Edmonton? A trucker had taken me from Saskatoon to Edmonton, dropping me off at a no-tell motel sort of place outside Edmonton at three in the morning. The night clerk had seen me get dropped off by the trucker and assumed the worst about me. The jerk propositioned me—a free night in a room if I'd blow him. I told him to go fuck himself and turned to leave, and then thought better of it. I turned around with a proposition in return. I'd work for free cleaning rooms the next day in exchange for a room for the night.

He agreed because his cleaning lady had quit the day before, and he was facing the prospect of having to make up the rooms himself before he could go home after his shift. I sweetened the deal, telling him I'd stay on for a few days, cleaning rooms in exchange for the room for the night and some cash under the table.

I did that job for almost a week, sleeping in a room as far from the creepy-ass night clerk as possible, with the chain on the door and a chair propped under the doorknob. I cleaned rooms all day. Oddly, or perhaps not so oddly, the motel's business was even more brisk during the day than it was at night—mostly cheating assholes meeting their side pieces for afternoon sleaziness, drug dealers selling their wares, and prostitutes selling theirs. Being a place that rented by the hour as well as by the night, I often ended up cleaning the same room several times in a day, which was fine by me, as it meant I got paid. And sometimes, I even got tipped by the patrons.

That week in the motel outside Edmonton netted me enough cash to get me the whole leg from Edmonton to Prince George. By the time I'd gotten picked up by a kindly long-distance trucker named Mark outside Fort Fraser, my cash was nearly gone, which was the only reason I'd had to accept his charity in the first place.

I opened my eyes, blinking at the white snow-filtered light streaming in through the window over my head. The bed I was in was distinctly masculine—red-and-black checkered flannel sheets and a down comforter in a black duvet. The pillow under my cheek had a masculine scent—shampoo, a hint of cologne, and just that man-smell, which jarred memories of climbing into Mom and Dad's bed and sleeping between them. Dad's pillow always smelled like the one I was on, and there was something comforting and nostalgic about it.

Lucian.

Our hours of conversation last night flooded through me, hours spent pouring myself out to him. I avoided the touchy stuff—Mom and Dad's death, and those hellish weeks and months immediately afterward—but I told him things I'd never told anyone. I shared the small stuff, the minutiae, that in some ways defines who we are as people. I told him about eating a mushroom I found in the backyard as a little girl, and getting so sick I had to be rushed to the ER, about failing English class my sophomore year for refusing to read *The Scarlet Letter* because I'd found the book unutterably horrible and boring and stupid and irrelevant and hadn't wanted to be bothered with it, which I think the teacher had recognized. I told Lucian about my breakup with my best friend my freshman year, how we'd quarreled over a guy we'd both liked, and the fight had spiraled out of control, but by the time we realized how stupid the whole thing was, the damage had been done and too many nasty things had been said to overcome, and we'd never hung out again.

He, in turn, told me about growing up with seven brothers, being the second youngest, the struggle of being raised by an older brother who was still really just a kid himself, having an absentee alcoholic father. Lucian had idolized his father, until their mother passed, and then his father had shut down and Lucian had been disenchanted, to say the least. He told me a lot about the places he'd seen, how he'd walked across much of southeast Asia by himself, catching rides here and there, occasionally taking a train or bus, working for meals and living on a shoestring, as he called it. While his travels had been voluntary, as in he'd at least had a home to go back to, I still understood him on a visceral level, and he understood me the same way. Unless you've lived a vagabond life, you can't really understand what it's like, and Lucian is the only person I've ever met who genuinely understands.

I sat up, feeling more rested and refreshed than I had in…god, so long.

A glance out the window told me the blizzard was still in full force outside, perhaps even worse than yesterday. Snow was piled on the sidewalks several feet deep, and even higher in drifts in some places, and the snow was still flying so thickly the water across the street was totally obscured.

Looked like I wasn't going anywhere for at least another day.

There are worse places to be stuck—the thought popped up in my head and refused to go away. I mean, yes…Lucian has been kind. He saved my life, and he let me take a shower and got me clean clothes and fed me, and his family seemed to accept me without question, his brother's pushy interrogation notwithstanding.

And yeah, none of the Badd brothers were exactly hard on the eyes, Lucian especially.

God, that man. Those deep, dark, expressive eyes, and his long, thick, wavy brown hair? His features, thin and sharp and otherworldly in their beautiful perfection. He wouldn't need a wig or makeup to play an elf in Peter Jackson's *The Lord of the Rings*—just give the man pointy ears and he'd be an elf. Orlando who? Lucian was Legolas, but way sexier.

I mean, his name was *Lucian*, for god's sake. How

cool was that?

Why did my pulse thunder just thinking about him?

The entire time we'd been talking last night, I'd been tempted to hold his hand, which I'd refused to let myself do. I'd also wanted to trace those sharp, high cheekbones with my fingers, and the line of his lips. I'd found myself wanting another look at him without his shirt on.

None of those thoughts were even remotely like me. I wasn't that type of girl, and my life didn't lend itself to idle, unproductive nonsense like being attracted to guys. Surviving took every ounce of energy and every second of my day, and I didn't dare trust anyone that far. Not with my body, not with my safety.

I'd learned that the hard way, and wouldn't be making that mistake again.

A lesson I'd do well to remember around Lucian. Just because he *seemed* nice, *seemed* kind, didn't mean he was. It's possible that he might expect some gesture of gratitude from me at some point, the way some guys seem to expect something in return. Granted, I'd learned to trust my gut when it came to which trucks to get into—one look at a guy, and I could reliably tell if I should trust him. I'd also learned the hard way to trust my gut, and that I was never wrong about men.

Lucian was the real deal—that's what my gut told

me. His brothers were the real deal, too. His sisters-in-law, well…I had no real, recent experience with women near my own age. Should I be their friend? I wanted to be; they all seemed like smart, sophisticated, fun, funny, cool girls, not to mention drop-dead gorgeous. Of course, that made them as intimidating as hell. How could I measure up? I wasn't educated like they all seemed to be, and I certainly couldn't match Eva's flawless fashion sense, or Claire's brutally blunt and hysterical humor, or Dru's easy, competent grace, or the twins' effortless sense of worldly cool, or Mara's fiercely feminine aura of strength.

Ugh. I'm falling into my own head.

My stomach rumbled, shaking me out of my thoughts. There was no clock in the room, which didn't surprise me, as Lucian probably used his phone for an alarm, if he needed one at all. I had no concept of what time it was, not with the sun obscured, but judging from how stiff I was as I got out of the bed, and how hungry I felt, I suspected I'd slept really late.

I went across the hall and used the bathroom, and then made my way out into the living room, where I was greeted by a sight that stopped me dead in my tracks.

Lucian, wearing nothing but a pair of tiny, tight running shorts, was gripping a tension bar for pull-ups, hauling himself up in slow, smooth repetitions.

His body was coated in sweat, his chest was heaving, and his muscles bunched and flexed as he pulled up, lowered himself, and pulled up again. I counted eight reps, and then he dropped to the ground in the push-up position, and began running in place, his knees driving up to his chest, palms flat on the floor. His back was to me as he did the mountain climbers, and I tried in vain to not appreciate how tight and hard his ass was, but failed miserably.

I found myself wondering if it was as hard and firm to the touch as it looked.

Probably.

My breath caught as he finished the mountain climbers. He went back to the tension bar, leapt up and caught the bar in both hands, and now, instead of pull-ups, he pointed his toes and lifted his stiffened, outstretched legs until his toes touched the lintel over his head, and then lowered them again, as slowly as he'd lifted them. He did this twenty-five times before dropping to the floor, gasping for breath. He wasn't done, though. He dropped to the ground again and did pushups, fifty of them, slowly. His back rippled, and his arms flexed.

He saw me, I know he did, but his focus was total until he finished his pushups and leapt up to his feet. Facing away from me yet again, he squatted down so his butt was nearly touching the floor, and then leapt into the air with a single powerful spring, landing into a squat, and then leaping again.

This time, I didn't bother trying to stop myself from staring. I just owned it. I mean, what else was I supposed to do? The man had an amazing ass, and it was right there in front of me, in action. Flexing, hardening, going taut as he leapt. Good god.

Should I be this faint? Why were my thighs quivering?

Shit. Shit. Shit.

I leaned against the wall and watched as he finished his jump-squats, and went back to the bar and began the entire circuit again—pull-ups, mountain climbers, pushups, jump-squats. He did the circuit through twice more without resting, at which point he was gasping for breath, chest heaving, dripping sweat.

He was nowhere near as bulky as his older three brothers, especially—Bast, Zane, and Bax. They were each monstrously muscled, heavy with muscle, like bulls or bears, whereas Lucian made me think of a wolf, lean and quick and powerful.

I thought, after the end of his fourth round, that he'd be done, but he wasn't. He rested for a full sixty seconds—I counted—and then he dropped to the pushup position, did a pushup, and then jumped his feet underneath him, leapt into the air, dropped back down, did a pushup, and repeated the leap. After doing this twenty times, he collapsed on the floor on his back, gasping and sweating so bad I was honestly worried about him.

I couldn't keep my eyes off him—lying there gasping, each muscle of his abdomen rippled and flexed with each breath.

Finally, once he'd caught his breath, Lucian glanced at me. "Hi."

I blinked hard, and forced my eyes away from those abs. "Uh, hey."

He rolled to his feet in a lithe movement. "Hungry?"

I nodded. "Famished." Following him into the kitchen, I glanced at the clock on the stove: 1:25 p.m. "Holy shit, it's one thirty in the afternoon?"

He nodded as he began pulling out ingredients—some kind of flour, eggs, extracts, oil, baking powder. "Guess you needed sleep."

"Yeah, I guess so." I gestured to the ingredients. "What are you making?"

"Pancakes."

"You have a thing for breakfast food in the afternoon, huh?"

A shrug. "I have a thing for breakfast food in general." He glanced at me as he mixed the ingredients together. "You know how to make pancakes?"

I shook my head. "Um, no. Not really."

He smirked and shook his head as he set a griddle to heating. "What do you know how to make?"

I shifted uncomfortably. "Kraft Mac 'n Cheese?"

He made a disgusted face. "That is *not* food."

I flipped him off. "That shit was my *jam*, growing up, man. I made it every single day after school."

He sighed. "I'll make you *real* mac and cheese for dinner, tonight."

Now that the griddle was heated, he waved me over to the stove and handed me the bowl with the batter. "Ladle out some of this onto the griddle. Just big enough to be about the size of your palm, or less. These are going to be thick so we're making them on the small side. Do six."

I did as he'd instructed, making six small circles of batter on the griddle, the air immediately filling with the scent of frying pancakes. While I did this, he was heating up another pan and adding frozen breakfast sausages, which sizzled as they cooked.

"When do I flip them?" I asked.

"When the batter is mostly solid on top." He glanced at them. "Another minute or two."

I started to panic—what if I messed them up, and ruined them? He didn't seem worried, focusing instead on making coffee and turning the sausages.

"Should I flip them now?" I asked. "They look

like what you said."

He glanced again as he filled the carafe with water and dumped it into the coffee maker. "Yeah, they're good. Go ahead and flip 'em."

I carefully and nervously flipped them one by one, and felt an absurd burst of joy in the sense of completion. Lucian made sure I removed them when they were done, and then I managed to make the second batch all on my own, flipping them when they were a perfect golden brown. By the time the pancakes were done, Lucian had finished the sausages, and the coffee had finished brewing. We sat down together at the table, across from each other, took turns drizzling syrup and spreading around butter, and dug in.

"Damn—these are *amazing*!" I said.

He grinned at me. "You made 'em."

"All I did was cook them, you made the batter."

He finished a bite. "Wanna know the secret?"

I nodded. "Of course."

"The flour I used was a mixture of sprouted oats and almond flour, rather than traditional pancake mix. Makes them denser, and if you get the mix right, they'll be just as fluffy, but twice as filling."

"Well, damn. I had no idea you could even make flour from almonds."

He shrugged. "I'm kind of the health food junkie

of the family. Bax eats pretty healthy too, being an athlete and all." He eyed me, hesitating. "How is it you don't know how cook? I know I said I wouldn't ask questions, but I'm super curious about this one."

I ate in silence, not answering right away. I took a sip of coffee, breathed a deep sigh, and set my fork down.

"I can make a hell of a latte," I said. "I just never learned how to cook."

"You worked in a coffee shop?"

I shrugged, tilting my hand side to side. "Yes and no."

He frowned at me. "You'll have to clarify that one."

"It's complicated."

He sighed as he finished his pancakes and took two more. "Seems like an innocuous enough of a question."

"You'd think, but it's not."

"You really won't tell me a damn thing about yourself, will you? I mean, not the real stuff."

"I told you things last night that I've never told anyone. Seemed pretty real to me." I felt anger rising, my quick-burning temper flaring.

"I know, I know—I'm sorry." He held up his hands to forestall my impending outburst. "I just—it's just that you dodge the weirdest shit."

"My parents owned a cafe—a coffee shop and a bookstore. Mom shelved the books, Dad worked the espresso machine, and they took turns with the register. They were the only two employees, so they worked all day every day. I'd come home from school, do my homework, make a snack, and eventually head over to the cafe." I let out a shaky breath. "As I got older, I helped out after school. Dad taught me to how to make lattes and cappuccinos and mochas and whatever, and I'd shelve the books and help with inventory, stuff like that. I'd stay with them until they closed at nine, and then we'd all go to dinner at this little mom-and-pop diner down the street, owned by friends of my parents'. Mom didn't cook, and neither did Dad—although Dad would make us eggs or pancakes on Sunday mornings, the only day they opened late. I never learned, though. Dad would make them before I woke up, and he'd come in and get me up— waking up to breakfast on Sunday mornings was...it was magical."

Lucian just stared at me, his gaze understanding, compassionate. "That sounds awesome."

I nodded. "It was. It really was. But we were open from nine to nine six days a week, and from noon to seven on Sundays, which meant Mom and Dad never had time for home-cooked meals. I'd figure out my own breakfast, eat lunch at school, and dinner with them after work, at the diner. Breakfast on Sunday mornings, and then dinner again. I usually stayed home and caught up on homework or went to Maria's for the afternoon on Sunday. But…cooking just wasn't part of our life."

"I grew up on bar food. Burgers, chicken tenders, fries, shit like that. When I was little, Mom would cook for us, but like I said before, she died when I was nine, and food for our family that wasn't grilled or deep fried disappeared when she passed away."

"Is that why you like healthy food?"

He nodded. "Partially. I got in shape and cleaned up my diet while I was overseas, and when I came back, I just had no interest in going back to living off bar food. I worked as a cook on several boats, so I learned how to make a lot of different stuff, and I just tweaked the ingredients to make them healthier."

I couldn't help the question. "How did your mom die?"

His eyes searched mine. I knew we're both aware of the hypocrisy of my question—I asked him a question I wouldn't answer myself.

"Brain cancer," he said, eventually. "It was fast. She was fine and healthy, and then one day she had a headache that wouldn't go away, and then she came home from the doctor's office, crying, and then, just a couple months later, she was gone."

"God, that's awful. I'm sorry."

He toyed with his fork, his eyes downcast rather than on me. "It was...pretty gnarly." He slugged back coffee, which was still scorching hot, but he didn't seem to notice. "She went from beautiful and healthy to frail and skeletal in a matter of weeks. There wasn't a damn thing anyone could do. The tumor was too big to cut out, and chemo and radiation wouldn't have saved her, only prolonged the inevitable, so she refused treatment. Which means we just...sat in a hospital room and waited for her to die."

The pain in his voice was very carefully modulated, hidden behind words carefully enunciated, his tone too calm. As an expert in that same tactic, I saw through it.

"Lucian, I'm sorry."

He stood up abruptly. "You'd think after eleven years that I'd be less affected by it."

He walked back toward his bedroom, and I was torn between following him and letting him go.

But my legs didn't seem to be conflicted at all, because I found myself following him. He was in his room, removing clothing from the drawers under his bed. He stood up and turned around, finding me standing in the doorway, watching him.

"Lucian, I—"

"In case you're wondering, Dad died of a heart

attack," he interrupted. "But don't worry, I won't ask about your parents."

He twisted to slip past me, and I breathed in his sharp scent, tensing as his body brushed up against mine. I felt his chest against my breasts, and his breath on my face, and his hips and his thighs against mine, and every muscle in my body froze, tensing. I stopped breathing. My heart hammered in my chest.

His eyes met mine for a split second as he slid past me, and then he was gone, into the bathroom.

And then I found myself chasing him yet again, emotions rampaging through me—anger, confusion, desire. I shoved the bathroom door open without thinking, without hesitating. He was naked, the water running, and just about to step in. When I slammed the door open and entered, he turned around to confront me.

"The fuck, Joss?" His voice was surprised and not a little angry.

Ohhhh shit. Oh Jesus. God, he was perfect. I couldn't look away. Every muscle was defined, not an ounce of fat anywhere on his body. All lean, hard muscle and masculine angles and planes. And then... my eyes wandered downward.

To say I blushed wouldn't be doing the fire on my cheeks due justice.

I didn't have a lot of experience with male

anatomy, but…oh my god. HUGE. Long and thick and pink, hanging down his thigh, curled to the right ever so slightly, with a thatch of dark pubic hair in a spray around the base. I swallowed hard, trying like hell to tear my gaze away, to leave, to act, to say something, anything.

"Get a good look?" Lucian snapped.

His voice shook me out of my trance, and I spun around, covering my face with both hands. "I'm—I'm sorry. I'm sorry." I just—" I had no good way to finish that, so I didn't, instead took a deep breath and started over. "I wasn't thinking. I apologize."

"Turn around." His voice was quiet, but firm. Not angry, anymore.

I shook my head. "Um, no. Thanks."

"I'm covered, Joss." His voice was amused, now.

I turned around, and he had a towel around his waist, the water still running, the curtain open.

He gestured at me. "You barged in here like you had a hair up your ass. Might as well say what you were gonna say."

I shook my head. "Doesn't matter."

"Joss."

"No."

"*Joss.*"

I took an aggressive step forward. "They were killed in a car accident, okay?" I shouted the words, the first time I'd spoken of it since it happened, and then I continued more quietly, once the initial outburst was out of me. "We were on vacation in Yarmouth, Nova Scotia, three years ago. I was seventeen. They wanted to go hiking the Evangeline Trail, and I didn't want to. I was on my period and had horrible cramps, and hiking sounded like complete hell, so I stayed at our hotel. They were driving to the trailhead. It was eleven o'clock in the morning. We'd just had breakfast together. An older guy was driving the opposite direction, had a stroke, and crossed the centerline. Hit my parents head-on. All three of them died instantly, although I think the old guy was already dead from the stroke."

"Shit." He turned off the water and then stepped toward me, mere inches between us, and his hands came to rest on my upper arms. "Joss, I'm sorry."

I kept going, because now I had to get it out. "The cops found me at the hotel. I was in my pajamas watching a comedy special on my iPad. I'd ordered dessert from room service, and I'd...I'd just pigged out. I was eating Key lime pie when they knocked on the door. I answered it, and I saw them standing there, and I knew. I just...I *knew*. I fell to the floor crying before they'd even said a word. 'Miss Mackenzie, your parents have been killed in a head-on collision. I'm so sorry. Can you come with us, please?'" I choked as I repeated the words I won't ever forget, in the same flat, emotionless, robotic tone they'd been spoken to me. "He was a kid, the guy who delivered the news. He looked scared. Probably his first time doing a notification call, or whatever it's called when you have to tell someone their family is dead."

I blinked away tears, swiped at them angrily, because I don't cry. I *don't* cry.

I sucked in a breath, and shook my head, and forced them away. I kept going. "My dad was from Jamaica, and his family was all still there, but we never saw them. He left when he was nineteen and never went back. I never met any of them." I flipped up the end of one of my dreads. "My dad was black. Where the name Mackenzie came from, I never knew. It was his legal name, I know that much, because it was on his driver's license. I don't know. Maybe he picked it at random to distance himself from his family...that's what I've always assumed. Mom was from upstate New York, where I grew up. We lived less than half an hour from my grandparents, and I was pretty close to them as a kid, but they died when I was young. Which left Mom's brother, Uncle Derek, as my only family, and he was—or still is, I guess—the quintessential permanent bachelor uncle. Nice guy, loved hanging out with him on the holidays, but...there was no way he was going to take me in. Not a seventeen-year-old girl."

"Jesus, Joss."

I let Lucian hold my arms, because the feel of his hands on me wasn't a bad thing; it grounded me, reminded me that I wasn't there anymore.

"I identified them. And then they brought me into a room with some Canadian government official, and someone from the US government, since we were on vacation in Canada. They were discussing what to do with me. Deciding my fate, as if I wasn't there and didn't get a fucking vote. Just doing their jobs, I know that now, but then? I was still in shock. But I'd physically *seen* Mom and Dad's dead bodies, so it had been hammered home that they were dead, they were gone. That I was alone. Uncle Derek never even crossed my mind as an option, I just remember sitting there listening to them talk about foster care and the difficulty in finding a family to take me, given my age. They left, at some point, I don't know why. To discuss my fate in private, maybe. And I was like, no, fuck no, I'm not going into foster care. Fuck that. I knew a kid in my high school who was a foster, and...his stories did *not* inspire confidence, to say the least." I closed my eyes, inhaled, held it, and let it out slowly. "So...I left. I just walked out of the police station, walked back to the hotel, packed some shit in my backpack, and left. I didn't think about it, I just knew I wasn't going to sit around while some random government dudes decided what happened to me. So I just...I started walking, and I never stopped. Otherwise, I would've just... I would have laid down under a bridge somewhere and just...stopped."

"I'm glad you kept going."

I finally met his eyes. "I didn't have a plan. A goal. Nothing. I just...I walked because I didn't know what else to do. I should've tried to get back to the States; I realize that now, but I just...I wasn't thinking. I followed the road away from Yarmouth and walked for...I don't even know long. Hours. All the way to the next village on the coast, don't remember its name. I needed to get away, as far away as possible and as soon as possible—away from the accident, away from the death of my parents—it wasn't a logical decision to run, it was an emotional one. So I bought a bus ticket. And then another bus ticket, and another, and somehow, almost a full day later, ended up in Québec. I don't even know how I got there. There were a lot of transfers, and I was operating on autopilot or something. I had a lot of cash, since Mom and Dad had left their cash behind when they left to go hiking, and I'd taken it. But that bus trip to Québec cost me a lot of money, and I realized I couldn't keep taking buses everywhere, especially if I didn't have a plan. I just knew I needed to get away. So I got to Québec, and just kept walking west."

"Just because to get as far away from everything as possible?" Lucian said, his voice gentle.

I nodded without looking at him. "Yeah, pretty much."

"And now?"

Something in his voice made me look up, and the mocha of his eyes was warm and kind and gentle and inquisitive and hypnotic. Once I met his gaze, I couldn't look away. He was tall, so much taller than me that I had to tilt my head up to meet his eyes. His chest was bare, and he was clad in only a thin towel cinched around his waist. A mental image of his... um...manhood...flashed through my mind, and I blushed again. Maybe he noticed, maybe he didn't— my skin is dark enough it can be hard to tell when I'm blushing.

"And now...what?" I swallowed hard.

"Now that you're here, what are you going to do? You're as far west as you can go, and you're back in the States. So...now what?"

Was his face closer than it had been? Were our bodies pressed closer together? Why was my pulse going so haywire? What was happening to me? I don't react this way to anyone, about anything. Ever. Even when I had that crazy crush on Nick Wellesley in tenth grade I wasn't affected by him like this, and

we got to what Maria called "second base" before I
realized Nick was dating three other girls at the same
time as me.

Wait. He'd asked me a question. What was the
question?

His chest was hard and soft and the same time—
the skin was soft and warm, but the muscle underneath was hard as a rock. Wait…why did I know that?
Oh, because my palms were both resting on his chest.
And his face was closer to mine because either he was
leaning down, or because…oh—or because I was up
on my tiptoes.

A tableau, then: his eyes on mine, his hands sliding from my arms down to my waist, my fingertips
digging into his pecs, just above his nipples.

And then he huffed gently, a sound of frustration, or relief, or of him giving in to something he'd
been fighting, I wasn't sure which. A huff, and then
his mouth was slanting across mine, and his lips were
warm and damp and soft and gentle, and my heart was
crashing in my chest, and the feel of his body against
mine made me dizzy, and his mouth was intoxicating.
His kiss was intoxicating. This wasn't Nick, an eager
but clumsy boy—this was a man, and *god*, could he
kiss. It swept me away, and I lost myself in it. I heard a
soft whimper, a breathy sound from my throat.

Yes, it was a kiss so potent it literally made me

whimper involuntarily.

And yet, that sound, the whimper, it snapped me out of the hypnosis his kiss had put me in.

I stumbled backward, fingers on my lips. "Lucian, I—"

"You are so damn beautiful, Joss." His voice sounded awed.

I blinked hard, my throat closing, heart still hammering in my chest so hard it hurt, my hands shaking, lungs finally sucking in a full breath. "I can't—we—I… shit."

I turned and ran into his bedroom and closed the door. I collapsed on the bed, my mind spiraling, emotions running on high-octane, adrenaline crashing through me.

He kissed me.

I kissed him.

Which was it? Does it matter?

That kiss was the most amazing experience ever. It felt as if, for a few incredible moments, all the worry and stress I had been feeling was lifted from my shoulders, and I felt light and free. Amazing.

Too amazing.

I want to kiss him again. I want to kiss him again so badly I have to grip the duvet under my hands to keep from getting up and crashing in on his shower again.

I fell backward on the bed, laughing into my hands, hysterical.

I saw his penis…and it was beautiful. I want to see it again. I want to touch it. I want his hands on me.

Shit, shit, shit, this was bad.

I can't feel this way about Lucian. He's too much like me, and yet so different. His family is so…*much*. Overwhelming and amazing and fun and welcoming.

I belonged. For a few minutes there, I had known what it felt like to be part of a family. More than just that, but part of…something big and complicated and messy. Even with Mom and Dad, it had been neat and orderly and lonely. Dinner was always a quiet affair. I spent a lot of time alone, or with my best friend Maria, before we argued over that idiot Tim Ennis. After that, my life was even more lonely. And then, after Mom and Dad died, I was just…alone all the time.

So to be surrounded by all those people, who all knew each other and loved each other, making fun and teasing and joking, laughing, drinking together, just…being together…that was something I would never forget.

But the kiss, though.

Holy shit.

My thighs clenched together involuntarily at the memory of his mouth on mine, and the possessive way his hands had moved to encircle my waist.

I wanted more. Desperately, I wanted more.

But this was dangerous territory. If I wasn't careful, this could get out of hand very quickly, and I don't think I could handle anything else going wrong in my life. I can't let myself have him. I can't let myself *want* him. Because there's another problem, another secret I'm not ready or willing to reveal, to him or to anyone.

But that doesn't stop me from being totally under his spell. I kept seeing his eyes as he closed his for the kiss, kept feeling his lips on mine, his strong hands on my waist, kept seeing that long, thick organ dangling between his thighs.

Need was an overwhelming drive inside me, and I only knew one way of alleviating the pressure... something I rarely had the privacy or opportunity to indulge in...

I shouldn't.

God, I shouldn't.

But my body was going crazy, my mind whirling. My nipples were hard, my thighs quaking. Heat was pooling. It wouldn't take much, and it had been so long...

FIVE

Lucian

I WENT THROUGH THE MOTIONS OF SHOWERING ON autopilot, but my mind was still stuck on the kiss. How silky her lips had felt, how soft her waist felt in my hands. The way her breasts had crushed against my chest as she lifted up on her tiptoes to kiss me. Her fingers on my chest, short, rounded fingernails digging into my skin.

Just a kiss, but holy shit—what a kiss.

I twisted off the water, but didn't get out of the shower right away. I couldn't. How could I leave the bathroom like this? I had a hard-on so vicious it hurt.

Yet, she was only mere feet away, in my room. Thinking about me? About our kiss? She hadn't been unaffected by it—I heard that moan.

I stood in the shower, back against the cold wet tile wall, and fisted my cock. Unbidden, an image of Joss filled my mind—the way she'd looked in that brief glimpse I'd gotten of her, naked and soaking wet. A line from a Sam Hunt song popped into my head—*hips like honey, so thick and so sweet.* Yeah, exactly. Her hips were wide, curving down to strong thighs. Narrower in the waist, and then, god, her breasts. My cock throbbed—her breasts were perfect. Heavy, big and round and teardrop shaped, her lush skin a few shades darker than caramel, wide dark areolae and even darker nipples.

Fuck, fuck, fuck—no.

I'm not jerking off to her. I'll never be able to look at her in the eyes if I do that.

I released myself and breathed forcefully for a few seconds, and then roughly jerked on my clothing; even with tight boxer-briefs and jeans, it was obvious I had a hard-on, but I wasn't hiding in the damn bathroom. I exited, but then cursed when I realized my stupid hairbrush was in my room—living with so many people for so long had taught me to keep all of my belongings confined to my personal space.

One thing I wasn't used to was sharing my space, so I didn't think twice about going into my room, forgetting momentarily that Joss was in there.

I twisted the knob and pushed the door open, took two steps in before I happened to glance at the bed.

And stopped, literally, midstep. My jaw dropped, and any chance I had of getting rid of the hard-on was erased instantly.

Joss was on my bed, one hand shoved under the waistband of the yoga pants, moving vigorously. She had the hoodie shoved up, baring her breasts, and she had two fingers pincered around a nipple, rolling it. Her hips were gyrating, and she was biting her lip to muffle the moans she was making…which had disguised the sound of my entry.

She hadn't noticed me.

Her eyes were closed, a rictus of ecstasy turning her beautiful face into a mask of erotic release as she fingered herself.

Shit, I should leave.

But I was paralyzed in place by the image of her, like that—thrashing, hips flying, moaning, breasts bared, pinching her own nipple.

I forced my eyes closed, backing up a step. Another. My shoulder blades hit the doorpost, and I couldn't keep my eyes closed anymore.

God, I was a piece of shit, and I knew it, but I couldn't look away.

Right then, as my eyes flew open, Joss came.

Her moan flew out past her teeth, and she tensed, hips flexed upward, fingers moving inside her pants, and then she was undulating crazily against her fingers and groaning past clenched teeth. Flopping back down to the bed, she gasped breathlessly, withdrawing her hand and lowering the hem of the hoodie.

Her eyes flicked open and immediately fixed on me. "You—you saw."

I'm never speechless; I never stumble on my words...except right then. "I—uh. My hairbrush, and you were...um."

I squeezed my eyes shut and breathed slowly, counting to ten; this usually calmed me, centered me, but in that moment, all it did was let visions of an orgasming Joss fill my libido-flooded mind.

"I'm sorry, Joss. I should've left—I shouldn't have watched. But I—shit. I'm sorry." I spun around on my heel and left, inadvertently slamming the door behind me.

I made it down to the studio and slumped onto the couch they keep there. I put my head in my hands, trying to get myself under control. My erection throbbed, aching painfully. There was no hope for control, no hope of getting it to go away—erotic visions of Joss danced in my skull, teasing me.

"FUCK!" I shot to my feet, pacing away, fruitlessly adjusting myself in an attempt to alleviate the aching pressure behind my zipper.

I heard a step, stopped in my tracks and turned to find Joss in the stairwell, watching me through the open door, the hood drawn up over her dreadlocks. "Lucian?"

I jerked my hand away from my cock as if burned, shoved my hands in my back pockets. "Hey."

She took a step toward me. "Hey. So, about what you just saw—"

I held up my hands to stop her. "Joss, I am *so* sorry I walked in on you, more so for not walking back out like I should've." I wiped my face and turned away. "I'm a piece of shit for watching you like that."

"No," she murmured. "Don't say that. You're not."

I laughed bitterly. "I kind of am. That was a dick move."

"We're both guilty of staring longer than we should have, then. So let's call it even."

I shook my head. "Not quite. Slightly different situations. You caught me getting into the shower, I caught you…" I trailed off.

"Masturbating."

"Yeah."

She took a step closer to me. "What's going on, Lucian? Between us, I mean. What is this?"

I let out a breath. "No fucking clue."

She shoved her hands into the pouch pocket of the hoodie. "But you feel it, too."

I nodded. "Yeah."

She stared up at me. "You asked, before, what I was going to do now." She ducked her head, dropping her eyes to her bare feet. "When I was passing through Winnipeg, I happened to wander into this little bookstore. It was cold, and I was looking for somewhere to sleep for the night, and was just kind of killing time. This bookstore was just this tiny little place, maybe half a dozen shelves, mostly used sci-fi, westerns, and mystery paperbacks. The owner was this middle-aged black guy, and he had a tiny espresso machine in the back, and if you asked, he'd make you a latte or Americano or whatever. And it just...I don't know. I felt them there. My mom and dad, I mean. I sat on the floor between two shelves and cried because I missed them so much. And the owner helped me to a chair and made me coffee and got me talking about Mom and Dad, how they owned a little place like his, and how I missed them so much. And he... he said something so simple and so profound it just... changed me. 'So open your own place.' Like it was the most obvious thing in the world."

"That's what you're doing next?"

She nodded. "That's my dream. I sat in that little bookstore, sipping coffee out of a chipped mug, the smell of books everywhere, and I had this vision of opening a place like Mom and Dad owned. Nothing big, nothing fancy. Local books, bestsellers, whatever I like. A nice espresso machine, maybe some baked goods. Somewhere you can go and sit and sip and read, where students can do homework and writers can write and locals congregate. That's what Mom and Dad's place was, and I had this vision of me, in my own place like that."

"What's stopping you?"

She shook her head, sniffling, dreadlocks moving in serpentine waves. "I don't know. Everything. Life. Being homeless. Being broke. Not having a high school diploma. Where do I even start? I don't know. But that's my dream, and I'll get there someday. For Mom and Dad."

"What would you call it?"

She smiled, hesitating over her answer. "I would call it home."

"I meant—"

She looked away with a shrug. "I know. And I have no idea—I haven't thought about it."

I frowned at her. "Bullshit."

She fiddled with a dreadlock, and then glanced at me. "The Garden."

I laughed. "Really?"

She sniffled again. "Mom and Dad fought over

the name for months when they opened their place, and that's what Dad wanted to call it. Mom thought it was silly, and insisted on the more pedestrian Pete's Cafe, which Dad always hated. But Mom insisted, and Dad could never tell her no, so that's what they called it. But Dad always told me one day he'd get her to change it to The Garden."

"Why that?"

"He said it was because a bookstore is really a garden of sorts. Each book is a seed, for ideas and thoughts and dreams, and I always thought it sounded like a cool, unique, even romantic name for a bookstore."

"I like it."

"Really? You don't think it's stupid?"

I shook my head. "No, not at all."

She looked up at me again, and her gaze was hesitant. "About the kiss…" She shifted her feet, shoved her hands in the hoodie pocket again. "I'm not sure I'm ready for that."

I felt the sting of rejection, even though I knew it was stupid—she was a girl with a dream, a wanderer, and I knew better than anyone that when she was ready to leave, there would be no stopping her, certainly not me, or a kiss, or even the hint of attraction, or whatever it was between us.

"Ready for what?" I stepped toward her. "It was

just a kiss."

Her gaze dropped down to my zipper; my erection was subsiding, but it was still very much obvious that I was, or at least had been, aroused as hell. "Not *just* a kiss."

I passed a hand through my damp hair. "Joss, come on. It doesn't have to be a big deal."

"We kissed, and then you caught me masturbating because of it, and unless I'm mistaken, you either did or wanted to do the same thing."

"I didn't," I admitted. "It didn't feel...I don't know."

"But I did." She laughed bitterly. "Now I feel even more like shit."

"Joss—Jesus. It's not like that. I'm sorry I walked in on you...I should have realized you'd be in there and I should've knocked."

"That's not what I'm pissed off about, you idiot!" She barked another bitter laugh and turned away, pacing the room. "We had this kiss, this moment, and yeah, it was crazy hot—and then you caught me jilling off while thinking about you, and that fucking kiss. And now you tell me you *didn't* jack off when clearly the kiss was just as hot for you, because that goddamn python in your pants makes it pretty damn obvious. But you didn't jack off because it didn't feel right or whatever, and I did because I'm fucking *weak*."

"Joss, it's not like that. It's not a big deal. You're allowed to do whatever you want and you don't need to give me or anyone explanations." I moved toward her, standing behind her; she was facing away, hands shoved in the pouch pocket, hood still up.

She must have felt my presence, because she took a step forward, out of reach. "Just...let it go."

I sighed. "Fine."

She turned around. "Lucian, I don't want you to think—"

I held up a hand. "You said let it go, so fine, let's just let it go."

A long, tense moment of silence between us.

"Can we go to the other place, where the bar is?" Joss asked, after a while.

"That stressed out you need a drink, huh?"

She glared at me. "That's not what I—"

I waved a hand to stop her. "I was kidding. Let's get shoes and coats and go."

"I don't have shoes here, all my wet stuff is in the other apartment."

"You can shove your feet in a pair of my boots. They'll be big but it'll work for the short distance we have to go."

These exchanges were tense and uncomfortable, each of us feeling out of sorts.

I found her a pair of thick wool socks, which

came up to her knees, and an extra pair of snow boots her feet swam in, but between that and an extra puffy coat I found in a closet, she was fine to make the short trek down the sidewalk. Of course, that didn't take into account the insane amount of snow we'd gotten—something like three feet in less than seventy-two hours. The city was doing their best to keep the streets and sidewalks clear as it fell, but we never got this amount of snow, so they didn't have the infrastructure necessary to keep up. Which meant snow had blown in from the water and was piling up against the buildings in drifts taller than me, in some places—and snow was still flying thick and hard in a blinding, stinging wall of white. We left through the front door of the studio, and I had to shove the door hard to clear snow away enough to let us out, and then we immediately sank into snow up to our thighs, and had climb out over the drifts and into the street where the snow was *only* up to our knees.

Joss clung to my arm and put her mouth to my ear. "This is crazy!" she shouted, and the wind even then tried to snatch her words away. "Will we even find the bar in this shit?"

I pulled Joss close and shouted in her ear. "Stay close! Hold on to me!"

She clutched the back of my coat and followed in my footsteps as I stomped and slogged through the knee-deep snow, clearing a bit of a path for her. It was brutally difficult, and I was out of breath by the time I caught a glimpse of the front door of the bar. I angled us onto the sidewalk, and caught a shovelful of snow in the face, thrown by one of my brothers. It was Bast, decked out from head to toe in layers of clothing, a scarf around his mouth and nose, a pair of goggles on his eyes, a shovel in his hands as he dug out the door.

He saw us coming and stuck the shovel into the snowbank, hauled open the door, and we both ushered Joss in before us.

I leaned close to Bast. "What the fuck are you doing?"

He gestured at the snow with his mittened hands. "Shoveling snow, dumbshit. What's it look like?"

"I know, but why?"

"Because if I don't keep it at least somewhat clear, we'll get trapped in, if this bullshit keeps up." He gestured up at the second-story window. "You wanna jump out from there and dig us out when it stops snowing?"

"Good point."

"No shit."

I left him to it and went inside. It was weird, seeing the bar empty and dark like this in the middle of the day, all the chairs up on the tables, only the hanging lights over the bar turned on. Joss was standing just inside the doorway, stomping snow off her feet and shaking it off her arms.

I gestured at the empty room. "Well, we're here. Now what?"

She shrugged. "Hang out upstairs with whoever's here?"

I shook my head. "So you just don't want to be alone with me."

Joss's shoulders slumped, and she turned to look up at me. Her golden-brown eyes were soft, hesitant. "Lucian, that's not—I mean, it is, but not how you're taking it."

"Then enlighten me, because I'm confused."

"I'm not staying, Lucian. I'm not getting into a relationship, or joining your crazy but amazing family." She shook her head and shrugged, hands lifting, palms up. "I can't get into anything. I just *can't*. Not with you, or anyone. Not now, and maybe not ever."

I backed away from her, away from her scent, from those eyes, from the temptation her lips presented. "Fine. I get it."

"Lucian…"

I shook my head. "Don't. I get it, I really do." I gestured at the stairs. "Go hang out."

"What are you going to do?"

I shrugged. "I dunno. Help Bast shovel, probably."

"Lucian, I don't want you to be—"

"I'm not anything. I'm fine." I tugged the hood of my coat up over my head and exited the bar before I said or did anything else.

I didn't have a hat or gloves or anything, but I didn't care. I just needed to be away from Joss and her eyes and those words, and my own stupid hurt feelings.

Bast saw me come out and rested on the end of his shovel. "Okay, Luce?"

I nodded. "Fine. Let me see the shovel."

He held it out to me. "Wanna take over? This shit is hard-ass work, man."

I took the shovel. "Yeah, I'll go to work on it." I made a gimme gesture with my hand. "Let me have your hat and gloves and shit."

Bast ripped the hat, goggles, and gloves off and handed them to me. They were damp with his sweat and from the snow, but I didn't care. My hair was still damp and my ears were cold and my fingers were stinging. But it was better than having to look at Joss and act like I didn't care that she'd just rejected me. I tugged the cold-weather gear on and attacked the snow with all the hurt and anger I had.

As I shoveled, I tried to keep my mind off of Joss, but it was a losing game. Every second or third shovelful of snow, she kept arising in my mind—naked, her lush dark skin wet; standing in the bathroom doorway, her eyes raking me, tongue sliding hungrily across her lower lip; on my bed, spine arched, heavy breasts swaying as she thrashed, her fingers between her thighs as she brought herself to orgasm.

"Fuck!" I shouted, frustrated, aroused, and angry.

I threw the shovel down and collapsed back against the door of the bar, gasping breathlessly. I glanced at my handiwork and discovered that in my angst I'd gone a little overboard, shoveling out into the street rather than just around the doorway, clearing a huge swath of sidewalk.

I went back inside, then, panting, sweating, heart hammering, fighting yet another hard-on I wouldn't do anything about.

I found Joss upstairs on the couch in front of the TV, a PS4 controller in her hands, tongue protruding from the corner of her mouth as she played the newest *Call of Duty* with Canaan, Corin, and Xavier. Bast, Bax, and Brock were in the kitchen talking, and I could hear the other women somewhere, chatting.

Joss was having fun, it looked like, ducking her head as shots whipped past her on-screen avatar's head, moving the controller around as if that would move her character faster, shrieking in triumph when she scored a kill against Corin.

"Goddamn, Joss!" Corin crowed. "You're good at

this shit. Sure you haven't played recently?"

Joss didn't take her eyes off the game. "Nope. First video game I've played in...oh god, five or six years? My ex-best friend Maria's younger brother had one of these games, and we used to play with him once in a while, but like I said, that was a long time ago."

Tate was sitting at the island, her Nikon plugged into a laptop as she sorted through photos; she glanced at Joss quizzically. "*Ex*-best friend? What happened there?"

I noticed Joss's hesitation, but I don't think anyone else did; it was a subtle thing, just a hunching of her shoulders, a tightening of her jaw. "Um...nothing too interesting. There was a boy we both liked, and we were both immature teenagers. We fought over his stupid ass—who liked him most, and who would get to date him, blah blah blah. It got so out of hand that we stopped talking, and never really figured out a way to get over it."

Tate made a sympathetic noise. "So who got the guy, after all that?"

Joss snickered self-deprecatingly. "Neither of us, which is the truly shitty part."

"Ohmygod!" Tate exclaimed. "You and your best friend broke up over a guy neither of you ended up even dating?"

Joss nodded. "Yep," she said, and then cursed good-naturedly as Xavier sniped her from across the map.

"Wow. That sucks, hardcore."

Joss shrugged. "Yeah, it does. But…it's old news so, whatever, at this point."

Joss scored two kills in a row, nailing Xavier and Canaan with a single grenade. She stood up, controller held over her head, cackling. "What now, bitches!"

Corin glanced at me. "Luce, buddy, your girlfriend is kicking our asses at our own game, man."

"Yeah, well…you guys suck at that game anyway." I grabbed a stool at the island beside Tate and watched her scroll through black-and-white photos of various locations throughout Ketchikan. "Those are awesome, Tate. You're really talented."

She smiled at me and turned the laptop so I could get a better look, and clicked to a different window to show me a photo she was editing in Photoshop. "I've been experimenting with retouching black-and-white photos with a single element of a bold color. It's nothing groundbreaking, obviously, but it's a lot of fun and really compelling."

The photo she was working on was of a big, bearded man kneeling down on the sidewalk, tugging a winter hat onto his daughter's head, while the daughter laughed and reached up to tug on her dad's beard. The only element of color was the hat, which Tate had turned to a vibrant royal purple, drawing the eye to the little girl's head, and the grin on her face. It was an incredible photo, and I found a little knot of jealousy forming inside me.

"I got the father to sign a release for the photo, so I'm gonna sell this at Eva's studio."

I breathed out between pursed lips. "That's... a *really* incredible piece, Tate."

She met my gaze. "You think so?"

I nodded. "It's amazing. For real."

Her grin brightened even further. "Thanks, Luce. That means a lot."

I squirmed inside, hating the jealousy I felt for her obvious talent. I'd never found my *thing*, aside from traveling. From sports to flying to athletics, my brothers all seemed to be happy with their career choices, but me? Nothing.

I had gone to the docks at every opportunity just to escape the house, the bar, and the enormous shadows cast by my brothers, and had found a measure of peace and quiet there, with the water lapping against hulls, ropes clinking against masts, the cry of the gulls and the honking of cruise ship horns. Dad's friend Clint had taken to me, for some reason, and let me spend my every free moment on his boat, and he never seemed to get tired of my questions and my presence. I loved the sea and I loved traveling, but was that a skill or a talent? Not really either. It wasn't something I could translate into a passion, or a career, unless I wanted to buy a boat and become a fisherman. But I don't love the fishing; I just love boats and the water, the freedom and quiet of coursing across the waves, far from anything.

Tate, Aerie, Eva, Mara, Claire, Dru, they all have their things.

Even Joss has something she's interested in.

I clamped down on the unsettling disquiet running through my brain. I stood up and left Tate to editing her photographs, and everyone else to their conversations.

Where did I fit in?

I slipped back downstairs to the bar, unnoticed, and sat alone at the bar, in the dark, nursing a glass of whiskey and my private inner turmoil.

SIX

Joss

I DON'T EVEN KNOW HOW LONG I SAT ON THAT COUCH, playing that stupid but fun video game. It was so dumb, but so fun. Relaxing. Easy. I wasn't in a shelter or a bus station, or on a bench in a park, or in an alley trying to rest while keeping one eye open. I was just… hanging out with people who seemed ready and willing to simply accept me. Bring me into the fold.

I want this.

I want this kind of atmosphere all the time, and these people around me. A sense of home. A sense of family, a sense of belonging.

But I don't. I don't belong here, and I don't belong with them. This was just an accident, a situation brought on by a freak storm. I'm just biding my time here.

And Lucian?

I don't even know what to think about him. Every time my mind goes there, I shy away from it, unable to think about him, or how he made me feel.

It's too raw, too real, too scary. Too much.

It's not meant for me. I don't know what to do with it, with him, with my feelings for him, which are developing so fast. These thoughts are so intense and I'm not in the least prepared for any of it. Meeting someone like Luce was the last thing on my mind when I arrived here in Ketchikan in the middle of a blizzard.

I'd tapped out of the game and Bax had taken over for me, so now I was sitting on the couch sandwiched between Bax's enormous, hard-as-marble bulk and Corin's long, lean frame. The boys were all shouting insults at each other as they killed or died in the game, talking smack and jostling each other. In the bedroom, down the hall, the girls were shouting strings of profanity at each other and then cackling—playing Cards Against Humanity, it sounded like, with the baby, Jax, providing baby babble commentary at the top of his little lungs. Brock, Zane, and Bast were in the kitchen where Brock was refereeing an arm-wrestling contest between the other two, where again, there was a lot of shouting and cursing and good-natured smack-talking.

The noise in the apartment was deafening and overwhelming.

My emotions were raging, my heart was hammering, my hands were shaking, and I couldn't take it anymore.

Where was Lucian?

I couldn't see him—my initial instinct was to find Lucian and let him calm me down, and somehow, I knew he would. This instinctual need for and trust of Lucian only added jet fuel to the flames of my anxiety.

I shot to my feet, unearthing myself from the pile of elbowing, shouting Badd males, and made my way around the couch and toward the hallway, trying to remain at least visibly calm while I sought somewhere to catch my breath and get a grip on myself. There was a bedroom door open across the hallway from the room the other women were in—it looked vacant, the bed neatly made with a blue down comforter and a couple of pillows. Judging by the orientation, I guessed it would overlook the city, but I could see nothing through the window except a wall of howling, blowing, drifting white snow. It was nominally quieter in here, so I sat down on the bed, threw back my hood, and cradled my head in my hands, trying to catch my breath and calm my nerves.

I left the door open; through the doorway and across the hall to the other bedroom, I had a direct line of sight to Dru, sitting cross-legged on her bed, sideways, her back to the wall, a pair of black and white cards in her hands, with Jax on her lap wiggling and shouting nonsense and trying to grab either the cards or Dru's fiery red hair, or both at the same time. Dru glanced at me, and then held my gaze. Her grin turned to a carefully blank expression, and she played her last two cards before handing Jax over to someone else and sliding off the bed.

She crossed the hall and hesitated in the doorway, one hand on the doorpost. "Hey. Care for some company?"

I didn't, really, since I'd come in here to be alone, but I didn't say that. "Sure."

She swung the door closed all but a few inches and sat on the bed beside me. "Overwhelmed?"

I nodded. "Yeah, a bit."

She laughed. "Our tribe is…a lot. Especially if you come from a small environment."

I focused on slow, deep breaths. "You come from a small family?"

Dru nodded. "Yeah. My mom left Dad and me when I was eleven, and he raised me by himself. But he was a cop—he's retired now—so he was gone… pretty much all the time. I was a pissed-off and confused eleven-year-old who took care of myself most of the time."

"That's rough," I said.

She shrugged. "It was just Dad and I after that. He never dated again, and I never trusted again, so I was alone a lot. I mean, I had friends, but no one I really trusted down deep."

I searched her open, kind green eyes. "You married Bast, though."

She nodded, smiling. "He's the first person I ever really let in. And let me tell you, it's been a hell of an adjustment, going from living on my own, holding my own counsel, no real friends to…" she waved at the apartment, "to this. Of course, I was the first to date one of these big, rough, gorgeous hunks of Alaskan beefcake, so, except for me, there was literally zero estrogen around here until Zane snagged Mara."

"Do you trust her?"

"I do now. I didn't at first. I mean, we were friends, sort of, but more out of necessity than anything else, being the only two women in a family of eight men all living under two roofs and working in the same bar. We were thrown together, in a way. Thank god we got along right away, but did I trust her right away? No, of course not. I was still working on really, truly trusting Sebastian. That shit takes time, you know?"

I picked at the edge of the duvet cover. "What do you mean you were 'working on trusting Sebastian'? You either trust someone or you don't."

Dru's smile was gentle. "See, I disagree. And I say that having thought the same way my whole life." She pointed toward the kitchen. "I knew I loved that man, like fucking *hard*, but loving someone and truly trusting them aren't the same. I loved him, but trusting him—and I mean, like, living with him all the time and letting him see my vulnerabilities and trusting him to compromise when we fight and all that? That's a process. You don't just *have* that, you have to build it, and that takes a step of faith."

"Oh."

Dru laughed. "'Oh', she says."

I sniffed, a sound that wasn't quite a laugh, but almost. "I don't know. Sorry. I'm just...I got stuck here because I fell into the water and then the storm escalated, and no one seemed to think it was safe for me to leave. And after the walk here from the other apartment, I agree about the safety. But I'm just stuck here, and you guys are amazing and fun and *so* fucking loud, and kind of crazy, and a lot overwhelming, and you all seem to think I'm *here* now, like somehow I've been adopted or something, and I'm just—" I stopped before I said something really dumb.

Dru just gazed levelly at me. "You just want to

get out of here, because you're overwhelmed and your fight or flight reflex is kicking in."

"I guess."

"Where are you going to go?"

I shrugged. "I don't know. I never know. I was heading west for Alaska, and now I'm here, and I don't know anymore."

Dru's gaze sharpened. "Are you backpacking? I didn't see a real backpack, like for hiking the PCT or something."

I squirmed. "I…um. No, I'm not a backpacker. I don't know where I'm going. I'm just…going."

"Drifting, you mean." Dru hesitated, opened her mouth, stopped, and tried again. "Joss, I don't mean to pry, because god knows how I used to feel about people asking me personal questions, but…do you *have* anywhere to go?"

I shrugged again. "Um. I've been…I've been on my own for a while. I'm fine."

"Joss." She shifted closer on the bed. "I'm asking, do you have anywhere to *go*?"

"I *said* I'm fine," I snapped. "I've made it this far. I started in fucking Nova Scotia and fucking walked here, so I think I can survive Ketchikan."

Dru sighed, and let the silence build for a few minutes, thinking. "So that's a no. Nowhere to go back to, and nowhere you're really trying to get to."

Her eyes met mine. "You're drifting."

"Yeah, I'm drifting," I said, hot, sharp, spiky emotions rising inside me. "I'm not a goddamn hobo, though, okay? I'm not going to steal your fine china or anything."

Her eyes narrowed. "That's not what I meant."

"Yeah, well, that's how it sounded—*you're drifting*, like there's something wrong with it. It's the life I've got, okay?" I heard my voice rising and couldn't stop it. "I'm homeless, is that what you want to hear? I'm just choosing to spend my life going somewhere rather than sitting on a street corner somewhere begging for spare change, or turning tricks for somewhere to sleep at night."

The door opened, then, and Bast's massive, six-foot-four-inch frame filled the doorway, darkening it. His thick, ropy, tattooed forearms were crossed over his thick chest, and his dark hair was messy, a strand hanging in one eye, weeks of scruff that didn't quite make a beard darkening his craggy jawline. Jesus, the man was sexy, in a rough, brutal, menacing sort of way. He stepped in, kicked the door closed behind him, and leaned against it, scrubbing a hand through his hair.

"Bast, baby, we're talking," Dru said, her voice sweet but firm.

"I heard you." Bast's ursine brown eyes flicked to

me. "Heard you say you were homeless."

"Fuck me," I groaned, tugging on a dread. "Should I make a fucking announcement so everyone knows they've got a *transient* in their midst? Hide your purses and wallets, it's a homeless girl!"

"Joss, shut up." His rumbled order took me by surprise.

I frowned up at him. "Excuse me?"

"You heard me." He lifted his chin, gazing evenly down at me. "I said shut up. Means shut up and listen."

I glared at him. "This had better be good, you big macho fuckstick."

The corners of lips quirked in a stifled grin. "Only my wife gets to call me that." He slid down the door to a squat. "We got a lot of people in this crew, you may have noticed—"

"No? Really? You *think*?" Sarcasm couldn't have dripped anymore thickly from my words.

Bast just quirked an eyebrow at me, jaw ticking, and I promptly shut up—this clearly wasn't a man to ignore.

"But recently, we've had a lot of shifting around in living situations. Brock and Claire have a place; Bax and Eva have a place, and Zane and Mara have a place, which just leaves the two sets of twins, Luce, Xavier, and me and Dru. Canaan and Aerie are touring most of the year, so they don't need a permanent room, which takes them out of the equation."

I made a face. "For a grunty orc of a man, you sure are talking a lot. Get to the point."

He continued like I hadn't spoken. "We've got six bedrooms between the two apartments—and only four rooms are being used right now. It's the first time since everyone came back that we've had more rooms than we do people staying in them." He tapped the floor between his huge, wool-socked feet. "This room's empty."

My heart started to pound. "What's your point?"

"Point is, we own both buildings free and clear, no rent, no mortgage. The bar is pulling a profit. And we got extra bedrooms."

"Don't bullshit me." I blinked hard.

"I don't bullshit." He waited until I met his eyes. "This room is yours. No rent, no utilities, no nothing. You wanna work, we always need help downstairs, and I'll pay you average restaurant wage. You want to get a different job, whatever, fine with me."

I swallowed hard. "I'm not—I can't…"

"Don't have to be homeless, Joss." For such a large, gruff, imposing man, his voice was shockingly gentle as he said those six little words, and then hardened again. "You wanna walk away when the storm clears tomorrow, be my guest. But you'll be walking away from a roof, a bed, and safe place to figure your shit out, free and clear."

"I don't take charity." I managed to get it out through the knot in my throat and the conflict in my head and heart.

"I look like a fuckin' philanthropist to you?" he snarled. "We got space, you need space—problem solved."

"It's not that easy—"

"It can be," Dru said. "If you let it."

I blinked hard, swallowed again past the burning lump in my throat. "I...um."

Dru stood up, patting me on the shoulder. "Take your time. Think about it." She reached down, took her husband's hands, and hauled him to his feet. "Come on, you big sexy lummox. I'm gonna kick your ass at *Mario Kart*."

They left me alone and when they were gone, the door closed behind them, I slid onto my back on the bed, and stared up at the ceiling.

Sebastian had offered me a place to live. No conditions, nothing. Just...*hey, stay here for a bit. Get your life together. Figure things out.*

Could I do it? Should I? I'd been drifting, traveling for so long I wasn't sure I knew how to stop. Previously, I would sometimes stop for a few days here and there, sometimes a bit longer if it was a good situation, but I always worried about overstaying my welcome. And besides, being a US citizen loose in Canada without a visa…well, staying put in one place too long risked drawing attention to myself. I'd have landed back in the States, but I didn't want to deal with any difficulties so it was easier to just keep moving, work for cash, and keep my head down.

Keep moving; don't trust anyone. That was my mantra.

But it's a free room! A bed to sleep in every night. A safe place to actually *live*. I could stop drifting and start working toward opening The Garden. How could I turn that down?

Plus, if I stayed here, and Lucian was at the other apartment, I'd be less likely to get myself mixed up with him. Which would be a danger and a distraction I didn't need. A temptation I didn't dare give in to.

I tried that once, and nearly didn't survive the experience. No thanks, not doing that again, no matter how nice and kind and sexy the guy may be.

But I could stay here. I could get a job. Save money. And maybe, eventually, find a little spot, put a down payment on it, and work on opening my own place.

It doesn't have to be here—after all, I've seen nothing of this town except snow and water. But I could pause here, take time to breathe, to feel safe, to put money aside and formulate a plan for opening the cafe.

The thought of actually living here brought tears to my eyes, which I couldn't stop. I didn't try—I was alone, I was safe, so I could indulge in a little emotional weakness.

Although, the last time I'd *indulged*, Lucian had caught me with my hand in my pants, and had watched as I'd had my first orgasm in...well, since that four-day stretch in a little cabin near Thunder Bay—an older couple had picked me up on ON-17 outside a little place called Hurkett, and they'd taken me to their rustic little "resort" on Lake Superior. It was a handful of ancient, tiny log cabins with decor, appliances, and electric wiring from the Eisenhower era—or whatever the Canadian equivalent would be—but it was cute and quiet and quaint. They'd let me stay there in exchange for helping them catch up on some maintenance chores. They'd fed me, let me watch TV in their main house, talked to me, and told me to stay as long as I wanted—clearly they were lonely and missed their grandkids or something like that. They were sweet, and I started liking that little cabin a bit too much, so I'd moved on. There'd been one other person staying at those cabins, a guy in his midthirties, alone. Muscular, bearded, attractive. We'd spoken a few times, and he'd been nice enough.

Then I went outside late one night, unable to sleep, and had caught a glimpse of him diving naked into the frigid water of Lake Superior. I'd gone immediately back inside, but my imagination had gotten the better of me and I'd given myself an orgasm.

That was the last time.

Until today. And today was…utterly unlike that previous time.

Today was…shit. *SO* much more than that. I'd NEEDED to release the insane pressure kissing Lucian had incited in me. Just thinking about him, about that kiss, about walking in on him in the shower got me all jittery and flustered and made my pulse pound.

And when I think about him catching me touching myself? Yeah, there's embarrassment there. But beneath it? There's something else. I don't dare examine it too closely, though. And when I'd found him in the music studio, it had been clear what he'd seen had affected him, too.

I'd affected him.

In a *huge* way.

I snickered at my own mental joke, because if he'd been big when he was about to get in the shower, the glimpse I'd gotten of him aroused, confined in his jeans…well… that left me short of breath and a little delirious.

Why am I thinking about Lucian? I'm not

supposed to think about Lucian.

Or his penis.

Or his lips, kissing mine.

Or his eyes, when he looks at me like…like I'm something amazing, something he desperately wants.

Fuck, there I go. I'm going in circles, thinking about him, getting caught up in him.

From ONE kiss.

What if there was more…more kisses, or more than kissing?

NO.

Nope.

Don't go there, Joss. Remember Toronto? Remember Rob? That's what happens when you let a cute guy get too close, when you let a sexy smile and pretty eyes lure you in.

I let my mind drift.

I tried to imagine living here. Having Canaan and Corin around, Dru, Bast, Bax and Eva, all the others. Waking up to coffee, maybe sitting around with Dru and just chatting.

Not walking through the night on a deserted highway in the middle of nowhere, or sleeping under an overpass during the darkest, coldest hours of the night. No more sleeping on a bench in a bus station, or dozing in the corner of a library, a book on my chest to make it seem like I'd come in for a book and had merely fallen asleep. No more accepting rides from truckers and hoping they were nice. No more begging midnight shift waitresses to let me wash dishes for leftover food.

The thought of not having to go back to that choked me up all over again.

I thought about hitting the road again. Catching a ferry from Ketchikan to wherever…and just continuing to drift. Is that what I want?

My mind and my soul recoiled at the idea.

No. A hundred times, no.

I didn't have to stay here forever, but I knew I couldn't hit the road again with the same kind of drive and determination. At least not yet.

Some part of me was insisting I stay here, and dammit…I just *wanted* to.

I just have to keep myself uninvolved with Lucian.

Something told me that would be easier said than done, but I had to try if I wanted to stay here a while longer.

But a man that sexy, a man with that much power to lure me in with a look, a touch, a kiss, was a man who stood between me and staying here in Ketchikan.

I had to keep my distance.

Yeah…right, a tiny voice deep in my heart whispered.

SEVEN

Lucian

IT WAS XAVIER WHO FOUND ME SITTING AT THE BAR, nursing the same glass of whiskey. He sat beside me, sniffed at the amber liquid, made a face, and then leaned over the bar to pour himself a beer.

"What are you brooding about, down here by yourself?"

I shrugged. "Things."

Xavier rolled his eyes at me. "Come on, Lucian."

I could only shake my head. "Don't really want to talk about it."

He nodded. "Okay."

And so we sat in silence, sipping our drinks in the dark.

I glanced at him. "You know, I came down here to be alone."

Xavier didn't look at me. "I know."

I waited. "You're still here."

"Yes." He finally shot me a glance. "You *never* want to talk about it, or anything, ever."

"Just how I am."

"Maybe it should be different."

"Maybe not. But it's the way it is." I tossed back the last of the whiskey. "Good talk."

I stood up and went back upstairs, leaving Xavier behind, watching me go, a speculative look on his face. When I arrived upstairs, there was a bastard-ized, drinking version of a trivia game happening. Everyone was jammed into the living room and they each had a card in their hand, and there was a bottle of Crown and a bottle of tequila side by side on the coffee table, along with a cluster of shot glasses, cans of soda and bottles of beer as chasers, a container of lime wedges, and a salt shaker near the tequila. One person would read a trivia question, and the team that guessed the correct answer first won, with the losing teams all doing shots.

I sat down beside Joss.

"LUCE!" Bax hollered. "You're finally back from Broodyville! You're behind on shots, bro! Catch up!"

"Whose idea was this game?" I asked, ignoring

his jibe as I reached for the tequila, lime, and salt.

"Mine, bitch!" Bax shouted. "Snow's s'posed to stop tomorrow, which means the bar opens back up, so we might as well spend the last day of our unexpected mini-vacation getting naked wasted, right?"

"Makes sense to me," Corin said.

"Getting naked wasted always makes sense to you, babe," Tate said.

"Well *duh*," Corin said, chuckling. "I'm a rock star, that's what we do."

"Especially the naked part," Canaan put in, and the brothers bumped knuckles, cackling in unison.

I watched this exchange as I licked my wrist, sprinkled salt on it, licked it off, poured a shot of Patrón Silver, and drank it, then sucked the juice out of the lime. I felt Joss's eyes on me while I did this, but refused to glance at her. The rejection still stung and I wasn't quite ready to act as if it hadn't happened.

Xavier came up, then, and took a seat on the floor beside Canaan and Tate, and despite Bax's prompting, wouldn't do a shot.

"I tried doing shots once," was his explanation. "It...did not agree with me. At *all*."

Bax snorted. "What happened, you forgot how to do calculus long enough to actually have fun?"

Xavier twisted his head to stare at Bax. "I had calculus mastered by fifth grade, if you must know. My issue with drinking to excess is not about fun, Baxter, it is about control."

"Exactly!" Bax reached down and patted Xavier's head paternally. "It's about letting go of control, in safe situations, or with people you trust."

Xavier just shook his head. "It did not feel good. I have little enough by way of verbal filters and aware-ness of social cues when I am in full possession of my faculties. Inebriated, I become someone I...do not care for very much. It is entirely a personal choice, however."

Joss leaned close to whisper to me. "Did he really learn calculus in fifth grade?"

I nod. "He was into higher math by junior high, like the kind of math where equations take up en-tire blackboards and academic papers get written on theorems."

"So he's, like, really smart."

I actually snorted at that. "He has *The Odyssey* and *The Iliad* memorized...in the original Greek. He builds and sells robots in his spare time. He can speed-read a book in a matter of minutes, and then recite the whole thing to you, essentially verbatim. *Really smart* doesn't quite cover it."

"Oh." She glanced at Xavier, and I tried to see him from an outsider's perspective.

Same height and build as me—tall, lean, and

angular—with dark brown hair shorn nearly to the scalp on the sides with the top left long, loose, and messy in a mop of curls, and bright, arresting green eyes, the only Badd brother to get Mom's eyes rather than Dad's. His hair was darker than any of ours, more like Mom's black ringlets than Dad's messy thatch of brown hair the same shade as a grizzly's fur. He was wearing a tight red T-shirt with the logo of a robotics lab on it, and tight, ripped jeans; he had tattoos on his forearms, a series of interlocking geometric shapes and mathematical symbols, and both ears were pierced three times. He looked more like a rock star than a Tesla or Da Vinci level genius, and it was a look he could certainly pull off, although I doubted he realized how attractive girls found him.

She glanced at me again. "Really? In the original Greek?"

Xavier heard her, tilted his head to the side and glanced at the ceiling, then began reciting ancient Greek. He kept going until it became evident he hadn't just memorized the first few lines as a party trick.

Eventually Bast leaned forward and threw a lime wedge at his head. "All right, Homer. No one else knows what you're sayin', kiddo."

Xavier threw the lime back at Bast and repeated everything he'd said, except in English this time, until everyone groaned, and he finally stopped.

The game continued, and Xavier's team won any question that wasn't current events or pop culture, which meant my team was quickly losing the battle against sobriety. Joss had even taken a few shots of Crown, while I stuck to tequila.

I tried not to think about how much I wanted to lick Joss's wrist, put salt on it, and lick the salt off.

Or do body shots from her navel.

I squirmed on the floor, shifting, trying to tamp down the thoughts rifling through me.

Joss eyed me. "You okay?"

I nodded. "Fine."

Eventually, when everyone was pretty drunk—except Xavier and Tate, who was pregnant and thus not drinking—Xavier called a halt to the game and insisted on heading downstairs to make food. Bax and Brock went down to help him, while everyone else remained where they were, half a dozen different conversations going on at once.

Bast and Dru were murmuring to each other in low tones, and then Bast nudged Joss with his elbow.

"Yo," he said, with a jut of his chin. "Think about it at all?"

I tuned in to this.

Joss lifted one shoulder, but then nodded. "Yeah, a bit."

"And?" Dru reached across Bast to take her hand. "No pressure, but I'd like it if you stayed."

Stayed? I glanced at Joss, then, sharply, inquisitively, but she wouldn't meet my eyes.

"I'm staying," Joss whispered. "But I don't know for how long."

"I think it's a smart move, Joss." Bast patted her knee. "Welcome to the shitshow, babe."

Joss just nodded, seeming scared, or nervous. "Thanks." She glanced at Bast and Dru. "I mean, thank you. From the bottom of my heart. You don't know what this means to me. You really don't."

"Did I miss something?" I asked.

She finally glanced at me, her gaze hesitant, distant. "Um, your brother said I could stay here, in their extra bedroom."

"I see." I nodded, looking away. "There's an extra bedroom at the other apartment too, you know."

I didn't need to say that. She probably already knew that and I was just asking for more rejection.

Which I got.

Joss's whisper was low and meant only for me. "Come on, Lucian. Don't."

"Don't what?"

"I think I need distance and time, okay? It's not personal. I just…" She blinked hard, picking at a loose thread on the seam of her hoodie. "You, and me, it's...I'm not there yet, okay?"

I let out a breath, nodded. "Yeah, fine."

"Lucian." She tried to catch my gaze, but I avoided hers. "Don't make it weird."

"All I said was, yeah, fine. I meant it. It's cool." I shrugged. "Besides, we've been drinking. Not the best time for these kinds of conversations anyway." I got to my feet and went down to join Bax, Brock, and Lucian in the bar kitchen, and helped them prepare a boatload of food for everyone.

The rest of the day passed smoothly enough, if you ignored my moody, sullen silence. Which, to be honest, wasn't much different from any other day. But today, my silence was weighted with an irritated, pissed-off, morose glower.

Which I realize is stupid, and childish, but I couldn't seem to help myself.

Her parents died, leaving her an orphan. She was homeless, and she had literally walked across all of Canada, alone. She's survived, alone. So, yeah, intellectually, I completely understood how she wouldn't be in a place for a relationship, but shit, I wasn't asking for one, was I? All we did was kiss, and we both saw a few things we maybe weren't meant to see, but I haven't even touched any part of her body except her waist.

And she's pushing me away, because she needs

time and space, even though she's living with my brothers above the bar I work at?

Whatever.

———✶———

The snow stopped the next day, and the city eventually got the streets and sidewalks clear, but it took a couple days for business to pick back up to normal levels. For Joss, moving in was literally just putting her backpack into the bedroom, as she owned nothing else.

For the first week, she worked at the bar washing dishes, running food, and bussing tables, but in her spare time she scoured Ketchikan putting in job applications. Not that she minded working at the bar, she said, but she didn't really enjoy food service and wanted something of her own choosing, and after about a month of looking, she got a job at a bakery.

During that month I was restless, though, and unhappy. Unsatisfied. Something about Joss's presence threw my entire life into chaos, a phenomenon I couldn't quite understand. Nothing was different, on the surface of it—I wasn't doing anything different. I read books in my free time, worked out, and pulled long hours in the bar, slinging drinks, taking orders, and helping Xavier in the kitchen when he got swamped by food tickets—which wasn't often, as the guy seemed to grow six extra arms when he was in the kitchen, capable of doing seven or eight different things at once. Usually, he was utterly focused on the one thing he was doing, to the exclusion of literally everything else. But in the kitchen? He just…exploded into a frenzy of coordinated mania.

So…if my life wasn't different, why did it feel so thrown out of whack?

Or was it me?

Why did I feel so off?

I barely saw Joss, especially after she started at the bakery. Once in a while she'd stop in after her shift and would sit at the bar and sip hot tea if it was before close, or a pint if it was after, and we'd fall into easy conversation—easy, as long as we kept it light and didn't go deep or personal. We had an easy camara- derie, and I was able to talk to her in a way I couldn't with anyone else. Which made it hard. I'd leave those conversations wanting more. Wishing I could see her more. Wishing I could do dumb teenager shit like hold her hand, or see a movie with her, or just sit and hang out. But we never got that. Maybe she was keep- ing busy to avoid that? I don't know.

She was working crazy hours, I knew that much. Doubles almost every day, and frequently she worked the prep shift, which meant she was often heading to work when we were finally finished closing the bar at 3 a.m.

Late one night, while mopping the floors, it hit me. Joss was busting her ass, working sixty and seventy hours a week…saving money, and working to make her dream a reality.

I worked similar hours…but for what?

So why was I busting my ass? I had plenty of money stashed away—I'd put my portion of the inheritance in the bank and left it, adding it to my already sizable savings. I didn't LOVE the bar. It was a family thing, sure, but it was really just…something to do. I wasn't working FOR anything. I didn't have a goal, or a dream.

I was spinning my wheels.

While Joss was driving hard for the one thing she wanted, with singular focus.

What was I doing?

What did I want?

And suddenly it hit me—Joss had shown up and, without knowing it, had highlighted the lack of purpose in my life.

Two more weeks passed, and I became increasingly restless. Books ceased to be able to hold my attention for very long, a problem I'd never had before. I took Xavier's motorcycle out and rode for hours, going nowhere, just riding to feel the wind in my hair; I also found myself at the docks a lot, watching boats strike out to sea. Whenever a sailboat or fishing boat heads out for the open ocean, I find myself wistful, anxious, restless—*why am I still here?* I asked myself, quite frequently. *Why not get on a boat and go?*

My brothers need me, for one. Bast isn't ready to take on outside help yet, although that time is coming, and soon.

Even though I haven't really spent much time with Joss, lately, I still hold out hope that she'll have gotten the time and space she needs, that she'll find herself more comfortable in this new life.

I washed glasses and stocked the bar, watching her talking to Xavier, laughing at something he said, and I got jealous. She was sitting at the bar eating lunch between shifts, so I took a quick break to sit beside her and talk to her, inhaling the scent of the bakery on her layered over shampoo and woman, and desire flooded through me.

She seemed happy. Less prickly, less closed off. Having a home and a job has…not quite softened her, but smoothed out some of the edges. She's quicker to laugh, to smile.

Not at me, though.

Her eyes flick to mine frequently, and our eyes meet, and her expression goes carefully blank, as if she's afraid to give away too much of what she's thinking or feeling; I'd give anything to know what she's thinking and feeling, even once. To get one of those brilliant smiles and barking, enthusiastic laughs the others get when they say or do something funny.

Her smile lights up the room, and her laugh fills it with joy.

But none of it is for me.

The more time passes, the more restless I become.

The more dissatisfied with my life I become.

Working at the bar isn't a life, isn't a career—it's just a job.

Joss seems content to avoid me and work like a madwoman, burning the candle at both ends.

My brothers couldn't be happier—everyone has their thing, and those things are going well. Xavier recently received an order for several large crates of robotic parts he'd been saving for, and was working on creating larger-scale robots to sell, now that his business was booming. The women were all just as busy with their own jobs and hobbies and projects.

Everyone had something...

Except me.

———*———

Joss had been in Ketchikan for two months. We'd started spending a little more time near each other, if not actually together. Apparently she and Tate had taken a shine to each other, and so Joss would pop over to the apartment in the mornings on days she didn't work until late afternoon or evening, and she and Tate would sit and talk, or watch reality TV together and, oddly, play video games together. Tate, being pregnant, rarely wore anything except what she called her "preggers uniform," which consisted of capri yoga pants with an extra wide and stretchy waistband tugged up over her belly, and a tank top, sans bra. She was eight months pregnant by then, so her belly was huge and she waddled and peed every ten seconds.

With Aerie on tour with Canaan most of the time, Dru more involved than ever in her budding real estate business, Claire freelance programming, Mara with the marketing firm of which she was now a full partner, Eva doing her art, and Corin busy running the twins' record label, Tate often found herself at odd ends, alone and deprived of company, so Joss being around was a godsend for Tate.

It also meant I got to see Joss more. And, since Tate sat around wearing…not a lot, Joss tended to do the same. She'd show up in this pair of ultra tight, bright red yoga pants that came to the knee, and a scoop-neck T-shirt with nothing underneath—her comfy clothes. That T-shirt drove me absolutely crazy;

it tended to hang open at the neck, giving me tantalizing glimpses down her shirt. The pants, though…shit. Bright red, contrasting with her dark skin, and crazy tight, hugging her thick, muscular legs and highlighting the firm, round perfection of her ass.

I think she wore the outfit just to make me crazy.

If so, it was working. I often had to leave the room when the two of them were around, because they ended up laughing and teasing and causing a ruckus, and certain elements of their anatomy would be bouncing and jiggling and I wouldn't be able to keep my eyes off Joss, hoping for another look, another glimpse.

I couldn't handle how bad I wanted her, and I didn't know what do with it or how to squash it, or pretend I didn't feel it. But I also wasn't willing to risk another rejection by her again, so I just…plugged along miserably, like a pathetic teenager with his first crush.

She noticed me staring, too. She never said anything, but she noticed. She'd catch me looking, and then give me a steady gaze I couldn't read. Not reproachful, but not playful either, and certainly not inviting.

I didn't know what to do…

About Joss, or about my life. About anything.

One morning, nearing Joss's three-month mark

in Ketchikan, I was sitting at the kitchen table at the apartment over the studio, reading a book, listening to music, and trying to act like I was ignoring the girls while secretly stealing glances at Joss as she and Tate played the latest *Far Cry* game. They both had their favorite outfits on, and were cackling and teasing each other and being generally loud and playful. Corin breezed in from the studio, where he'd been working on the finishing touches of the Canary EP.

"Tate, babe." He stood behind the couch with his hands on her shoulders. "Get some shoes on, sexy, I'm taking you to lunch."

"Yay—food!" Tate squealed as she paused the game. "But I need a bra, too. Can you grab me one?" She glanced at Joss. "Sorry to bail on you, J."

Joss just grinned and waved a hand. "Go! Have lunch with your husband."

Tate glanced from Joss to me, opened her mouth, but then thought better of it. Corin brought her a bra, and Tate pulled her arms inside her T-shirt, put on the bra, shoved her arms back out, put on a sweatshirt and shoes, and then she waddled out of the apartment hand in hand with Corin, arguing with herself about whether she wanted a burger and fries, or a salmon Caesar salad.

And, just like that, for the first time in weeks, Joss and I were alone.

I paused my music, tugged out my earbuds, and set my Kindle down. Joss was still sitting on the couch, game controller in hand, toying with the buttons. Her eyes flicked over to me, down to her feet, and then back to me.

My heart was banging like a jackhammer. "You hungry?" I asked.

She set the controller aside and offered me a hesitant smile. "Yeah, actually."

I stood up, shoved my phone and wallet into my hip pockets, and sat on the couch next to her to lace up my boots. "You changing?"

She shrugged one shoulder. "I wasn't going to. You think I need to?"

I used the exchange as an excuse to sort of blatantly look her over. "No. Not at all. You look...amazing. I was just asking."

"I could probably use a bra, though."

I stood up. "Not on my account." I allowed a hint of a smirk on my lips, a foray into flirtation. "Doesn't bother me any."

"Yeah, I'll bet," she murmured, standing up and grabbing her backpack.

"What's that mean?" I asked.

She hesitated over her answer. "I feel you looking at me."

"Hard not to."

She stood facing me, chin lifted, eyes searching me. "Why's that?"

"Because you're beautiful." I held her gaze for a moment, and then slid past her to the stairs, getting away from her before I did something I'd regret, like kiss her.

She followed me down the stairs and out onto the street, tugging a hoodie on and zipping it as she caught up to me. "When you asked if I was hungry, I assume you were implying we eat together."

I nodded. "That was the idea, yes."

We walked a few steps in silence; I was heading toward a breakfast cafe I sometimes frequented when I didn't feel like cooking for myself.

"So is this a date, then?" She asked this quietly, her voice so low I almost missed it.

Well, damn, that was a loaded question. I looked over at her, searching her. "Do you want it to be?"

"Are you answering a question with a question?"

"Aren't you, too?"

She laughed, a musical sound that sent sparks of something electric through me. "This is stupid." She stopped, turned to face me, and met my eyes. "Just answer the question, Lucian. Is this a date?"

I held her gaze. "I would like it to be."

"So would I." She paused, as if hunting for the right words. "But can we just...it's *just* date, okay?

Can we take it slow?"

I nodded. "I can handle that."

We walked in silence to the cafe, sat down, ordered coffee and breakfast food, even though it was closer to noon than breakfast. After a few minutes of silence, Joss leaned forward, her hands wrapped around her mug.

"You've been avoiding me."

I nodded. "Sort of."

"Why?"

"Things felt...awkward."

She frowned. "Because of the kiss?"

"More because of after the kiss."

"It was unexpected. It surprised me, overwhelmed me. The kiss, I mean." She stared into her coffee. "And then after...it was just too much too soon. I'd just met you, I was with you and all these people I didn't know, and then being attracted to you, kissing you, and the other stuff that happened—you catching me, all that. It just..." She shrugged. "It was too much. I felt like I was jumping off the deep end and I wasn't ready for that."

"It was just a kiss." I waved a hand. "And the other stuff? It just happened. Doesn't have to mean anything."

"It wasn't *just* a kiss, Lucian."

I blew out a breath, eyeing her. "Then what else

was it?"

"A gateway drug." Joss leaned back in the booth as the waitress brought our food.

We ate in silence for a few minutes, and then I glanced at her. "You're going to have to explain that one. What do you mean, gateway drug?"

She quirked an eyebrow at me. "You know what I meant."

"Humor me."

"If the other stuff hadn't happened—if you hadn't seen me naked after I fell in, if I hadn't walked in on you in the shower, if you hadn't caught me jilling it—there may have been a chance of it being just a kiss. But that stuff *did* happen, Lucian, and now…" She paused to take a few bites, washed it down with coffee, and then continued. "And now we're both aware of…of the fact that we have chemistry."

I laughed at that. "Joss, that kiss alone would have been enough to make us painfully aware of the fact that we have *chemistry*."

"Exactly."

"Why is that a bad thing? What are you scared of?"

Her gaze hardened. "A lot of things, Lucian, and for good reason."

"Look, all I meant was—"

"What you said," she interrupted, and then she sighed. "And yeah, just for the sake of honesty, then, I should admit I've been avoiding you too."

I narrowed my eyes at her. "No shit."

"I just...I couldn't handle the complication. I still don't know that I could." She fixed me with a hard glare. "And what about you? I told you I wasn't ready for what seemed to be brewing between us, and instead of just being my friend, you spent the last two months all but avoiding me completely, while still staring at me over the top of your Kindle, like I wouldn't notice." She poked the back of my hand with her fork. "You know what that says to me, Lucian? It says you're scared too."

I couldn't deny that, but wasn't willing to admit to it out loud, and certainly not to her. The waitress came by at that moment, thankfully, and provided a distraction as I paid the tab. We left, walking in silence, and somehow ended up at the water's edge, standing side by side at the railing, watching a cruise ship come in.

Eventually, I found myself fumbling through an explanation. "If I have been avoiding you, it's because I'm not sure how to make an in-between thing work."

"Meaning...what?"

"How to be *just* your friend."

"So the only other option is avoid me altogether?"

"Pretty much."

"Or what?"

"Or I'll kiss you again."

She glanced sideways at me. "Just like that? Just kiss me?"

"Pretty much."

"What if I don't want you to kiss me?"

I straightened and turned to face her; she mirrored my action, so we were standing facing each other, about a foot of space between us.

"You don't?" I asked, inching toward her.

"I said *what if* I didn't. Not that I don't."

"You want me to." This was foolish. Reckless. I was pushing her, and she'd just said she wanted to take it slow.

But...god, I couldn't help it. I wanted to taste her lips again. I wanted to feel her pressed up against me. It didn't have to lead to anything else, I just...I *needed* to kiss her.

To know if I'd imagined how it had felt, how intense it had been.

"Lucian—" she protested, as I sidled closer, closing the gap between us.

I stared down at her. "Tell me you don't want this, Joss."

"Want what?" she breathed.

Moving slowly, deliberately telegraphing my intentions, I reached out and placed my hands on her waist, just above her hips, and moved so our bodies just barely touched—her breasts against my chest, soft and pliant and firm, our hips nudging, our faces inches apart. Her eyes went wide, and her breathing quickened. My hands slid around to her back, edging lower, to the upper swell of her buttocks, where they remained.

"This," I murmured.

She stared up at me, and her tongue slid across her lower lip. "Lucian—"

"Tell me to let go, Joss." I watched her tongue wet her lips, leaning closer. "Tell me not to kiss you."

Her hands lifted, rested on my chest, and then her fingers curled into the thick cotton of my sweatshirt. "I can't," she breathed. "You know I can't."

She was trembling—I felt it in her breath, in her hands. Scared, or excited, or both?

I'm not sure whether she lifted up or if I leaned down. Who kissed whom? I don't know. I just know our lips met in a tangle of wet warmth. She leaned against me, and her fingers released their grip on my sweatshirt to slide upward, carving over my shoulders and wrapping around the back of my neck. It was an effort of sheer willpower to keep my hands where they were, to keep them from descending lower and palming her luscious ass. I barely managed to restrain the impulse, instead letting one arm wrap all the way around her waist, my other hand lifting to her cheek. Her lips worked against mine, shifting and seeking, and then they parted and I felt her tongue teasing mine, questing.

She moaned, a low whimper in her throat, a sound of agonized rapture. God, what would she sound like if it was me making her quake, making her gasp and moan as she toppled over the edge? I remembered all too well the sounds she made as she came, and I couldn't suppress a vision of us together, of me, between her thighs, tasting her. Touching her. Bringing her to an orgasm she'd never forget.

I lost myself in the kiss, trying to banish the image I'd conjured.

In vain.

I felt us moving, and then she was braced against the railing of the dock and reaching up to pull me down, both hands on my face, lifting up on her toes to reach me, to deepen the kiss. I pressed harder against her, palming her cheek, and she gave me her tongue, unabashedly, hungrily. I groaned as my willpower ran out, and the thick, firm weight of her ass filled both of my hands, and her moan was one of surprise and pleasure. I kneaded and cupped and caressed, pulled her flush against my body, my hardness against her softness.

Abruptly, just like the first time, she yanked herself out of my grip, panting raggedly, her fingers trembling as they slid across her lips.

And then she was gone, bolting at a dead run back toward the bar.

EIGHT

Joss

I T HAPPENED AGAIN. ONLY...WORSE. OR BETTER. OR something.

That kiss had eclipsed the first one completely. It left me shaking all over, breathing hard, aching between my thighs, and unable to think straight. His hands had been on my ass, and I'd allowed it to happen. Enjoyed it, even. It wasn't until he'd ground against me and I'd felt the long, hard, thick ridge of his erection against me that I'd woken up, that I'd been shaken out of my aroused hypnosis.

That's really what it was, too—hypnosis.

I'm a strong, smart, tough girl—independent, a survivor. I don't get sidetracked or distracted or duped or tricked. But Lucian—once he got his hands on me, once his mouth met mine, he just…decimated me. Ravaged my ability to think straight. His lips were jet fuel on the fire of my libido, his hands on my body setting off the afterburner of my desire.

I ran like my life depended on it, seized by an odd mixture of arousal and the need to cry.

I made it to Badd's, slammed through the door and into the dim interior of the bar. I saw no one, nothing, heard a voice calling my name, but I ignored it, hauling ass upstairs to my room.

I collapsed into bed, sweating, peeled off my hoodie, gasping partly from exertion and partly from the overwhelming, emotional, visceral reaction to everything that was Lucian.

How could he have this effect on me? What did he do to me? What was wrong with me that I was so easily swept away by him? I didn't want to want him, but I did. I didn't want to feel a desperate need for his touch, his kiss, but I did.

I hated it.

It was weakness on my part, pure and simple. It would only sabotage my future. I was living a precarious existence, walking a delicate line. I was trying to not get too attached to the Badd tribe, because I couldn't stay here indefinitely. They weren't my family. This was just a pit stop on the road. A side quest.

A chance to get off the streets for a while, to be safe, a chance to put away some money—I cashed every check I made, banded the cash into tight rolls, and hid them in an old tampon box in my backpack, which I never let out of my sight. That backpack represented everything to me—my savings, my potential future. If I saved enough, I could start thinking about opening The Garden, someday, but to do that, I had to work every spare moment, save every penny. There was no time for a man. No time for attraction. No time for Lucian.

And even if there *was* time, I couldn't emotionally afford the risk of getting involved with Lucian. Losing my parents like I did had shut me down, emotionally, and being alone and homeless on the road had forced to me put up a hardened facade to the world, hiding myself within layers of walls. Lucian, somehow, got past those walls and saw the real me. But the damage he could do to my heart and soul from inside my walls? It was incalculable. I'd only survived this long, emotionally, by being cold and shut down. I couldn't care about him. Just COULDN'T. He would wreck me, ruin me.

I'd gone down that road once before, and it had nearly undone me. Nearly killed me, physically, and shattered any ability I had to trust men.

Lucian wouldn't be any different than Rob.

But he is, a small voice whispered. *You know he is.*

But what if he's not? What if he's the same?

I heard a door close, heard booted footsteps outside my room. A moment of silence, hesitation, and then a knock. "Joss?"

"Go away."

"Joss, please…talk to me." He sounded as out of breath as I was.

"I can't—I can't—Lucian, please, just…leave me alone."

My heart was urging me to listen to him, my mind was shackling me in place with chains of fear and distrust, and my body was screaming for me to open the door, to take more of what he was offering.

"Joss." I heard a thump, as if he'd thunked his head against the door, or a fist. "Let me in. Please."

"The door isn't locked," I murmured.

I rolled away to face the wall, curled into a tight ball.

I heard him enter, close the door behind him, felt him sit on the edge of the bed. His hand touched my side, and I flinched, even as his touch thrilled through me.

"Joss, I don't understand."

"You couldn't."

"I want to."

"No you don't."

He shifted closer to me, and I felt his body heat, felt him close, his hand on my waist. "Yes. I do."

"Why?"

"Because I—" he halted, and I heard him swallow. "I don't know how to put it. It's…it's *you*. I need—I want—*fuck*." He broke off with a strangled groan. "Joss, just let me in a little. Why do you keep pulling away from me? Do you not want me? Is there something wrong? Something I did wrong?"

At the confused pain in his voice, I rolled to face him. "Lucian, no. It's not that."

"Then *what*, goddammit?"

"It's everything. It's me. It's my life. What I've been through, where I'm trying to get—you asked me what I was so afraid of, and I told you everything. And that's the truth." I stared up into his conflicted brown eyes, hating the pain I saw there, only partially masking the desire also prevalent.

He just stared back down at me, as if he could divine the truth just by looking hard enough.

And the hell of it was, it felt as if he could. His eyes were so deep, so expressive, so piercing, and they bored into me, penetrating my defenses, making me want to tell him everything, the things I'd never spoken aloud to a living soul.

He was back inside my physical space, touching me.

"Don't look at me like that," I whispered.

"Like what?"

"Like you can see my every secret."

"If only I could."

"Why would you want to? What if you don't like what you see?"

His eyes raked over me, reminding me that I'd taken off my hoodie, revealing the fact that I wasn't wearing a bra—as if my recent run hadn't made that painfully clear enough as it was. His eyes on my body gave my question multiple layers of meaning and context.

"I see you, Joss, and I like what I see. I want more of what I see." He returned his eyes to mine. "So much more."

"Dammit, Lucian." I put my hand on his chest to stop him from getting any closer. "It's not that simple."

I shouldn't have touched him. Even as the conflict in my head and heart warred on, the act of touching him incited a riot in my body, sending sparks through my blood, setting me on fire all over again.

He was sweating slightly, a sheen on his forehead and upper lip. He had lost his sweatshirt at some point too, and was wearing just his T-shirt, a plain white V-neck stretched tight around his sculpted body. My hand was on his chest, dead center between his pecs, and I felt the heat of his skin under my palm. I had a mental flash of him naked, every ripped, shredded muscle on display, and my heart thundered.

Silence.

His eyes on mine—one hand on my waist, my hand on his chest; it was like the moment before a storm hits, when the air crackles with energy.

This time, it was all me.

I lunged at him, groaning a curse at my own weakness even as I gave in yet again to the desire I knew would only further confuse me, would only cause me to pull away yet again. This couldn't last. Fear would take the reins again—I kissed him knowing this.

But dammit, I wanted him. He kissed like he'd invented it, taking control of my mouth, guiding us to rapturous heights, until I was breathless with need for more.

I landed in his arms, and he fell backward to the bed, pulling me on top of him, and everything inside me became a roaring conflagration of desire for Lucian. My heart crashed and skipped beats, and my hands sought him, sought skin, pushing his shirt up so my palms and fingertips skated across his hot taut flesh and firm muscles. I felt that huge hard ridge between us, and it made my thighs quake with equal parts fear and need. It didn't stop me, this time, though. I was too lost in the fervor of his mouth, the debilitating, dizzying way his hands explored my body.

Oh god, oh god, how could this feel so perfect, so right, and yet so scary and so wrong at the same time?

His tongue demanded mine, and I gave it to him. Tasted him, felt him beneath me. His hands slipped under the hem of my shirt and his fingers danced up my spine, and then his palms skated back down. His hands were warm and strong and callused and gentle as they soothed in circles from shoulders downward to the small of my back. I shivered, broke the kiss to pull away to meet his eyes. All I saw in his gaze was need, desire as potent as my own. And then he was reclaiming the kiss, groaning as our mouths parted and our tongues tangled in a wild dance of furious passion. I felt him hesitate, felt his hands pause at the swell of my butt, and then, with a deep, raspy moan of pleasure, he cupped my ass. I arched my spine at his touch, my heart thrumming and crashing, heat and pressure roiling low in my belly, need building inside me with volcanic intensity.

His fingers clawed into the meat and muscle of my buttocks, and then released to caress, to explore the roundness and the weight, and I felt his touch like an electrical current searing through me, igniting my desire to mad, manic, explosive fury. I shoved at his shirt and he ripped it off, and then he was twisting against me, rolling, and I was pinned beneath him. His weight was centered at our hips, his erection hard against my core. I pawed his muscular back, exploring his broad shoulders, tugging his hair free from the ever-present ponytail to cascade around our lip-locked faces. Shoulders, spine, sides, I touched him everywhere I could find skin—chest, stomach, arms. I couldn't resist the temptation of his ass, cupped by just-tight-enough jeans. I pulled him closer, gasping into his mouth, whimpering at the strength and gentility in his touch, in the possessive ferocity of his kiss, and his exploration of my body.

And then he wasn't kissing my mouth anymore, but my stomach, my side, my diaphragm. He pushed up my T-shirt—it caught on my chin and then slipped off, vanishing, and his hands were sliding up my ribcage. I gasped, and then moaned breathlessly when his hands palmed my bared breasts, whined in my throat as his thumbs brushed over my nipples, sending currents of sizzling ecstasy through me. His mouth danced across my flesh, skipping and kissing and stuttering from navel to ribs, up my breastbone, to my throat, and then he was cupping my breast as an offering to his lips, and his hot wet mouth latched onto my nipple and his teeth and tongue were a frenzy of erotic attention, sawing, flicking, suckling, until

I was arched up off the mattress, shoving my hips at his, grinding against him wantonly, moaning, the edge of orgasm bearing down on me.

I caught at his bicep, the bulging power filling my hand, taut and thick. My mouth found his neck, and then his shoulder, and my tongue tasted the salt of his skin and my lips slid and my teeth dimpled the flesh as he shifted from the left breast to my right. His fingers pinioned my nipple, the one still slick from his mouth, twisting and pinching, and then his hand was caressing and lifting and squeezing the entire heavy mound of my breast while his mouth devoured the other. My spine was concave, pressing myself against him, offering myself to his lavish attention.

God, more.

More.

I felt the desperate cry within my body for more of his touch like a siren song. I *needed* more.

I buried my hands in his hair, running my fingers through the silky locks, and then cupped the back of his head in my palms, holding him in place as he licked and lapped and suckled at my tits.

He groaned, and then growled. His hips lifted from mine, and he shifted so his body was to one side of mine but still levered over me. He never stopped his mouth's attention to my breasts, one and then the other in alternating rhythm, one hand on whichever breast his mouth wasn't latched onto. His other hand, ohhh, that hand was sliding downward. Dancing down my belly, going past my navel to the stretchy waistband of my yoga pants.

Did he know I wasn't wearing anything under them?

Too late, now.

His fingers were teasing underneath the elastic cotton, and I was quivering in anticipation. Riding the edge already just from his mouth on my breasts, the prospect of his touch on my most intimate, most sensitive place had me shaking and too breathless to make a sound. I wanted his touch—I wanted this.

But yet, there was an undercurrent of something dark and subversive layered beneath the desire. I fought it. I didn't want that to hold me back—I knew what it was, and I didn't want to give it power over me anymore. But it was there. And it was growing stronger.

I palmed his cheeks and brought his mouth back up to mine, lost myself in kissing him all over again. Let the delirium of his mouth and tongue take me away again. Rolled my hips in invitation as he worked his fingers under the waistband. His tongue danced on mine, and I felt the first questing brush of his fingertip down my center. I whimpered, clutching at his shoulder with one hand and palming his cheek with the other, and the kiss broke, both of us gasping. My eyes flew open, and I met his heated brown gaze.

There was a moment of hesitation on his part then. Him, allowing me time to stop him.

I didn't want to.

I liked his touch. I enjoyed how beautiful his kiss made me feel, how wanted, how desired I felt in his hands. I knew what he was about to do, and I wanted it.

I lifted my hips again, and felt his touch slide against my seam, a slow, gentle foray. His eyes never left mine. And then, gently, slowly, he delved into me, eliciting a quavering whimper at the thick intrusion of his touch. In, then, deeper, gathering the wetness of my desire and sliding his touch outward and then upward, where his fingers circled, touching gently, delicately. I couldn't even gasp. Could only let my eyes roll back in my head, and let my hips roll at the slowly increasing speed of his circling fingers. The heat inside me was expanding and morphing into pressure, into desperation.

I felt myself coming apart, heard the sound of my voice crying out, muffled against his shoulder. My hands were claws, raking down his back as his fingers worked a sorcery like nothing I'd ever felt, sliding down to dip inside me, smearing my own essence on the bundle of nerves at my very core, manipulating me to wild, thrashing desperation.

His mouth was at my breasts again and I was clawing at one of his shoulders and my other hand was pawing down the hard rippling blocks of his abs, catching at the waist of his jeans. I felt outside myself, somehow, not in control. It wasn't me, I was some other Joss, a Joss free from the dark fear of the past. This Joss was hungry for Lucian, desperate to feel more of him, to take the pleasure he was offering and give him pleasure in return.

This Joss—the free one—was in control. I gave myself to the new version, gave her my mind, my heart, my soul, and let her lead me. My hands were at the front of his jeans. Popping open the cold brass of the button, sliding down the zipper.

Lucian's touch thrilled through me, seared me, like lightning striking again and again. I was beyond breathless, now, my thighs quaking, aching. His fingers teased and toyed, dove inside me and slipped out, circled my clit, drove me to the edge and left me hovering there, a gasping shriek escaping as an orgasm teetered inside me, a nuclear bomb an instant from exploding.

I welcomed it, my heels catching at the blankets, thighs quaking and falling open, hips driving upward into his touch. I buried my mouth in the side of his neck and let myself moan loud into his flesh as he circled my clit faster and faster now, until the heat and pressure and need and pleasure became too much, too much, and I detonated, biting down on his shoulder and screaming as I came.

Both of my hands seized his buttocks and clawed at the firm muscle—I was clutching flesh, somehow. Had I pushed his jeans away as I came apart under his touch? I vaguely recalled my fingers hooking into denim and elastic, and his body lifting. And now I had his skin under my hands, the soft smooth round hardness of his buttocks tensed against my palms. I was still shaking with the intensity of my climax, gasping, and whimpering as aftershocks racked me.

His mouth was lapping at my breast, his tongue flicking my nipple, but I was too sensitive for that, and nudged him away. Before I knew what was happening, my hips were lifting and he was tugging at the stretchy fabric of the yoga pants, yanking them down past my hips, and my feet kicked them away, and I was naked, totally bare, and he was on his hands and knees above me, shirtless, body hard and lean and toned, his jeans around his knees, hair loose. I followed the lines of his body, the broad sweep of his shoulders, the hard planes of his chest and the furrows of his abdomen, and the sharp V slicing from abs down to his manhood. Which was bare. Hard. Huge. Jutting upward flat against his belly. He shoved his jeans and underwear down to his ankles, where they caught on his laced-up boots. He tore at the laces and kicked his boots and everything else off, and then we were both naked together, and my heart was slamming in my chest at this.

His eyes stayed on mine, and I saw the fierce need in him, how he was riding the edge of his control.

My hands, resting possessively on his ass, slid up his back; he remained utterly still. My fingers grazed his chest, fingertips aiming downward, palm to his skin. Lucian shook, trembled, growling with each exhalation as I grasped his erection.

Oh.

My.

God.

He filled my hand, iron hard and silk soft at the same time. I squeezed him, and explored his length, stroking slowly downward and then back up.

He shuddered at my touch, holding still, allowing me to touch him at my leisure.

He felt amazing in my hand.

I wanted to make him feel even half as good as he'd just made me feel. So I touched him. Stroked him slowly, watching the way his thick pink erection slid between my fingers, protruding from above them, and then the head vanishing into my fist. He growled yet again, and his hips flexed.

"Joss—" His utterance of my name was a breath-less snarl.

He collapsed against me, as if his arms and legs couldn't support his weight, and for a moment, I was pinned beneath him, all his weight on me, his breath on my face.

In that instant, the past rose up like a venomous serpent and struck:

Helpless—

Pinned beneath a weight I couldn't shift, couldn't fight against—

A brutal hand wrapped around my throat, cutting off my oxygen—

The jingle of a belt, a rough voice telling me to shut up, that I knew I wanted it—

"Joss!" Lucian's voice snapped me back to the present.

I came back to myself, curled up on the bed, arms around my knees, throat aching, stinging. There was blood on my knuckles.

I blinked, looked around, and saw Lucian across the room, back to the door, naked, half-hard still, blood sluicing down his nose and mouth and chin and chest. He was gasping, breathing raggedly, staring at me in confusion.

"Lucian?" My throat was on fire, my voice hoarse.

"What the *fuck*, Joss?" he demanded, droplets of blood flying from his lips.

I'd left a bath towel on the floor after my shower yesterday; he bent, lifted the towel to his nose and wiped away the blood, and then held it against his face, pinching his nose and tipping his head back.

I shook my head, unable to formulate words, to understand what had just happened.

I was naked. I couldn't face him like this, naked. I couldn't face myself. I hauled the flat sheet up and wrapped myself in it, worked to a sitting position, and then slid off the bed on shaky, weak legs. Lucian watched me warily, his head still tilted back to halt the flow of blood.

There was a knock on the door, Mara's voice, worried, frightened. "What the hell is going on? Joss? I heard you scream, honey—are you okay?"

Neither of us answered.

"Joss!" Mara said, panicked now.

"I'm okay," I managed, raspy, each word pained.

"What happened?" Her voice on the other side of the door was worried.

"Just—just give me a minute," I said.

"Are you sure?"

"I said I'm *fine*. Just give me a minute," I snapped, and then gentled my tone. "Please."

"Okay," Mara said, sounding dubious. "I'm here

if you need me."

Lucian drew up to his full height, shoulders going back, eyes searching mine. "What...the...*fuck*... was that?"

I shook my head, tears now streaming down my face. "I don't know—I don't know—I'm sorry, I'm sorry."

"You don't know." His voice was flat with disbelief. "One second we were...you were enjoying what we were doing, and then you were screaming and punching me. You just...snapped. And you don't know what happened?"

I fumbled on the floor for my clothing, not daring to look at Lucian. I dropped the flat sheet, turned away from him, stepped into my pants and shrugged into my shirt, and then turned back to Lucian. Still holding the towel to his nose, he used one hand to tug on his jeans and zip them. Snagging his shirt off the floor, he tossed it over his shoulder and stood in the middle of the room, just staring at me. Waiting.

"Joss." He took a hesitant step toward me. "Talk to me. Please."

I shook my head, crying too hard to see or breathe or talk or function. The images from my attack, the memories that had so violently ruined the moment with Lucian, were flashing through my head, as fresh and raw as if they'd happened yesterday instead of more than two and a half years ago.

He took another step and I felt myself freeze, tensed, fists clenched. "Joss, come on. Talk to me. Tell me what happened."

"I can't—I can't."

"Joss, come on." He reached out a hand, intending to…I don't know. Comfort me?

"Leave me the fuck alone!" I shouted in a rasp, my scream having shredded my vocal chords. "Just… just go away."

"Jesus, okay, fine. I'm sorry." He backed away. "I'm sorry for whatever I did. I thought you—I'm sorry, Joss. I wouldn't have—" He shook his head, cutting off and turning away, hand on the doorknob.

It's not you, it's not you—

The words wouldn't come out.

He twisted the knob, opening the door, but paused in the opening. "Joss, I—"

I forced the words out, and it was like forcing myself to vomit. "It wasn't you, Lucian. It wasn't you. It was nothing you did."

"Then I'm *really* fucking confused."

"I'm the one who's sorry," I whispered.

"Then explain. Help me understand."

I shook my head, unable to get the truth out, unable to make myself trust him with it, with any of it. I saw the anger and the hurt blossom in his eyes, and

I hated myself for putting it there.

He pulled the towel away from his nose, dabbing, and, satisfied he wasn't bleeding any longer, held the blood-soaked towel loosely in his fist. His eyes were closed off, angry.

"Fine, don't fucking tell me." He spat the words furiously. "Whatever. I'm done being teased and fucked with and jerked around. Do whatever the fuck you want."

And then he was gone. I heard Mara calling after him, concerned, and the slam of a door. Mara appeared in the doorway, Jax on her hip, the baby chewing on a toy, drooling, and whacking her shoulder with a fist.

"Joss?" She hesitated in the doorway. "What happened?"

Again, I could only shake my head. "I'm fucked up, Mara. That's what happened."

Mara's eyes narrowed. "Lucian, you and he— nothing happened? He didn't—" She stopped, unwilling to finish articulating the idea.

"No!" I protested. "It wasn't like that."

"It's just…it's been a long time since I've heard anyone scream like that." Mara entered the room and set Jax down on his butt on the floor, and then sat on the edge of my bed. "Someone hurt you."

"Not Lucian." I swallowed hard and sat down, a

million conflicted feelings raging inside me. "Don't think that."

"None of these boys are capable of that, but a scream like that? It only comes from a very particular brand of fear and pain, Joss. I know what that sounds like. I've seen it, I've heard it, I've treated it."

"Treated it?" I asked, curiosity getting the better of me.

She nodded. "I was a combat medic. I did tours in Iraq and Afghanistan."

"I didn't know."

"You wouldn't. It's not something I talk a lot about." Her eyes met mine. "But Joss, if there's one thing I know, it's that you can't avoid or suppress your problems forever. At some point, you have to face things so you can move on from them."

"Easy for you to say." I watched Jax playing on the floor of my bedroom. "You have all of them." I waved a hand at the walls, my broader meaning obvious.

"Yeah, but I didn't always." She eyed me. "And for that matter, you have them, too. All of us."

"I don't. I really don't."

"You could, if you'd let yourself."

I shook my head. "It's not that easy."

Mara sighed, standing up and scooping Jax up off the floor. "Trust doesn't just happen, Joss. You have to work at it. It's not easy, god knows I know it's not, but it's worth it."

I had no answer to that, and Mara left.

I heard Dru's voice. "Is Luce okay? He had blood all over him."

"I don't know. I can go check on him. Looked like a broken nose, though."

"Do you know what happened?" Dru asked.

"I think things got out of hand faster than she was ready for," Mara answered. "Something triggered her, and she socked him or something. I don't know for sure, I'm just guessing."

"She wouldn't talk about it?"

"Nope. She's walled up like Fort Knox."

They moved out of earshot, then, and now that I was alone everything came slamming through me— the reality of how far things had gone with Lucian, and how they'd ended. He'd been slow, and careful, and patient, making sure I wanted what we were do- ing at every step. His touch had been gentle, his kisses passionate. He'd been voracious and eager, but cau- tious. He'd done everything right. I'd *wanted* it, want- ed *him*.

And then...exactly what I'd anticipated had happened. I'd ruined everything with my fucked-up baggage.

Fine, don't fucking tell me. Whatever. I'm done being teased and fucked with and jerked around. Do whatever the fuck you want.

I heard his voice snapping at me, and I saw the hurt and the anger.

Teased and fucked with? Is that what he thought I was doing? Teasing him? Jerking him around?

He had no *clue* what I'd been through, what I was dealing with.

I was angry at the insinuation that I was intentionally messing with his feelings, that I'd—

Like I could fake the reaction I'd had? Clearly I'd been reacting to something traumatic, and he had the gall to make it about him? To accuse me of fucking with him?

I tried to keep it in, to keep it down. Tried to remain where I was, which would have been the smart thing.

The problem is, once my temper is up, there's no stopping me, no calming me down until I've thoroughly vented my rage.

Anger coursed through me, burning hot and implacable, propelling me to my feet and out the door, a vitriolic tirade on loop in my head.

NINE

Lucian

I KNEW I'D REACTED LIKE AN ASSHOLE. SHE'D OBVIOUSLY been triggered by something I did—unintentionally, but still. And I'd freaked out, snapped at her. Stormed off like a petulant dick.

But holy shit, her sudden violence had shocked me witless. One second she'd been stroking my cock like it was her favorite thing in the world, shaking post-orgasm, staring up at me as if she couldn't believe we were doing what we were doing. She was *into* it; there was absolutely no doubt in my mind. It had been 100% consensual. She'd been the one to reach for my fly, to take me in her hand. I'd have been utterly content to give her an orgasm and leave it there, if that's what she wanted—I had zero expectation of reciprocity. Hope, yes; expectation, no.

Her small, soft hand had been gliding up and down my cock and she'd been watching intently, mesmerized, lower lip caught between her teeth. Her touch had been…beyond perfect. Exquisite. Incredible. I'd lost myself in her touch, in the silky slide of her hand around my cock. I'd collapsed onto her, turned sideways slightly so she could continue touching me.

That's when she'd just…snapped.

She'd frozen, tensed completely, and stopped breathing. I had immediately begun backing away, wondering what had upset her so suddenly. And then, without warning, she began screaming—an ear-piercing shriek of agony and rage and terror the like of which I'd never heard before. Her fist had shot out, connected with my nose in a blast of shocking, unexpected pain, and she'd kicked at me, shoved me, thrashing wildly, screaming at the top of her lungs.

I'd scrambled off the bed, blood dripping down my nose, my whole face throbbing. When I turned to look at her, she was curled up in the fetal position, silent, shaking, arms around her knees.

I could not have been any more baffled. Then, or now.

I had my shirt on my shoulder, my boots in my

hand, socks shoved into them. My nose, mouth, chin, and chest were sticky and crusted with blood. My balls ached and my cock throbbed—I'd been moments from coming when she'd freaked out. My head spun, and my heart clenched, twisting with confusion.

What the fuck, though? I didn't get it.

My bare feet slapped on the sidewalk as I stalked from the bar toward the studio and the apartment above it. Despite the chaos inside me, I was lucid enough to notice that the travel agency, which was usually open from eight to five each day, was darkened. I paused, glancing inside. The shelves were empty, and boxes were stacked in clusters. The owner, an elderly man named…God, what was his name? I'd only met him a few times. Dave…Lipinski? Something like that. Dave was in the doorway, an armload of boxes towering past his head, one foot trying to kick open the door. I tossed my boots aside and hauled open the door.

"Here, let me help," I said, taking the boxes.

An aging Honda crossover SUV was idling at the curb, hatch open; I set the boxes inside and pushed them as far forward as they would go.

"Thank you, young man," Dave said. And then he frowned, looking at my face. "Looks like you were on the losing end of a disagreement."

He was on the far side of sixty, neat and trim,

graying hair swept over a bald spot. He also sported a silver goatee.

"Something like that, yeah." I gestured at the rest of the boxes, half a dozen more or so. "I can grab the rest for you."

"I'd be grateful."

I loaded the rest of the boxes into his car, and then snagged my boots off the sidewalk. "Closing up shop, huh?"

Dave sighed, glancing back at the dark and empty interior. "It's time. My wife passed away last June, and I just can't stand to be in there without her anymore."

"Yeah, I heard about your wife. I'm sorry to hear that."

"Thanks." He jingled change in his pocket with one hand. "Heading to Florida. My brother lives down near Sarasota."

"Well, good luck and have a safe trip," I said.

He nodded. "Appreciate your help, son." He turned away and leaned into the front passenger seat, pulling out a FOR SALE sign and a roll of tape. He taped the sign in the window, locked the door, got into his car, and drove away with a wave out his window.

I stood for a moment, eyeing the spacious interior of the empty shop, and the FOR SALE sign, which read: "For sale: 1500 sq.ft retail space and 1500sq.ft living space above. Sold as a unit. Cannot be split."

The price he was asking for the place was…well, low enough that it was obvious he just wanted to unload it as quickly as possible. "Priced to sell" would be a generous assessment, although I wasn't a real estate expert by any means, and had no real concept of the comparables in the area; Mara would know, I was sure.

Why was I wasting my time considering it? I had no use for a retail space, or my own living space.

But if we owned this unit, we could connect the living spaces, and I'm sure someone could find a use for the retail space.

I got my phone out and snapped a photo of the sign with Dave's phone number on it, just in case, and then headed back to the apartment above the studio. Corin was on the couch, playing a video game while Tate lay with her head on his lap and her feet propped up on the armrest, her hands laced on top of her belly. As I entered, they both shot me a glance, and then they both did a double take.

"Jesus fuck, Luce!" Corin paused the game and shot to his feet, helping Tate to sit up. "What the hell happened to you?"

I kept walking right past them toward my room. "Don't wanna talk about it."

He caught at my arm and spun me around. "Too fucking bad, dude." He gestured at my face. "Your nose is broken."

"No shit."

He braced his fingers on either side of my face, preparing to set the broken cartilage, but I knocked his hand away.

"Don't need your fucking help, Cor. Thanks anyway."

Corin frowned at me. "When did you become such a grouchy asswipe, bro?" He stepped away and held up his hands. "Fine, though. Whatever. Have a busted-up face. See if I fuckin' care."

I growled in my throat, tilting my face up to the ceiling, realizing I was, in fact, being a grouchy ass-wipe. "Sorry, I'm sorry. I'm being a dick, and I apologize." I gestured at my nose. "Go ahead. Please."

Corin braced his hands on my face again, and then glanced at me. "Deep breath. This doesn't feel great, just in case you've never had your nose broken."

"Nope, this is my first—*FUCK!*" I broke off with a shout as he jerked my nose straight forward so it settled back into place. I could immediately breathe more easily, and the pain, while still an intense throb, faded somewhat. "That does NOT feel awesome."

Corin slapped me on the shoulder. "Welcome to the broken nose club, Luce." He grinned at me. "You're a real man now, son."

I couldn't help a smirk. "Fuck off."

He jutted his chin at me. "Seriously, what happened?"

At that moment, Tate appeared with a wet washcloth and a gallon Ziploc bag of crushed ice. She gently used the washcloth to wipe away the blood from under my nose and my chin, and then shoved the bag of ice into my hands.

"Put that on your nose," she ordered, and then cleaned off my throat and chest.

I held the ice to my nose and stood still as she wiped me off. "Thanks. Both of you." I turned away and headed for my room.

Corin sighed in irritation. "Fine. Don't tell us why you're showing up shirtless and barefoot with a broken nose."

I paused in the doorway of my room. "Sorry. I just…I don't want to talk about it."

Corin waved at me in dismissal. "Fine. Whatever. Be all closed off. It's not like I'm your fuckin' brother or anything."

I hesitated, but couldn't find the words to explain, or the will to trust him with the truth. I shut the door and collapsed onto my back on the bed, holding the ice pack in place.

Alone, I replayed what had happened, and tried to make sense of it.

She clearly had a hang-up about a physical

relationship—that much had been obvious from the start, from the first kiss and how she'd reacted to it. She also, just as clearly, struggled with trust issues, and had no intention of letting anyone get close to her. But all that was easily understood from everything that had happened before today.

Her violent reaction to whatever I'd done…that was different. That was something else.

She'd snapped when I put my weight on her, pinning her to the bed.

Realization slammed through me, making my blood run cold and my heart sink. There was only one rational explanation for her reaction, and now that I saw it, I regretted my angry outburst even more.

I owed her an apology. A big one.

I'd no sooner levered upright and swiveled to sit on the edge of the bed when I heard the front door of the apartment open.

"Joss!" Tate's voice. "Is everything okay? Luce came home a minute ago—"

"He's here?" Joss's voice cut in.

"Yeah, he's in his room." Tate, more subdued now. "But Joss—"

Seconds later my bedroom door flew open and Joss stood in the doorway, eyes sparking and spitting anger. She took two steps into my room and kicked the door shut.

"You're an asshole," she barked.

I stood up and tossed the ice pack onto the bed, remaining a few feet away from Joss. "I know. I owe you an apology."

"How *dare* you call me a tease? How fucking *dare* you act like I'm messing with you on purpose!" She didn't seem like she'd heard me. "You have no fucking clue what I've been through, Lucian. No clue! So fuck you for—"

"Joss!" I snapped, loud enough to be heard over her diatribe.

"What?" She bit out.

I held up both hands palms out. "I apologize for my reaction. I'm sorry, okay? I should have realized why you would freak out like that, and I should have been more understanding. I was an asshole, and I'm not excusing it."

She deflated. "I'm sorry I attacked you. I just—"

I risked a step closer. "Joss, I know I have no idea what you've been through. I'm aware of that okay? But I'm also not stupid. You don't have to tell me anything if you don't want to, but just know that I understand where your reaction came from."

"You understand." This was a flat, disbelieving statement.

"As much as I can, yes. Like I said, I don't expect you to tell me about it—"

She moved past me and sat on my bed. "Sit down and listen."

"Joss, you don't—"

"Just listen and don't interrupt. I've never told anyone this before." She sat in silence, just breathing, gathering her thoughts. "It was about six months after my parents died. I'd made it as far as Toronto. I had this idea I would stay there. Like, get a part-time job and sleep on the streets until I could afford a place. Something like that. It started out fine. I found a job at a hole-in-the-wall Chinese place, washing dishes for cash under the table. Shitty work and long hours and shitty pay, but it was something. I found a shelter nearby where I could sleep at night and take showers. For a few weeks, it was fine. I thought—I thought I had that shit figured out, you know? But then...I met a guy at the shelter. He volunteered there. Nice guy. Young, only a little older than me. Seriously cute, like he was...he was hot, and I was just this naive teenage girl. He seemed interested in me. We started hanging out. He'd meet me outside the Chinese food place after I got off work and we'd walk around and talk. He would buy me food. I was wary, because you know... guys, right? But he was just...*nice*."

She hesitated again. "So I...we got closer. He'd sit on the same side of the booth as me when we sat down to eat. He'd put his arm around me. I'd hold his hand as we walked. Innocent enough stuff, right? This went on for weeks. I was close to having enough money for a deposit on a shared place with some students. The room was tiny, but the place was central and the girls seemed honest. I hadn't thought about my visa or passport or anything, I just…I figured if I had the cash it would work out since the girls were from all over Canada and the U.S., and no one gave a second thought to me being a 'foreigner'. I was seventeen, almost eighteen, and I was naive."

She hesitated again, toying with the end of a dreadlock. She was quiet for a few moments, and then she continued, haltingly.

"His name was Rob—the guy from the shelter was Rob. One day we were walking around after having eaten, and we came to a big park—Trinity Bellwoods, I think it was. He said he wanted to walk through it, so we did. It was late, like two or three in the morning, because I worked at night and didn't get off until after midnight. I knew enough to know that wasn't a good idea for me to wander around places like this by myself at night, so I usually stayed away unless it was daytime. Anyway, I figured Rob was with me so it should be safe enough, right?"

She laughed bitterly. "He took us off the path, into this little grove of trees where there were some big rocks and stuff. Isolated. Silent. I knew, immediately, that I'd made a mistake, but it was too late. He—he looked around, checking for people, and then he just...changed. Like he'd taken off a mask or something. The nice guy just vanished, and he...he grabbed me. Threw me to the ground. Sat on top of me. Put his hand around my throat, choking me. He kissed me, but it was...rough, I don't know how to put it. Not really a kiss, more just him mashing his lips on mine. I couldn't fight him. He was too strong, too heavy, and I couldn't breathe. I was trying, but I couldn't get any leverage to hit him or knee him."

"Shit," I breathed.

"He got his belt open—I still remember the jingle, that sound. He had me pinned to the ground, choking me just enough to subdue me but not enough to make me pass out or anything. He had done this before—I remember thinking that as clear as day, he's done this before. He had his thing out, and was pawing at my clothes. I had a lot of layers on, you know? I tended to wear pretty much everything I owned because it was late spring and it got cold at night. So he was trying to get through the layers."

She paused, swallowing hard, a dread wrapped around a finger, tugging on it in agitation. "He...he got me to where he could, you know—rape me. In the moments before he did, though, he paused. He looked down at me, right in the eyes." Her voice dropped an octave and went rough, mimicking a male's voice. "'You want this, don't you? You know you want it, you little slut.' I felt him—I felt—he had me pinned, and he was breathing on me, and his belt buckle was jingling, draping on my leg. The metal was cold, I remember that. He stank. He was so heavy. And his thing—he was trying to get at me. But he hadn't pulled my layers of pants down far enough."

She laughed again, a bitter huff of breath.

"Those layers saved me. He let go of my throat a little, focusing on trying to get my clothes off enough that he could get to me. He moved off me, and that allowed me enough leverage that I could get my knee between us. Once I had my knee up, I was able to kick at him. I hit him, kicked him, bit him. I fought like a fucking tiger." She glanced down at her hands, clenched into fists, and forced them open, shaking them out. "I, um, I found a rock in the grass, and I hit him with it. A lot of times. He fell over and I got up, got my pants back up, and I ran. I have no idea what happened to him. If he—if I'd hit him enough with the rock to—to, you know, kill him, or just hurt him. I ran and I didn't stop until I couldn't run anymore, and then I walked." She shook her head. "I vowed then that I'd never stop again for more than a few days, and I'd never trust another person again. Certainly not a guy."

She sighed. "I, um. I was a mess, obviously. This woman, Val. She, um—she was walking by, talking on a cell phone. She saw me, and she just—she ended her call without even saying goodbye, and—and asked if she could take me somewhere safe I could get cleaned up. I was in shock, I think, because I just went with her. She took me to a place called Covenant House. It, um—they let me stay there." Joss stared at her feet. "Covenant House literally saved my life. After Rob, I think I would have…I don't know. Offered counseling to help me past what happened, food, safety." She blinked hard. "They had this little library. It was a couple shelves in a corner, with a folding table and chair in front of them. I was put in charge of checking books out and in and shelving them. That…it gave me something to…to do."

"How long did you stay there?" I asked.

"A little over a year. I knew I couldn't stay forever. I didn't want to leave, but…otherwise I'd just be trapped there forever. I remembered Dad telling me while he made pancakes one Sunday morning that he'd always wanted to go to Alaska. So when I left, my goal was to come here…for Dad."

My room was filled with another silence I didn't dare break.

"Joss, I—" I really didn't have any idea what to say, though.

"I trusted Rob," she cut in. "When I first got to Toronto, I thought I had a chance at figuring out a normal life. Get a job, get a place, maybe even a boyfriend. I was naive and stupid, and it almost got me raped. So yeah, I don't trust anyone." She finally glanced at me. "Least of all a man."

I sighed. "And when I put my weight on you, it triggered you."

She nodded, looking down at her feet. "Yeah. But you didn't deserve that. I just—I was triggered, and I couldn't help it."

"I get it."

She twisted on the bed, looking me. "Lucian, I—I need you know something." She reached out and took my hands in hers. "Before that, before I freaked out—I wanted what we were doing. You had no way of knowing what would happen, that I'd react that way. I enjoyed what we were doing, Lucian. I promise you I did."

I swallowed hard, grabbing the ice bag, removing my hands from hers. "I thought I'd misread things or something. I mean, I know I didn't get actual verbal consent every step of the way, but when someone initiates contact, that's pretty clear consent, right?"

She shifted closer to me. "Lucian, god—please don't think that. I wanted it. I really did."

"Did." I sighed. "You *did* want it."

She groaned. "Lucian, don't."

"It's fine." I felt myself shutting down, closing off.

She flipped her dreads backward and flopped onto the mattress with a groan. "Lucian, I'm just not there."

"I get it."

She sat up. "Please don't be mad at me. I'm sorry I'm so—back and forth with you, I just—it's hard, okay? I don't know how to do this, how to trust you, how to be the kind of person that just…" she trailed off with a huff. "I'm just not there, okay? I tried, and I couldn't do it. I like you. I'm attracted to you. But I can't do this with you. I'm sorry."

I nodded, and tried to act nonchalant, like there wasn't a cold hard pit at the bottom of my stomach. "It's cool. Whatever." I lay back on the bed and set the ice pack against my nose once more, closing my eyes.

"Don't 'whatever' me, Lucian. I'm trying to be honest with you here. I told you what happened—and that's a big deal for me. I don't talk about myself with anyone, ever. I don't trust people. I don't stay in one place. This isn't me. I've been trying, but I can't do it."

"Okay."

She fell silent, and I expected to feel the bed lift as she stood up, but it never happened.

"Okay?" Her voice was tiny, soft. "That's it?"

"Well…what is it you want of me, here?" I remained on my back, ice pack on my nose, eyes closed, even though my instinct was to turn to her, to comfort her, to tell her how much I wanted her, how not okay all this was. "You said you couldn't do this—whatever *this* is. And I'm saying okay. Fine."

Another long silence. "Whatever this is."

"Yeah. Whatever this is, because I sure as fuck don't know."

"Neither do I! What do *you* want from *me*? How am I supposed to know how to navigate this shit? I'm fucked up, Lucian! My life is fucked up." She went from loud to quiet in an instant. "What do you want from me?" This was more of an echo, a repetition out of exasperation.

"Nothing. I don't want anything from you." That was a damn dirty lie—I wanted *everything* from her.

I wanted to kiss her and never stop. I wanted to feel her beneath me, feel her legs wrapped around me. I wanted to go sleep with her and wake up next to her. I wanted all this so bad it fucking hurt, so bad it scared me stupid. But she couldn't do this. She just wasn't there. Which meant there was no fucking way in hell I could even let myself think any of that, much less say it to her.

Problem: I had already thought these things to

myself, but it was too late to put the genie back in the bottle. Now I just had to live with it, and live with knowing it wasn't going to happen.

I felt Joss beside me—her physical presence, yes, but also her energy.

"You don't want anything from me."

"Nope."

"Bullshit!" she shouted. "Fucking bullshit!"

I sat up and threw the ice pack across the room so it smacked against the door and hit the floor. "You want to know what I want? I want you to quit fucking with my head!"

She reared back as if I'd hit her across the face. "Fucking with your head? The fuck is *that* supposed to mean?"

"It means you're a goddamn tease! You said it yourself—you're back and forth every two seconds! One minute you're all no, go away, leave me alone, don't touch me, and the next moment you're all over me, kissing me like you've never been kissed in your fucking life, like you can't get enough. And then you run off on me, all upset about who the fuck knows what!" I gestured angrily at the door. "And this is all *before* you broke my goddamn nose! What do *I* want! How about you figure out what the fuck *you* want! Do you want me, or do you *not* want me? You let me kiss you, and then you bolt. You let me give you an

orgasm, and then you break my nose. And yeah, I understand the trauma of what you just told me about,
but that doesn't totally explain how hot and cold you
are with me."

I saw the anger in her, but I ignored it and kept
going, letting out the fears and doubts I'd been harbor-
ing, that had been percolating inside me for months.

"This thing with you, to be honest, it's the last
fucking thing I needed. You've thrown my entire life
into chaos, you know that? And I mean *everything*. You
make me doubt myself. You make me doubt what I'm
doing in life, where I'm going, and why. Like, why am
I here? I mean in Ketchikan, not in some metaphysi-
cal sort of way, but shit—yeah, that way too. Like, all
my brothers have...a *thing*. A purpose, a talent, or a
career path set out in front of them. Every single one
of them, except me. And I was fine with that until *you*
showed up."

"How in the hell does any of that have anything
to do with me?" she demanded.

"Because you and I are a lot alike. We both have
trust issues, we both have done a lot of traveling—for
different reasons, but still. But you—you're different.
You have..." I hesitated over admitting this to her, to
anyone, to myself. "Even you have something. You
have that cafe bookstore you want to open. And I...
don't have any aspirations like that. Nothing. And I

didn't realize that until I met you."

"Oh, poor you, poor Lucian. You don't have a purpose? You can't find your talent? Boo fucking hoo. Try losing both parents at the same time! Try being totally fucking alone in the world! Try being homeless in a foreign country, a girl, and a teenager! You have seven brothers who love you and take care of you! Not to mention Dru, Mara, Claire, Eva, Tate, and Aerie! You have a home, a family, a place to fucking *be*, a place that's yours!" She stood up and backed away, facing me, in a full rage, now. "And how fucking *dare* you call me a tease! I'm not teasing you! I've never teased you!"

"Sure as fuck feels like it!" I snapped back. "You get me all worked up and let me think you're into it and you want it and then all of a sudden you're freaking out, running off on me, panicking, acting like—like—I don't fucking know! Like you're scared of me, or something! And all I can think is, what the fuck is *wrong* with me? What did I do? What am I doing wrong? I'm fine waiting, I'm fine going slow. But then we start kissing and you get into it and make me think you want to take things farther, so I do, and I try to be careful and make sure you're with me every step of the way, but then you freak out all over again! What the fuck else am I supposed to think? Either you're scared of me, or I'm missing something."

She turned away from me, shoulders tensed as if expecting a blow, hands fisted at her sides, breathing hard as if restraining herself from physically attacking me again.

A beat passed in silence; the only sound was her ragged breathing.

Then, she whirls on me, eyes blazing. "It's not *about* you! It's about *me*!" She stomps closer, leaning forward. "I'm scared of you because you make me feel things I can't afford to feel! You make me want things I can't afford to want!"

"What is it you can't afford to feel or want? Explain that much at least."

"YOU! This! Us!" She gestures with both hands at me, at the door behind us. "EVERYTHING! I can't afford to want you; I can't afford to want to stay here. I can't—I don't belong here! I want all this and I can't have any of it!"

"Why not?"

"Because—fuck, you wouldn't understand."

I stood up, now. Angry, frustrated. "Why not? And why not at least try me?"

"I can't."

"Why not?"

"I just *can't*!"

"You're just scared."

"Yes! I am! I already said I was, goddamn it!" She

steps toward me, stomping a foot and glaring up at me.

"What are you so scared of?"

"We're going in circles, Lucian."

I groaned, spun away, ripping my hair out of the ponytail and running my hands through it, and then whirled back to face her. "Because you're not actually answering me. It's obvious you're scared of me, of how I make you feel, but I don't know why. You're scared of things getting physical—that much is obvious, but I don't know why. You're scared of letting yourself belong here, but again, I don't know why! And you won't explain any of it." I sighed, the anger going out of me. "You're going to leave, right? So just go. Quit playing games with me, and just do what you do—run."

"I'm not running! I haven't been running, Lucian, I've been surviving!" She said this through a veil of tears she couldn't hold back.

I want to hold her, comfort her, but I don't let myself. "Yes, you are! And I get it, Joss, I really do. Your parents died, and you did what you had to do to survive. And then that shit in Toronto happened. I get it, okay? Trust is hard. I don't really trust my own brothers, and they're—they're great. They're amazing. Which is part of the problem, if I'm being honest, but that's not what we're talking about, is it? We're talking about you. All this shit happened to you, and it was horrible and you're scared and you don't trust anyone. Totally understandable. But how long can that continue? Are you going to live your whole fucking life like that? It doesn't have to be me. That's fine. But someday, you have to trust someone."

"Oh, like you're one to talk? You just said you don't even trust your own brothers! Which is…that's batshit crazy to me. I mean, what have *you* been through to make you so scared of trusting anyone? Unless there's something you haven't told me, something I'm not getting."

"You're an only child, you won't understand."

"I'm an only everything, Lucian! I'm alone! I'm fucking *alone* in this world. So no, maybe I don't get it."

"You've met all my brothers. You've spent time around them. You see what they're like! Well, try being a quiet, introverted kid with brothers like that. Bast, Zane, Brock, and Bax were fucking legends in this town while I was growing up. They were the big dogs wherever they went, whatever they did. They were big, loud, brash, and cool. They had all the friends, they played football and basketball and soccer. They came home with black eyes and bloody noses at least once a week, bragging about the epic fights they'd gotten in. Zane knew he was going to be a Navy SEAL by the time he was a sophomore, Brock had his pilot's license by the time he graduated, Bast was basically running the bar by himself by the time *he* graduated, and Bax was setting state football records left and right."

I paced away, hair flying around my face, seething, now, venting all the shit I'd kept inside for so long.

"The twins were in a garage band by middle school, had paying gigs by high school, got signed by a label and put on a world fucking tour by the time they were nineteen. And don't even get me started on Xavier. That kid is going to be the next Steve Jobs or Nikola Tesla. He was talking at nine months, reading at two, doing algebra by five...and on top of all that he's a fucking rock star on the soccer field, although that's just, like, an extra little thing he likes to do, it's not even anything he finds important." I paced, paced, paced, ranting.

"And then there's *me*," I said, bitterly. "I'm not an athlete. I'm not a musician. I'm not a pilot or—or a genius. I don't even *like* working at the bar, but it's all I fucking have so I do it. My brothers are all larger than life, and I'm just...I'm not like any of them. I've never been like any of them. I don't fit in. I'm quiet and introverted. I'd rather read than hang out with them. I left home because I couldn't handle living in their shadows any longer. Everywhere I went, I was

Bast's little brother, or Zane's, or Brock's, or Bax's. I was the kid brother of the rock stars, or that really smart kid's older brother. That's how everyone defined me—by the way I couldn't even begin to fill the shoes left by my goddamn brothers! And yeah, I know they're great guys. Solid, kind, dependable, generous, all that. But that only makes it worse. It'd honestly be easier if they were douchebags, because then I could just dismiss them as good-looking and talented assholes. But they're not! They're good men. They'd do anything for me. I was a dick to Corin earlier and he still set my nose for me. That's just how my brothers are."

I choked on my own emotion, my own flood of words. Breathed through it, got it under control.

"And I'm not anything like a single fucking one of them. I don't fit. I never have." I shook my head and sank down onto the edge of the bed. "Once you're gone, I'll probably just leave too. I'm not good at fucking anything but that, so I might as well just…" I fluttered my hand vaguely. "Just go…somewhere. I don't know."

She sighed, and sat down beside me. "Lucian… Jesus. I had no idea you felt like that."

"No shit. No one does. I don't talk about me to anyone, ever." I laugh. "I didn't even really know I felt like that myself until you showed up and fucked my world all to hell."

"I didn't mean to."

I nod, not looking at her. "I know. But you did. You showed up, threw my whole life into question, made me more attracted to you than I have been to anyone else in my entire fucking life, made me want you so bad it hurts, but you never let me get anywhere with you. Or if you do, you just rile me up and then run away. Again and again you've done that with me." I wave at the room. "Even now, you get me to say all this, but I know exactly what's going to happen—you're gonna fucking bolt. I feel it. I know it. And you're not gonna answer for shit before you do."

"That's not fair."

"Yeah, well…life ain't fair, is it?"

There was a long, long silence. I stole a glance at Joss. She was sitting on the edge of the bed, perched there as if ready to flee at any moment. Her eyes were on her feet, picking at the cuticles of one hand with the fingers of the other. She was frowning, biting her lower lip. Her dreads hung around her face in thick black ropes.

"I…" she began, and then trailed off.

I waited.

"I was a good kid, growing up. Obeyed my parents, didn't stay out late, didn't party. I never smoked weed, never got drunk with friends. I dated Nick

Wellesley in the tenth grade, but then I found out he was messing around with three other girls and I just…I refused to date any of the guys at my school after that because they all seemed the same." She rubbed her palms together, knees bouncing restlessly. "And then we went on vacation in Nova Scotia my senior year, and my parents died, and…and the one guy I tried to get to know, the *one* guy I was starting to trust…almost fucking raped me, and would have if I hadn't fought him off. How am I supposed to trust anyone after that? After Nick, after Rob?"

"Joss—"

"You wanted to hear this, so shut up and listen." She hesitated a few moments, and then continued. "I'm a homeless orphan without a high school diploma or GED. All I know is survival, emotionally and physically. I walked across all of fucking Canada, because yeah, I was scared to stop. So yeah, I've avoided guys, avoided people, avoided letting anyone get to know me."

"Joss…what are you saying?"

"I'm saying there's a pretty damn good reason I've been…wishy-washy with you. I like you. I'm attracted to you. I like how you make me feel. Trust issues aside, you make me crazy. Physically, you make me lose all sense of reason or self-control. You kiss me, and I just…I lose myself, and that scares the ever-loving shit out of me! I don't know how to handle that. I don't know what to do with it." She gestured at the door. "Just now, in my room, with you—that was as far as I've ever gone, and if I hadn't gotten triggered, I would've gone farther, because I *like* you more than I know how to deal with. But I don't know how to stop, Lucian. I don't know how to stop moving, I don't know how to stop wanting you, and I don't know how to stop being scared of you."

"Joss—"

"I'm scared to fucking death of having sex with you because I'm a fucking *virgin*! Does that answer your question? I'm not a tease, I'm a virgin! I'm scared of how you make me feel, and I don't know how to fucking *do* this with you because I've never *done* it before!"

She bolted, then, finally. Yanked my door open so hard it slammed against the wall, denting the drywall. I heard the front door squeak open and then slam closed, and then there was silence.

She was a virgin?

That explained…well…everything.

And made me feel like even more of a grade-A asshole.

Fuck. What a mess.

Everything was a mess, and I had no idea how to fix any of it.

TEN

Joss

I RAN BACK TO MY ROOM AT A DEAD SPRINT, HEART hammering so hard it hurt, so hard I thought I was going to have a heart attack.

I'd told Lucian the truth. All the truth, everything I'd been hiding from him and from myself.

I couldn't face him. Not after that. How could he want me, after that? Twenty years old, uneducated, homeless, and a virgin. How could there be anything between us, now?

There couldn't be.

I changed into my wandering garb: a pair of thick leggings and baggy jeans, thick socks, combat boots, a long-sleeved T-shirt, a sweater, and a thick hoodie, and then shoved the remaining few items of clothing I had laying around my room into my backpack, and headed out the door. Three months here, and packing to leave took thirty seconds. I'd always been planning on leaving, though. The Badds weren't my family.

I made it to the door at the top of the stairs before anyone stopped me.

"Going somewhere?" Dru asked, sitting at the kitchen table with a laptop open in front of her.

I kept my eyes on the door and my hand on the knob. "Yeah. I'm leaving."

"For good?"

I nodded. "Yeah."

"Can I ask why?"

I sighed, a tremulous sound. "It's—it's time. It's past time."

"This is about Lucian." She grabbed something from the table next to her and walked over to me. "Isn't it?"

"It's about a lot of things." I forced my eyes to hers. "You'll never know how grateful I am to you and Bast for letting me stay here."

"I don't know what happened, and it's none of my business, but…" she hesitated, a lock of red hair falling into her eyes. "I don't think you're making the right choice."

"This is what I do. It's all I know."

"So learn something else."

"I can't." I whispered it, barely keeping my voice from breaking. "I can't. Don't you see that?"

She searched my face without a word for several long beats, and then nodded. "I guess I do." She lifted her hand, extending something to me. "Take this. It's connected to our family plan. Unlimited calling and data. All of our numbers are programmed into it."

It was a cell phone, a brand new, latest generation iPhone, a glossy black screen with a thick red rubber case to protect it from falls.

"I can't take this, Dru."

She lifted an eyebrow. "You can and you will."

"Why?"

"Because you're going to get out there, and you're going to realize how wrong you are. You're going to realize that home is where you choose to be, and that family is who you choose to surround yourself with. You're going to realize that *we* are your family and *this* is home." She tapped the phone. "And when you do, you're going to call me. Day or night, no matter where you are. You're going to call me, and we're going to come get you and bring you *home*." She reached past me and opened the door for me. "You can leave if you want—"

I resorted to sarcasm as a defense against how she was making me feel. "Oh, I can, can I?"

She ignored me. "You can leave if you want, Joss, but you'll be back."

I took the phone, shoved it into the pocket of my hoodie, and pushed past her. "Whatever."

I ignored Bast's questions as I swept across the bar and outside. I headed for the nearest mode of transportation out of here: the ferry to the airport. I had to get away, had to get as far from here as I could, as fast as possible. I had the cash, so I may as well use it.

I sat alone at the front of the ferry, clamping down hard on the rampage of thoughts and emotions boiling inside me. The ride was short, and soon I was facing a clerk across a counter, trying to figure out where to go next.

"Where does the next flight out of here go, and how much is it?" I asked.

The clerk tapped at her keyboard, consulted her monitor, and then glanced up at me with a flat attempt at a smile. "Seattle…five-fifty." She glanced at her watch. "It's twelve forty-eight now, and the flight leaves at one thirty-six, and it's almost sold out, so if you want this flight, you'd better decide quickly."

I blinked at her. "Five hundred and fifty dollars?"

"Round trip, yes."

I swallowed hard. "One way—how much?"

"Two seventy-five for a one way."

I twisted my backpack around, dug around for the box with my cash in it, withdrew enough to cover the fare, and handed it to her. "I'll take it."

"Luggage?"

I shook my head as I slung the backpack onto my back. "Nope. Just this."

She processed the purchase and printed out a boarding pass, giving me directions to the gate. And then came the look I'd been waiting for. "One-way trip, no luggage. Running away, are we?"

I gave her a *die-bitch* glare until she blanched and hurriedly handed me the boarding pass. "Have a nice flight. Next!"

It was less than two hours to Seattle. I deboarded the plane, splurged again, recklessly, on a cab to downtown Seattle. I was barely avoiding a breakdown at this point, forcing myself to breathe slowly and keep my thoughts off of Lucian, off of Ketchikan, off the bar, the brothers, the girls, the bakery...and how I'd been closer than ever to The Garden. If I'd stayed in Ketchikan, could I have saved enough to find a place?

God, stop, Joss, just stop. It's not happening. It could never happen.

Eventually, the cab let me off downtown, and I was back on familiar ground—on foot, alone, with no destination. Only this time, niggling in the back of my head was a tiny, quiet, but subversive thought:

I may not have anywhere to get to, but I do have somewhere to go back to.

It was not a comforting thought.

I wandered Seattle for hours.

And I came to an uncomfortable and unsettling realization: I had no desire to be there. There was nothing here for me. Just…buildings and people, structures that meant nothing and faces I didn't know, and would never care about.

So, I started walking. Out of Seattle, heading south for the first time, instead of west.

Darkness fell on me somewhere between Seattle and Tacoma. I wasn't as comfortable in the darkness as I used to be. The highway became ever more deserted as night expanded and darkened around me. I walked on the side of the I-5, passing through evenly spaced pools of light, the occasional car or semi whooshing past me.

My feet began to hurt after only a handful of miles.

I'd never felt more alone in my life.

I kept going until there was a tinge of gray on the horizon. My feet throbbed, and I had several blisters. I was cold. I was hungry. I was exhausted.

I just want to go home.

The thought struck me, unbidden, like a lightning bolt, and I began to cry. Just a tear or two trickling down now and then, but eventually I was bawling like a baby, sobbing, and I couldn't stop. I couldn't see for the tears. I staggered off the shoulder of the highway and into the tall grass. Bright white lights buzzed above me—a billboard; I stumbled through the grass and caught up against a low chain link fence, on the other side of which was an RV dealership, the white rectangular bulks of the RVs lit up along the fence line by three tall light poles. I sagged against the fence, gulping down sobs, my fingers grasping blindly at the chain link, my eyes blurred by tears.

I don't want to wander anymore.

I want to go home.

I sank to my butt in the cold, dew-damp grass, slung my backpack around to my lap, and rested my back against the fence. I unzipped the outermost pocket of the backpack, and, with trembling fingers, withdrew the cell phone Dru had given me.

ELEVEN

Lucian

S HE WAS GONE. I HESITATED FOR ABOUT TEN MINUTES, doubting and debating whether to go after her, and then I realized I was being a dumbass, so I jogged to the other apartment.

I was too late.

Dru was sitting at the kitchen table with her laptop, working. She looked up when I entered. "You're too late, Luce. She's gone."

"Gone? Where?"

Dru shrugged. "Didn't say. I don't think she knew."

I sagged against the closed door, my head thunking backward. "Fuck."

"What the hell happened between the two of you?"

I banged my head against the door. "I fucked up."

"Clearly. How?"

I shook my head, scrubbed my face. "It's complicated."

"Life is complicated, Luce. Sometimes you gotta talk about it."

I scraped my hair back into a ponytail and let out a breath. "And sometimes you don't."

I turned and jogged back down the stairs before Dru could question me any further, and found Xavier coming up out of the basement of the bar where the weightlifting equipment was kept. He was sweaty, hair damp and dark with sweat, with earbuds trailing up from his phone to his ears. He saw me, tugged one earbud out, and waved at me.

"Hi, Luce."

I jutted my chin at him. "Hey."

He stared at me hard, for a long moment. "You are in a worse mood than usual, I think."

"Worse mood than usual? What's that mean?"

He shrugged. "You have a tendency to be… somewhat moody."

"I'm not moody, I'm introverted."

"I disagree, brother. I think you are simply a victim of your own self-isolation." He blinked at me for a moment. "I am going for a run. Care to join me?"

"Victim of my what?"

He waved a hand in dismissal. "Forget it." He headed for the door. "Run with me, Lucian."

I growled. "Fuck. Fine. A run might do me good." I joined him at the door. "Gotta stop by my room so I can change, though."

Xavier only nodded and accompanied me back to my room, waited in the living room watching Corin play PS4 while I changed into running shorts and shoes, and then we exited through the studio.

We stretched out on the sidewalk together, and then trotted off down the docks at a swift jog. The pace Xavier set was punishing, a six-minute mile at maximum, if not faster. I wasn't a regular runner, but my usual workout routine kept me fit enough that I could keep up with him, although I felt the burn in my lungs after a couple of miles. We ran together in silence for a while, maybe through three or four miles, and then Xavier slowed to a stop on the outskirts of town, at the bottom of a short, steep hill.

I bent over, hands on my thighs, gasping. "What are we stopping for?"

Xavier was as out of breath as I was. "Running sprints up that," he said, gesturing at the hill.

"What?" I gasped. "You're crazy."

He nodded. "I am a little crazy, I suppose. Hill

sprints are brutal but effective."

"A four-mile run, hill sprints, and then a four mile run back?"

He nodded, grinning at me. "I've done a few free weight sets with Bast already."

I rebound my hair into a tight topknot and scrubbed sweat off my face. "Crazy fucker." I swung my arms and shook out my legs. "Let's do this, then."

For the next fifteen minutes, we sprinted up the hill, walked gasping back down, rested a moment, and then sprinted back up, repeating until we were both holding stitches in our sides and pouring sweat.

Xavier pointed at a fallen tree on the side of the road. "Let's rest before we run back."

We sat down, breathing raggedly.

After a few minutes of silence, I glanced at my brother. "What did you mean, before, that I was a victim of my own self-isolation?"

He wiped sweat off his brow with the back of his wrist. "How honest would you like me to be?"

I frowned at the question. "Um, very?"

"Then you have to respond in kind." He met my gaze, his fierce jade eyes piercing. "No avoidance."

I actually hesitated. "Xavier, I—"

He flicked his gaze away, shaking his head. "See? You cannot even agree to that much."

"Fine, Jesus. Just tell me what you meant."

He picked up a twig at his feet and began peeling the bark off of it. "Ever since I was young, you have held yourself apart. As if you were...separate from the rest of us, somehow. You never entered conversations, never interacted with the rest of us. Canaan and Corin would play with me when I was little, and so would the others, but you...you never did. You just seemed...disinterested. In me, in all of us. As if whatever was going on in your head was more interesting to you than your own family."

I fought the urge to respond defensively, and thought about what he was saying. "It wasn't like that."

"I am only saying how it seemed to me. I cannot speak for our brothers, obviously, but they have all made similar comments at some point. None of us really...*know* you. You will not let us."

The shell was coming out, the walls shooting up. "What do you want, my life story?"

He quirked an eyebrow at me. "You only prove my point with your use of sarcasm as a defense."

I growled, picking up a pebble and tossing it angrily at a tree trunk. "Asshole."

He ducked his head, picking up another twig. "Am I an asshole because I am right, or because I said it at all?"

"Use a contraction once in a while, man, shit." I

flung another pebble. "Both."

"The use of jargon and slang makes me feel uncomfortable. I prefer a more formal manner of speech."

"Because you're uncomfortable with this conversation. You don't always talk like this."

He nodded. "That much is true." He glanced at me. "Will you answer a question as truthfully as possible?"

"I'll try."

"What happened with Joss? Why did she leave?"

"I don't know," I muttered, miserable and annoyed.

"That is a lie."

I sighed, and picked up a twig of my own, using it to chisel more pebbles out of the earth at my feet. "You're an annoying little shit, you know that?"

"We are the same size, Lucian."

"Latch onto the wrong thing, why don't you," I said, chuckling. "Joss left because that's what she does, okay? She leaves."

Xavier's gaze was sharp. "I do not think that is the entire truth, Lucian."

I eyed him sideways, and then tossed several pebbles as hard as I could, hitting a tree trunk about six feet away. "Goddammit, Xavier. Can't you let it go?"

"Why is it so hard to tell me what happened?"

"She left because of me, okay? She left because—because things got fucked up. She and I are both a mess, and it was never going to work between us."

"You cannot know that for certain. I think unless you try, you will never know what could work." He snapped the twig into halves, and then quarters. "But I think you are too trapped in your own self-isolation that you refuse to see possibilities."

"There you go again with the self-isolation bullshit."

"It's not bullshit, it's the truth!" For a moment, he lapsed into informality. "You isolate yourself. For some reason, you feel as if you are separate from us, and thus keep yourself held apart, alone. You perpetuate the myth of the lone wolf within yourself."

I frowned at him. "The fuck's *that* mean?"

"You are smart enough to know what it means, Lucian. You just have to be honest enough with yourself to admit it."

I stood up and paced away, Xavier's razor-sharp insights cut through me. He remained where he was, watching me, and eventually I sat back down on the log, breathing a long, resigned sigh.

"You're awfully observant for a guy with zero social skills."

He laughed good-naturedly. "You are not one to talk, Lucian. I may be awkward socially, but at least I

try. You don't do even that, the majority of the time."
He chose another twig. "You cannot avoid the issue
by insulting me, you know."

I groaned, and rubbed my face with my hands.
"Goddammit. Why is this so hard?"

"Because you are trapped in your own—"

"Self-isolation," I said in unison with him. "I
know, I know."

"As with most things in life, I think the only way
out, here, Lucian, is through."

"When did you get so wise?" I asked.

"By virtue of facing many challenges in a very
short life."

"I see." I met his gaze. "So what is it I'm supposed to be opening up with, here?"

Xavier shrugged. "What happened with Joss and
why she left, why you have always been so solitary
and unwilling to connect with the rest of us, why
you're so unhappy all the time…pick one."

"It's all mixed up into one big mess," I said. "You
really want to know all this bullshit?"

He nodded. "Yes. Very much."

I was silent for a long time. "I don't fit. I never
have."

"You do not fit where?"

"Anywhere. With anyone. In this family. With
you guys." I pinched the bridge of my nose. "I've

always felt that way. It's why I am the way I am."

"In what way do you feel you do not fit with us?"

"Because I'm just…not like any of you. I'm not loud or big or cool like the older boys, I'm not a rock star like the twins, or a genius like you. I felt…shit, I don't know how to put it. I felt trapped in my own head. Lost in myself. A small person in a big world, and a useless addition in a big family."

Xavier didn't answer right away. "Lucian…how can you not see your own value?"

I laughed bitterly. "What value?"

"You have always been effortlessly cool, simply because you are so…mysterious." He held my gaze. "You speak little, but when you do, what you say is worth listening to. You project an air of capability, as if you could do anything you decide to."

"That's a nice observation, but—"

"But nothing." He held my gaze. "Self-worth comes from within. It does not come from a talent, or a skill, or a calling. No one can give it to you."

I nodded, and tore my gaze away. "That's my deep secret, I guess, what the whole lone wolf thing is meant to hide—that I don't…" It was so, *so* hard to say out loud. "That I'm intimidated by all of you guys, and always have been, and I got so caught up in feeling left out and feeling like I didn't fit that I…" I trailed off with a shake of my head.

"You what? Say it."

"I've always felt…extra." My voice dropped to a whisper. "Worthless."

"It hurts me deeply to hear you say that." He pinned me with his gaze. "Because you are *not*."

"Xavier—"

"You *are not* worthless, Lucian." He twisted to sit facing me, straddling the log. "You are our family. Our brother. By blood, yes, but also by choice. We value you. We love you."

I stood up and paced away, agitated, emotional. "Dammit, Xavier."

He followed me. "Emotion is not weakness, Lucian." He went around to stand in front of me. "To have emotions is to be human."

"It's fucking hard. It hurts."

"*No man is an island, entire of itself; every man is a piece of the continent, a part of the main. If a clod be washed away by the sea, Europe is the less, as well as if a promontory were, as well as if a manor of thy friend's or of thine own were: any man's death diminishes me, because I am involved in mankind, and therefore never send to know for whom the bells tolls; it tolls for thee.*" Xavier glanced at me, waiting to see if I recognized the quote.

"I've heard that before, but I don't know who it is," I admitted.

"John Donne."

"Huh. And how does that relate to me?"

"Well I'd think the first part was pretty self-explanatory." In more familiar territory, Xavier loosened a little. "No man is an island, entire of itself. You're not alone, Luce—that's what it means. You *cannot* be alone. We are not meant to be alone all the time."

"And the clod being washed away? What's that mean?"

"Well, that's what I love about poetry—its meaning is not fixed, it is not immutable. A number is a number, it is what it is and cannot be changed. A poem? Well, the meaning of a poem can be…twisted, you might say, to suit the moment. For example, John Donne was speaking of death, yes. 'Never send to know for whom the bell tolls; it tolls for thee.' Meaning, we are all connected. When someone dies, it affects everyone. We are all made less for the loss. But take it back to the concept of connection, Luce: when you feel you have no value, you subtract that meaning from us. We feel you have value—immense value. Disclaiming that makes futile the value we have placed on you."

I stared at him. "Jesus, Xavier."

He glanced at me, baffled. "What?"

"You are something else, you know that?" I

laughed, ducking my head. "What else does John Donne have to say about me?"

Xavier thought for a moment. "Ah, I know." He paused, and then quoted. *"But we know ourselves least; mere outward shows our minds so store, that our souls no more than our eyes disclose but form and color. Only he who knows himself, knows more."*

I laughed again. "And the explanation?"

"We are each of us the poorest judges of ourselves. We cannot see ourselves from without, and so cannot judge our own worth."

"Goddamn, dude." I sighed. "Maybe you're right."

"Perhaps." He glanced at me. "But being right is meaningless if it doesn't push you into allowing yourself to become *more*. To connect. To claim your own worth and find your sense of self and meaning."

I let silence fill the space, and realized he was right. I've been so lost and trapped in my own sense of isolation, as Xavier put it, that I've never let myself even see what I'm capable of. And if I don't force myself to change, I never will.

And the only place to begin is by trusting Xavier.

"Neither Joss nor I were willing to trust each other. We were always dancing around how we felt. And when she finally did admit the truth about certain things, it was...too late, I guess. She ran off."

"And how do you feel?"

"I…" I choked on my thoughts. "I feel…a *lot* for her."

"It's a start," Xavier said. "But it's not everything."

"I want…I want her here. I want a future. I want *us*." I admitted it, out loud, and it sent a shock of exhilaration through me. "I just don't know what that looks like, or how to get it. Or if it's possible."

"Why wouldn't it be?"

"Because she left! She's gone, and I have no idea where she is."

Xavier eyed me thoughtfully. "And if you could find her…what then?"

I ducked my head and sighed. "I'd tell her how I felt. I'd ask her for a chance to…to at least try."

Xavier stood up. "Come on. Time to head back before our muscles cool off completely."

"Just like that?"

He shrugged. "There is not very much we can do much from here, is there?"

"I guess not."

The run back was more leisurely, an easy jog. Good thing, too, because my head was spinning, and my heart trying to germinate a seed of hope.

———✦———

When we got back, Tate was outside the studio, camera in hand, trying to bend down far enough to take a picture of a dandelion growing up in the gap between the squares of concrete. She was so hugely pregnant, however, that she couldn't get the right angle and she was getting frustrated.

"Dammit." She straightened, and then rested the camera on her belly while she scrolled through the photos she'd taken, none of which seemed to suit her. "These are all shit."

Xavier vanished into the bar, on a mission of some kind, leaving me with Tate.

"Photography problems?" I asked.

She sighed, shoving the camera at me. "More pregnancy problems. I want this photo of the dandelion, but I can't get the angle right. If I get down on the ground to get it, I'll never get up. In fact, to be honest, I couldn't even get down that far."

I tapped the button to scroll through the last few photos—all of the dandelion from different angles. Something clicked in my head, and I glanced at her. "I see what you mean. Want me to try? I'm no photographer, but I think I see what you're going for."

"Sure. Go for it."

I slung the strap over my neck and got down on my belly on the sidewalk and snapped a photo. I adjusted the lens, snapped another. It needed to be closer, bigger—I shifted forward and zoomed in as far as the lens would allow, until the bright yellow center filled the viewfinder entirely, out of focus. The lens zoomed and whirred, and then the focus clarified, and I snapped several shots.

Standing up, I handed the camera back to Tate. "See if any of those work."

She took the camera and flipped through the shots I'd taken. And then did so again, more slowly, stopping on the last few. Eventually, she glanced up at me with an odd expression on her face. "Lucian…?"

"Tate?"

She pressed a button on the back of the digital Nikon, and then pivoted to stand beside me, showing me the photos I'd taken. "Look."

She'd changed the display so the photograph appeared in black and white, but it was so close that it was nearly impossible to tell what it was at first. It was almost abstract, in a way.

I blinked at her. "I took that?"

She grinned. "Yeah, you did."

I stared at the photo with an odd, unsettled, squirming kind of excitement bubbling up inside me. "It's weird…but kind of cool."

Tate tilted her head and stared at me. "Kind of—Lucian…are you kidding me? It's amazing! Edit that in Photoshop, bring out the shadows and sharpen the contrast, blow it up, print on a big sheet of glossy photo paper...you could frame that and sell it."

I snorted. "Oh, come on."

She smacked my arm with the back of her hand. "Lucian, I'm serious! You think I don't know what I'm talking about?"

I shrugged. "Your own photography, maybe." There was too much going on inside me, and I was falling back on avoidance and defensive distance. "That's just...I don't know."

Tate smirked at me. "You liked it, didn't you?"

I held a carefully blank expression. "A little, I guess."

She stared me down until I looked away. "I see you, Lucian Badd." She grabbed my hand and tugged me toward the studio. "Come on. I want to show you something."

I followed her upstairs to her and Corin's room, where they had a small desk set up against the wall, on which was a top-of-the-line iMac and an expensive-looking printer. I stood in the doorway while Tate waddled to the desk, slumped laboriously into the chair, booted up the computer, and plugged a cord into the camera, connecting it to the computer. She transferred the photo from the camera to the editing program, and I watched as she touched up the photo, not altering it, but improving it so carefully it wasn't obvious anything had been done, until the photo looked...almost professional. And then she printed it out, stood up, and pointed at the photo sitting in the printer tray.

"Grab that," she ordered, "but don't touch the glossy part, it's still damp."

I followed her into the kitchen, carrying the photo on my fingertips. She gestured at the table, and I set it down; Tate slid a storage crate across the floor, flipped off the lid, and sat in a kitchen chair to dig through the crate, which was full photography supplies.

I watched, fascinated, as she placed the 8x11 photo onto a pre-cut mat, and then fit the matted photo into a thin black frame. I thought she'd hand it to me, then, but she didn't.

"Come on," she said, reaching for me. "Help me up."

We saw Corin again as we passed through the studio; he was on the couch, bass guitar in hand, idly hammering out a riff. "Where you two goin'?"

"The gallery," Tate said. "I have a point to prove."

Corin set the bass aside, shut off the amp, and stood up. "Ooh, I love it when you prove points, especially when it's not to me. I'll tag along, if that's okay."

The gallery? Eva's gallery? What point could she

be trying to prove?

We walked the couple of blocks to Eva's gallery, which also had a painting studio in the back, and found Eva at an easel with a brush in one hand and a palette in the other, wearing a long white button-down of Baxter's, the huge sleeves rolled up half a dozen times, the hem hanging to midthigh. She was painting a portrait of Bax, done in a single thick, dramatically swooping black line, a side profile that was almost abstract but also unmistakable as being Bax.

Eva glanced up as we entered via the private side door that led directly into the studio. "Hey there, kids!"

She scraped the paint off of her brush onto the palette and set both down on a nearby table, which was littered with tubes of oil paint in every hue imaginable, wiped her fingertips on her shirtfront, and glanced at the three of us in turn.

"Lucian, hi," she said her smile fading. "Where's Joss?"

Corin blew a raspberry. "You're wasting your breath, Eva. He won't say shit about shit."

I glared at him, and turned to Eva. "She left Ketchikan," I said.

"Why?"

"Again, you're wasting your breath—" Corin started.

Tate whacked Corin across the chest, hard. "Shut up, Cor."

I swiveled to face him. "I get that I haven't been the most...communicative or open, as of late."

"Or ever," he said, crossing his arms over his chest.

"I had a long talk with Xavier today, and..." I sighed. "I'm going to work on being more..." I waved a hand, hunting for the right word.

"Talkative?" Tate suggested.

"Gregarious?" Eva added, at the same time.

"Not an asshole?" Corin said.

I sighed and rubbed the back of my neck. "Yeah."

Corin laughed. "Not off to a real strong start, bud, with that one-word answer."

I did a fake, toothy, sarcastic grin and flipped him off. "Better, dickhead?"

"Hey, you got two words out in a row!" He pretended he was talking to a puppy. "Good boy, Lucian! Good boy!"

"That's enough, Corin." Eva put her hand on Corin's shoulder, silencing him as effectively as if she'd put a ball-gag in his mouth. "I think it's wonderful you're trying to turn over a new leaf, Lucian."

I groaned, face-palming myself. "Just don't use that phrase anymore, or I'll feel like I'm in a self-help book."

Eva laughed. "Starting a new chapter on life?"

"Starting with a blank slate?" Tate said, giggling.

I couldn't help a grin. "Now you're just trolling me."

Eva patted me on the top of the head. "Yes, Lucian, we are." She turned serious, then. "What happened, though, for real?"

I sighed. "I don't even know where to start." I scuffed at the floor with the toe of my running shoe. "I think things just got a little too…real…for the both of us."

Eva's gaze was knowing. "Someone used the 'L' word?"

I stared at her. "God, no. We've been on one actual date, and we've kissed, like, three times."

Corin looked at me with something akin to horrified embarrassment. "And that's all it took for her to run away from you? Jesus, Luce. Either you're a really shitty kisser, one or the both of you has *serious* trust issues, or when you say 'kissed' you mean went from zero to sixty-nine *way* too fast."

Tate snorted, covered her mouth with a hand, and then smacked Corin on the chest again. "CORIN!"

"Um. The latter two," I said. "Definitely not the first one. At least, not according to Joss."

"So mostly the second one," Eva said. "Trust issues."

"Yeah, as in we're both drowning in them," I said.

Eva just smiled at me. "Those can be overcome."

"How?"

"Simple—you take a huge, terrifying leap of faith, and just…trust each other."

"Just like that?"

"Just like that. No guarantees you won't get hurt. No assurance that it'll work out, just…hope, faith in the other person, and a whole lot of love." She smiled at me. "I came here with nothing. I left my family behind, the entire massive fortune I was set to inherit, and an easy life of idle wealth…all on the hope that the love Bax and I have for each other will be enough."

I blew out a breath. "Damn, Eva. That takes balls."

"You think I wasn't scared out of my mind? I was! For months, I had these middle of the night fears that everything would just…vanish, that he'd stop loving me, that it would get taken away from me, somehow." She shrugged. "I still get those, sometimes, but then I look at Bax, and I know it's going to be okay. He's proven time and again that I can trust him. But let me tell you, that first step? It's a hard one."

I blew out a sigh. "I've talked more about me and my love life in the last couple hours than I have in my entire life."

Corin, uncharacteristically serious and genuine,

just wrapped an arm around my shoulders—still bare, as I never put a shirt on after my run. "Luce, buddy, it's a good thing, trust me. I like this new you. Now we just gotta get you to crack a joke and a smile now and again, and we'll really be cooking with gas."

Eva clapped her hands. "Okay, therapy session is over. I need to paint. What brought you guys here?"

"Oh! Damn pregnancy brain." She lifted the framed photograph. "What do you think of this, Miss Princeton Art Major?"

Eva took the frame and examined the photograph critically. "This is wonderful work, Tate. I'm impressed." She glanced at Tate. "This is kind of outside your usual style, though. Are you experimenting with macrophotography?"

Tate gave me a grin that fairly screamed *I told you so*. "Actually, I didn't take this." She shoved it at me, and I took it automatically. "Luce did."

Eva eyed me with a new appreciation. "You did?"

I shrugged. "I guess I did."

"You guess you did?" Eva asked. "Or you *did*?"

"Yeah, I took it." I admitted it almost as if ashamed, which was ridiculous.

She clapped her hands in delight. "Another artist in the family! Yay!"

"I wouldn't say artist," I protested. "I took one photo. Beginner's luck, that's all."

Eva snorted derisively. "Bullshit." The curse held weight coming from Eva, as she rarely used profanity, unlike the rest of us, who swore like sailors. "This has a wonderful sense of proportion and subject, Lucian. It's just one photo, but to the trained eye, it reveals a lot. If you want my advice, I would say, pursue this. Take a million photographs, of everything. Figure out what you enjoy shooting the most, and shoot the heck out of it."

"I don't have a camera."

Eva walked across the studio to an antique roll-top desk she was in the middle of refinishing. Opening the top, she grabbed a large black rectangular bag and brought it to me. I opened it, and whistled at the contents: a huge, bulky, expensive-looking Nikon camera and several lenses of varying sizes and shapes.

"Eva, now come on. I don't know cameras, but this has to be—"

She cut me off. "My parents sold their estate recently and, in doing so, went through all of my things, and ended up sending me a semi full of my old things. I've donated most of it, but this I kept. It's a professional grade DSLR with a standard lens, a telephoto lens, a wide angle, a fish-eye, several prime lenses, a macro lens...and, oh, um...some filters, a flash, a spare battery pack, the charger block, a light meter, and maybe some other odds and ends. That's almost twenty grand worth of photography supplies."

I handed it back to her. "No. Thank you, but no. You can't just give this to me."

Eva shoved it back to me. "Yes, I can. It was a gift from Thomas, meant to butter me up into accepting one of his silly marriage proposals. I don't want anything to do with it. What's more, I'm not a photographer—never have been and never will be—I prefer a more hands-on medium. I like getting dirty, I like getting paint in my hair." She smiled at me. "Lucian, please. Just accept it."

Tate was fairly drooling. "If you don't take it, I will. That's some seriously sparkly shit right there, Luce."

I glanced at Tate. "Can you teach me that editing program?"

She shrugged. "Sure. I've only taken a few classes myself over at the university, but I'll show you what I know."

I zipped the case and slung it by the strap over my shoulder. "Eva, thank you. Maybe I'll give it a try. Thanks."

Corin, Tate, and Eva all stood staring at me expectantly.

I stared back. "Um…what?"

Corin waved at the door. "Hello, McFly? Go after Joss, dumbshit!"

"I—she's gone. I don't know where she is."

Corin rolled his eyes. "Xavier can track a fly fart across the Mojave if he wants to. I'm pretty sure he can get a bead on Joss. So that excuse ain't gonna pass muster."

"Do you care about her?" Eva asked.

I nodded. "Yeah, I do."

"Will you regret it the rest of your life if you don't find out if you guys could have been great together?" Tate asked.

"Yeah," I answered.

"Are you gonna actually die if you don't get her naked and screaming your name?" Corin asked.

Tate smacked him across the chest. "CORIN! RUDE!" She glanced at me. "But really. Are you?"

I blinked at Tate and Corin, waiting for my answer. "Well...yeah." I grinned. "It was pretty hot the first time."

They both howled in laughter, and Corin high-fived me. "That's my boy!" He shot me a surprisingly sharp and serious look. "For real, though, bro—don't let her get away. That girl was one of a kind."

I still hesitated. "She ran away, guys. Like, bolted as fast as she could. What if she doesn't want the same thing I do?"

Corin put both hands on my biceps and stared me earnestly in the face. "Lucian, I'll only say this once, okay?" He waited until he was sure I was listening. "You ready, buddy?"

I rolled my eyes at him. "Out with already, Cor."

"DON'T BE A FUCKIN' PUSSY!" he shouted, his face inches from mine.

Tate buried her face in her palm. "Corin, you lack any semblance of subtlety, you know that?"

He nodded. "Yep. Sure do. Fuck subtlety." He shoved me, hard. "Go. Get the fuck out of here. Find your girl, throw yourself at her feet, and tell her you fuckin' love her."

"Could you maybe throw a few more fucks in there, Corin?" Eva asked. "I don't think there were enough."

Corin, without missing a beat, started over. "Fucking *go*, Luce," he said, shaking me dramatically. "Get the fuck out of here! Find your fuckin' girl, throw yourself at her fuckin' feet, and fuckin' tell her you fuckin' love her." He glanced at Eva and winked. "Better?"

Eva cackled, slapping him across the shoulder. "You're so bad! Bad, but funny."

Corin shoved me toward the door again. "Go, Luce. For real. Go get your girl."

As I walked out the door, for the first time in more than three months, I felt I was finally getting my shit together.

TWELVE

Joss

THE SUN WAS RISING.

I was still sitting in the grass, holding the phone in both hands, watching the sunrise and thinking…hard. I had Dru's contact information queued up on the screen, so all I had to do was wake up the phone—Dru hadn't assigned a PIN yet—and hit the phone icon. I could call her. Tell her she was right. Tell her I wanted to come home.

But Lucian was back there.

What if he didn't want me anymore? What if he didn't actually care about me? What if he just wanted sex? I'd sat in plenty of train and bus stations listening to girls crying into their cell phones about guys who had fucked them and then ghosted. If Lucian was like that, I'd be stuck in a hell of a situation.

And if he wasn't like that? Was I just supposed to hang my entire future on some physical chemistry with a man I'd known a little more than ninety days? Was a relationship with a guy I'd known all of three months going to work? Was I going to hang my future on the way I felt about Lucian?

But god, what chemistry! It was *so* intense, and we'd barely scratched the surface. I may be a virgin, but I could feel, just from those few brief encounters, that there was a maelstrom of life-changing passion waiting to be unlocked, if I was to let things with Lucian develop.

But what if I couldn't? What if I freaked out every time we got close to having sex? He'd never shown any sign of expecting me to do anything to him in return. He'd given me an orgasm, and I knew—and had known at the time—that if I'd said the word, he'd have backed off immediately. But eventually his patience would give out. He would only be able to deal with my ambivalence for so long. And if that were the case, I couldn't blame him for feeling I was playing with him, teasing him. Dear god. What if I kept freezing, kept replaying the past?

What if…what if…what if…?

There were a million of them. The longer I sat

on the side of I-5, watching the traffic rumble past, doubting myself, the more what-ifs cropped up.

I was paralyzed by doubts, by fears, by my own pride.

Which was a joke—what pride? Sheer stubbornness, that's all it was. I'd run, and now I was too stubborn to admit that I wanted to go back.

A tractor-trailer—a semi without a trailer—hauled to a stop some twenty feet away, brakes squealing and hissing, flashers blinking. The driver's side door opened and closed, and a short, stout middle-aged woman rounded the back end of the trailer. She walked toward me, lifting a cigarette to her lips along the way, spewing a trail of smoke. She stopped in front of me, gazing at me evenly. She was darkly tanned, with wrinkled, leathery skin, graying brown hair cut in a mullet Richard Dean Anderson would have been proud of, and a mouth permanently puckered from sucking on cigarettes. She was wearing dirty jeans, a baggy trucking company T-shirt, and orange Crocs with white socks underneath.

"Looks like you've seen better days, sweetheart," she said, her voice permanently hoarse.

I shrugged miserably. "Yeah, you could say that."

She took a long hard drag, and then spoke around the smoke. "Need a ride somewhere?"

I held my head in my hands and moaned. "I don't

know. Fuck, I don't know what to do."

"Mmmmm." It was, somehow, a sound that conveyed a complete understanding of my predicament. "I see. Well, come on. No sense just sitting here."

I stood up, hiked my backpack on one shoulder, and cradled my phone in both hands. Following the woman to her truck, I climbed up into the cab with practiced ease.

Reaching her seat beside me, the woman eyed me. "You done that before."

I just nodded.

"You runnin' away from some*where*, or away from some*one*?"

"Both."

She turned off her flashers, put on her blinker to indicate she was merging over, and watched her mirrors as she brought the truck up to speed. When traffic was clear, she got back onto the freeway. The radio was on, country music playing. The cab was, oddly, a comforting space. Familiar. The tattered, smooth leather bench, the hiss and crackle and staticky voices from the CB, the radio playing softly, the smell of cigarettes, the rattle of soda bottles and the crinkle of snack wrappers. I'd spent a lot of hours and many miles riding in cabs like this one.

"They hurt you?"

I sighed. "No."

"They want you back?"

"I—maybe. Probably." I groaned. "Yes."

She eyed me carefully. "Been crying, looks like." She held back a smirk. "I'd bet my bottom dollar there's a man in this somewhere."

I nodded again.

"What's your name, honey?"

"Joss."

"Joss. I'm Big Mama Thornton. Not the original, obviously, or any kinda relation, it's just what folks call me."

"Nice to meet you." I stared hard at the phone in my hands, willing it to ring, saving me from having to make a decision myself; it didn't.

"So. Runnin' from a man, but he ain't hurt you, and wants you back. I got that right?"

I snorted. "There's a bit more to it than that, but yeah."

"Always is more to it, baby-girl. But all that, the more to it? Just fluff. Distraction. Bullshit. You gotta sweep all that aside—" Here, Big Mama Thornton swept her cigarette in a wide arc, scattering flakes of ash, "—and just focus on the particulars."

"Focus on the particulars."

"Yep, the big picture. The important shit."

I laughed. "What is with truck drivers and roughly spoken wisdom?"

Big Mama Thornton cackled, snorting smoke out her nose. "'Cause we sit in these cabs all day with no company except our own, no one to talk to and nothing to do but think." She tossed the butt out the window and glanced at me, tapping her temple. "If I ever remembered to get that dictation software thingy, I could write me a bestseller with all the shit I got floatin' around up here."

"I bet you could," I said, smiling.

She nodded. "I could. I will, too, someday." She laughed uproariously and waved her hand. "Nah, I never will. I just think about it."

"You should. I'd read it."

"Awww, you're sweet." Big Mama Thornton eyed me steadily. "So why you runnin'? If he ain't hurt you, and he wants you, what's got you runnin' your fine little heinie away from him?"

I stared out the window, twisting two dreadlocks around each other. "Well, number one, my heinie isn't exactly little. And number two, I'm running because..."

All of the arguments I'd been using to justify my flight seemed to wither under her silent scrutiny; I could trot them out and explain them till I was blue in the face, but I had a feeling this woman would just slice right through them with a handful of words.

"The truth is," I said, finally, "I'm scared."

"Scared enough that bein' alone out on the side of the freeway at six in the mornin' is the better option?"

"Seemed like it at the time." I waved at the windshield. "That back there, and this here, being in this cab like this—it's the only life I've known since I was seventeen. After spending three months with Lucian and his family, suddenly I can't do it anymore. But I'm just so scared of…of…"

Big Mama Thornton lit another cigarette. "Of what you don't know," she finished for me. "Look, baby-girl, I don't know your story and I don't need to. But one thing is clear as shined-up crystal: you love that boy, and for whatever reason, that scares the smart right out of you."

I could only nod. "Yeah, pretty much."

"I had a man, years back. I was about fifty pounds lighter, had hair down to my waist, a figure you could put on magazines—yeah, believe it. I know it don't seem like it now, but it's true. I was one o'them stay-at-home wives, you know? Cookin' and cleanin' and waitin' on my man to come home." She smiled dreamily to herself, remembering. "Ohhhhhh honey child, I loved that man somethin' fierce. Then, one day, he just…didn't come home. Quit his job out of the blue and just…took off. Never heard from him again, not a letter, not a call, nothing. No divorce papers, nothin'.

He was just gone. Been thirty years and I still wonder where he is, some nights." Her gaze went to mine, sharp and penetrating. "My point is this, girlie—after he done took off on me, I got man-shy. Never could quite get myself to trust anyone after that. Tried, but just kept figurin' he'd end up leavin' like Ricky did, and so what was the point? Now I'm too old and fat and ugly and stubborn and set in my ways to pretend I'll ever change. It don't have to be that way for you."

I felt heat pricking at the corners of my eyes. "It's not that simple."

She just snorted smoke. "Bullshit. Sure it is." She took a long drag, held it, blew it out and then glanced at me. "People say it ain't that simple when they know what the right thing to do is, but they're just too damn scared or stubborn to do it."

"So I should just…go back."

"Yup."

"What if—"

"Now that shit right there? Asking what if? You might as well hogtie yourself and lay down on the side of the highway as a start down that slippery-ass slope. It'll paralyze you." She took another drag. "Met a guy once who used to work for one of those intelligence agencies in DC. He was tellin' me about a thing called 'analysis paralysis' where you get so bogged down asking what if and overthinking shit that you never get off your ass and actually DO anything. Sometimes—shit, most of the time—you just gotta jump and figure out where you gonna land on the way down. This is real life, sweetheart—there ain't no safety nets and there ain't no guarantees. You wanna make somethin' of your life, you're gonna have to quit runnin' and start *doin'*."

Big Mama Thornton tossed the cigarette out the window.

"I'm pickin' up a load in Olympia," she told me, "so think on what I told you till we get there."

I stared out the window, turning the events of the last few months over and over in my head.

———✳———

Forty-five minutes later, Big Mama Thornton brought her truck to a stop at a red light just off the exit from I-5 heading toward Olympia. "Best place for us part ways is right here," she told me. "You figure out what you're gonna do?"

I opened the door and climbed down. "I'm gonna go back," I said. "I just have to summon the courage to call him."

"Smart girl." She glanced at the light as it prepared to turn green. "Good luck to you, Joss."

I smiled at her. "Thanks, Big Mama."

She tipped an invisible cap, and then waved at me. "Safe travels, girlie."

"You too." I closed the door as the light turned green, and stepped off to the side of the shoulder.

The tractor-trailer groaned away with a roar and a belch of diesel exhaust, and I was alone again. Traffic whooshed past me, wind from their passage buffeting me.

Analysis paralysis—overthinking my situation… that's exactly what I've been doing. But the thought of calling Lucian and saying…what? *Hi, I want to come back, can you come get me?* Yeah…no.

I started walking again, my eyes burning from exhaustion, legs aching, feet throbbing, stomach rumbling. I didn't have a destination, other than to find somewhere to sit down, get some coffee, and summon the courage to call Dru.

That was the smart angle, I decided. I wasn't ready to face Lucian. I'd dropped a bomb on him, two bombs, actually, and then bolted. He was probably angry at me. He probably wouldn't want to see me, not after the way I'd jerked him around and then run off. But I was tired of running. Big Mama was right—I just had to *do* something. If I wanted to ever open The Garden, I would have to settle somewhere and work at making it happen. It had been a pipe dream for so long, nothing but an ephemeral sort of idea, a nebulous, far-off goal, meant more to keep myself moving than anything else. Now? It was more real. An actual possibility. I'd worked an hourly wage job for three months and had more money saved than I'd ever possessed in my life. I had no idea how much it would take to actually buy or rent a space, much less all the equipment and shelves and books and everything I'd need to make the store a reality, but...if I ever wanted to actually *do* it, I had to just...*do* it.

No more running.

As for Lucian? Well...I wasn't sure what to do about him.

First things first—coffee.

I walked until I started seeing gas stations and restaurants. When I passed a cafe on the same side of the road as I was on, I went in, sat at a table and ordered coffee and breakfast. As I waited for the food, I sipped coffee—nowhere near as good as Dru's—and stared at the cell phone Dru had given me. I woke it up and read for the hundredth time the contact information on the screen:

Dru Badd; 907-445-5555; When you're ready to stop running and come HOME, call me. Xoxo. Dru.

She'd used a photo of herself as her contact info photo—it was her in the kitchen, cup of coffee held up in one hand, flashing a thumbs-up with the other, smiling a wide, goofy grin.

Come home.

Ketchikan was home.

The Badds were home.

The Badds were *family.*

Lucian was…god, what I wanted him to be scared me so deeply my mind and heart just recoiled from even thinking about it.

Before I could second-guess myself, I hit the dial icon, held the sleek device to my ear, and waited through two rings, my heartbeat pounding as if I'd sprinted up a flight of stairs.

"Hi, Joss," came Dru's voice.

I choked on a sob. "Hi."

There was nothing but sympathy in her voice. "I don't know when the last time you heard this was, but—speaking solely for myself here—I love you, Joss Mackenzie."

Any hope I'd had of retaining some semblance of dignity vanished. "Y-you—you don't…" I breathed in slowly through my nose and exhaled shakily from between pursed lips. "You don't even know me."

"Sure I do." I heard noise in the background, voices and chatter and laughter, all of them familiar enough that I could identify the owners—Bax, Eva, Zane, and Mara. "You're Joss Mackenzie. You're an orphan who *used* to be homeless. You're a hard-ass, a tough-ass, a badass, and if you don't tell me where you are so I can get you home where you belong, a dumbass. You're beautiful, you're a hard worker, and smarter than you give yourself credit for. You resort to sarcasm when you feel on the defensive, and everything makes you feel defensive. But you belong with us."

I took a sip of coffee to buy time—it didn't make any difference. I was still crying too hard—again—to speak clearly. "I hate you."

"I think you pronounced 'love' wrong, babe," Dru said, laughing. "And listen, it's just me you're talking to, here, okay? No pressure, nothing to be scared of. Regardless of what else may or may not happen in your life, *I'm* your friend."

"Why?"

"Why?" Dru echoed. "What do you mean, why?"

"I lived in your house for three months. I'm just some orphan girl who fell into the water near your bar. I'm no one. So yeah...why?"

"Hell if I know," Dru said. "I'm not a psychologist, so I can't explain why we click with certain people and not others. I just like you, okay?"

"Lemme see that," I heard Bax say in the background; there was a muffled shuffle, and then I heard his voice on the line. "Yo, Joss, whassup my girl?"

"Hey, Bax."

"So here's the scoop, a'ight? People click or don't

click for a very obvious reason, psychologically speaking. I took a class on this shit back at Penn State, and I remember the basics. It works like this. We recognize something in a person that resonates in our psyche—something familiar that makes us feel comfortable, or something opposite that attracts us—or the reverse, for the same reasons. This works for friendships as well as romantic relationships. So, we see something in you that makes our heads, hearts, and souls go 'fuck yeah, bitches, this chick is cool! Let's be friends!' and it's really that simple."

I couldn't help a laugh. "Is that right?"

"Sure is, princess. I'm a smart mothafuckin' meathead, you feel me?" I heard his voice go distant again. "There. Fixed it."

Dru laughed louder as she took the phone. "Ohhh, Bax. You're something else."

"He sure is," I heard Eva say. "And that's why I love him so much!"

"Yeah, there's that," I heard Bax say, "but Eva, darlin', *you* love me for my really, really, really huge—"

"BAXTER!" Eva shrieked, laughing in embarrassment.

"I was gonna say heart, honey," Bax said. "You love me for my really, really, really huge heart."

"Well, you *are* a big softie, underneath that brawny exterior," Eva said.

"And also my cock." Bax, of course, got the last word. "You also love me for my enormous and talented penile appendage."

I heard Eva groan. "You're impossible."

"And incorrigible," Bax added. "Don't forget incorrigible."

I was laughing—I couldn't help it. They were just...ridiculous. Always funny, always entertaining, and just...impossible not to like.

"So." Dru said, serious now. "Are you ready to come home?"

I'd gotten my tears under control, but her use of the H word brought them back out. "Yeah, I think I am."

"Send me your location."

"Ummm..." I snagged a menu and read the address off the front.

Dru whistled. "Olympia? You went a ways in a short time." She laughed, then. "I had actually meant ping me your location from the messaging app, but an address'll work. I'll just find you on Google Maps." Dru was quiet a moment, thinking, and then I heard her snap her fingers. "I've got an idea. Just sit tight, okay? Stay where you are. We're coming to get you."

I frowned, though she obviously couldn't see me.

"I'm hundreds of miles away. How are you going

to just come and get me?"

She just laughed. "It'll be more fun if it's a surprise. So just stay there."

"For how long?"

"A few hours?"

A moment of silence passed between us, in which Dru was obviously waiting me out, knowing I had something to say.

"Dru?" I asked, my voice querulous.

"Mmmm-hmmm?"

"Lucian…do you think he…I mean, do you think there's a chance—" I couldn't get any more out.

"Joss, my brother-in-law is so in love with you he doesn't even know which way is up, or what to do with himself. It may take some finagling to get him to admit that to himself much less to you…" Dru paused, and I could hear the shrug in the texture of the silence. "But I think if you work at it, if you're honest and courageous in your vulnerability, you'll discover something amazing waiting for you on the other side."

"Honest and courageous in my vulnerability," I repeated. "I don't even know what that means, what it looks like, or how to do it."

"Simple, honey. You just trust him. Give him your heart, and give him a chance to show you who he is and what he's got."

"Oh." I swallowed hard. "That sounds… terrifying."

She chuckled. "Oh, it absolutely is. But it's also totally worth it." There was a commotion on her end of the line. "Oh, good, Brock is here." To me, then. "I've gotta let you go right now, so I can arrange to get you home. Just stay where you are and one of us will call you when it's time"

"Okay," I whispered.

"Bye, honey."

"Bye, Dru."

So just like that…I was going home.

———— ✳ ————

About four hours later the cell phone—my cell phone, I supposed it was—rang, startling me. It was *Brock Badd*, a photo of him in a cockpit of a plane, head-set on, aviator glasses on his face, the world spread out underneath him making it obvious the selfie had been taken when he was upside down.

I swiped the tab to answer it. "Hello?"

I heard a blast of white noise in the background, and then a familiar voice that sent a warm current through me. "Joss?"

"Yeah, it's me."

"This is Lucian."

"I know," I said. "You think I wouldn't recognize your voice?"

"I—yeah, I guess you would. I dropped my phone in the water when I was getting into Brock's plane," he said. "Which is why I'm calling you from his phone instead of mine. Just, you know, so you know."

I'd never heard him making small talk before. "Lucian, are you…rambling?"

He cleared his throat. "No?"

"You are. You're rambling."

A brief silence. "Can you get to the Swantown Marina Seaplane docks?"

"Um. Is that in Olympia?"

"Yeah. It shouldn't be too far from where you are. A cab or an Uber or something could get you there."

"I…um…I can figure it out."

"You're sure?"

"Yes, Lucian. Remember, I *did* manage to navigate my way across Canada…in case you, you know, forgot."

"We should be landing there in…how long, Brock?" A muffled answer I couldn't make out, and then Lucian's voice again. "About thirty minutes or so."

"And you're coming by airplane?"

"Seaplane, actually."

"How…how will I know it's you?"

Lucian laughed. "Oh, you'll know. It's a giant red-and-white twin-prop seaplane, with 'Badd's Air Taxi' written in black letters across the side. Hard to miss."

"Oh."

"See you soon?"

"Yeah," I said. "I'll see you soon."

I ended the call, more nervous now than ever. I paid my bill and left the cafe, bringing up a map of Olympia on the cell phone. I managed to acquire walking directions from the cafe to the seaplane docks and set out, trying not to think too hard about the fact that I was about to see Lucian in about thirty minutes.

What would I say to him?

Should I apologize for freaking out? Did he really, actually want to see me?

God, my head was a mess. My heart was squeezing and hammering, and too many thoughts were buzzing in my head like moths trapped in a lampshade.

I followed the app's directions to the marina, my anxiety increasing the closer I got to the docks.

God, I didn't know whether I was coming or going, which way was up—

I had no idea what I really wanted.

Or maybe I did, but I was scared to let myself even admit I wanted it.

I reached the seaplane docks in a little under half an hour and stood watching the skies. The sky was overcast and heavy, leaden, threatening rain. I heard a buzzing in the distance, but couldn't find the source. Thunder clapped. Raindrops pounded on me, spatting on the docks. The buzzing grew louder, and then I saw the aircraft heading toward the docks, nose up, going what seemed to be way too fast. I watched, my heart in my throat, as the huge red-and-white seaplane settled with precise gentility into the waters of the bay, throwing up a white spray from the floats. Then it taxied slowly away from the middle of the channel toward the dock.

By the time the seaplane arrived where I stood, I was soaked to the bone, the rain having arrived in earnest, hammering down in thick sheets. There was nowhere to take shelter, so I just stood and waited, growing colder and wetter by the minute. When the aircraft thumped to a halt, I was so nervous that I was nauseous.

What would I say?

What would he say?

Oh god, this was so dumb. This was a mistake.

He opened the passenger side door and climbed down onto the float and then to the dock, ducking his head as the rain battered him. He ran toward me. I was frozen, paralyzed, motionless.

He stood in front of me, soaked to the skin. "Joss."

I swallowed hard at the sight of him—tall and lean, long hair slicked wet against his back, a plain white T-shirt pasted to his skin, showing his hard muscles. His eyes searched me. What was he hoping to find?

"Lucian, I—" My voice cracked, broke. "I—"

"Do you want to come back to Ketchikan?"

I could only nod.

He took a step closer, so only inches separated us. "And…and me?"

I gazed up at him, my heart pulsing in my throat. "And you?" I asked, my voice barely a whisper.

"Am I…are we…?" he trailed off, wiping rain off his face with one hand.

"Are we what, Lucian?" I couldn't lift a hand, even though I wanted to.

I was afraid of letting myself want him, letting myself give in to the desire, until I knew how he felt. I could keep myself shut down if I didn't let myself want him. I could skate through life around him, but not with him, if I didn't allow how I really felt about him to come to the surface. If I kept it tamped down, shut off, the furnace of desire cold, I would survive, if he didn't want me.

He searched me with his piercing brown eyes. "Fuck it," he murmured.

And then he kissed me. His hands seized my

waist, hauling me up against his body, and I felt his heart slamming in his chest as hard as mine was, and I felt the trembling in his fingers as they clutched at my back. His lips were firm yet soft, crushing against mine as if helpless to stop himself from this.

A heartbeat…two…

And then it all came crashing through me.

Everything I'd been shoving down, denying, bottling up. All the need, the desire, the hope…

That sharp hot piercing…*need* for Lucian. For everything he was. The need to understand him. To know his foibles, to know his mood, to know his body, to possess his heart, to pierce the mysteries of his personality. The need to know he was mine and I was his. To know we *belonged* to one another.

All of it came crashing through me all at once.

I lifted up onto my toes, my arms encircling his neck. I leaned into him, pressed my breasts against his chest and my hips against his, pressing our hammering hearts together. The kiss became a sob, as the full onslaught of emotion hit me, and Lucian pulled away.

"Joss?"

"I want—" I choked on a sob and started over. "I want to go…I want to go home."

He held my face in his hands. "Home?"

"With you."

He sagged against me, cradling my head under

his chin, wrapping me up in his arms. "Thank fuck."

Lucian scooped me up, backpack and all, and carried me to the seaplane. He set me down and held my waist in both hands as I climbed from dock to float, and then from the float into the cabin of the seaplane.

Brock was waiting for us in the seaplane, sitting at the controls, headset on, one hand on the throttle, the other holding his cell phone. He had a goofy grin on his GQ-worthy, Hollywood-handsome face, staring at his phone screen. As I slipped to sit behind the copilot seat, I saw why: Claire had sent him a nude selfie, which I caught a glimpse of—it wasn't just a nude, either, but an…erm…action shot, shall we say. I looked hastily away, and Brock jumped, startled at my presence, and fumbled with his phone, clicking the lock button.

"Joss, hey." He wasn't blushing, exactly—men that gorgeous didn't blush, I was pretty certain—but he did seem at least mildly embarrassed. "You—uh… you didn't see anything, did you?"

The interior of the seaplane, originally meant for cargo, I surmised, had been converted to hold seating for passengers, and the walls had been insulated against noise and cold. There was a partition between the cockpit and the passenger area that could be closed, if needed, but it was open right now. I buckled up.

I managed a genuine smile for Brock. "Did I see anything? What would I have seen?"

He chuckled. "Right, exactly."

I winked at him. "She's beautiful, Brock."

"I know." He gave Lucian a thumbs-up when he tossed the line off and climbed in. "Okay, kids. Let's go home."

Lucian took the seat beside mine, buckled up, and met my gaze.

As Brock taxied back out into the middle of the channel and prepared to take off, Lucian glanced down at my hands, folded in my lap, and extended one of his hands.

I gave him mine, and he threaded our fingers together.

"Let's go home," Lucian whispered.

THIRTEEN

Lucian

JOSS SQUEEZED MY HAND SO HARD DURING TAKEOFF I thought she might break bones, squeaking in fear as our floats left the water. I didn't blame her; taking off from the water in a seaplane was a vastly different experience from taking off from a runway in a 747. Once we were airborne, however, she immediately relaxed. Within minutes, her eyelids were drooping.

"Tired?" I asked, mouthing the word since we didn't have headsets and would have to shout to be heard over the noise of the propellers.

She just nodded.

"Where did you sleep last night?" I asked, leaning close and speaking directly into her ear.

She shrugged, and shook her head. "I…I didn't, really."

"At all?"

She just shrugged again. "Couldn't."

"Well, it's almost four hours or so back home," I said. "Rest."

She tilted her seat back and closed her eyes, and within a few minutes, her mouth had fallen open and she was snoring, a soft, feminine huff of breath. I watched her sleep, hardly daring to believe she was here. There was so much to say, but I didn't know how to say any of it. I didn't even know where to start.

She tilted sideways, drifting slowly toward me as she fell into a deeper sleep, and soon her head was resting on my shoulder. She murmured in her sleep, nuzzling closer; my heart twisted into a knot at the soft, vulnerable sound.

I hadn't slept much myself last night, too worked up, too upset, my mind too occupied by thoughts and plans and fears and doubts and questions to allow for rest. There was no way I was sleeping now, though. I was hyperaware of Joss—her scent, the soft soughing of her breathing. I was hyperaware of the kiss—however brief it had been—she'd leaned into it, clutched at me. Kissed me back. Admitted she wanted to go home. She'd called Dru.

Did that mean she had changed her mind about us? She'd run away from me, from us, from...everything. But now she was coming back. With me? Was it with me? Or had the kiss just been one of relief? It didn't seem that way, but...she was so hard to read, sometimes.

I didn't dare let myself hope too much. Not yet. Not until we'd had a chance to talk alone.

I shoved my hand in the hip pocket of my jeans, fingers toying with the cold jagged metal keys I had. Had I been too impulsive? Was it too much? Should I have done it? But...it had made so much sense at the time, had seemed like the perfect gesture to communicate how I felt. Now, with her beside me, doubts assailed me. Would she be overwhelmed all over again when I told her what I'd done?

Maybe I'd misinterpreted things. Misread her feelings.

If she didn't want to be with me, I'd be stuck with the results of my impulsiveness.

I'd risked everything on this plan, staked my future and everything I owned on it, and now, with Joss beside me, her head resting on my shoulder, I began to wonder if I'd made the right choice.

———✳———

It was early afternoon when we landed and taxied to the docks across from Badd's. Joss slept through it all.

"Joss?" I said, as Brock powered off the aircraft and set aside his headset. "Joss. We're here."

"Mmmm." She nuzzled closer to me, resting on hand on my chest. "Mmmm-mmm."

Brock laughed quietly. "Just carry her, bro. She's done for."

I handed him her backpack, unbuckled the both of us, and knelt in front of her so I could scoop her up. Standing, I edged toward the door. Brock was there, standing half on the dock and half on the float, one hand out to steady me, the other gripping the wing strut for balance. Once I was safely on the dock with Joss in my arms, he shut the door and followed me up to my room over the studio. I settled Joss on my bed and covered her with the blankets; we'd both dried out most of the way on the flight home.

Brock set the backpack down in the corner of the room, and I followed him out into the hallway.

"You good, Luce?" he asked in a low voice.

I shrugged. "I hope so. I guess I'll see."

He frowned at me, puzzled. "She came back with you. And she kissed the ever-loving shit out of you back in Olympia."

"Yeah, but..." I shook my head, "she's been so back and forth about her and I, so I just...I have no idea what to expect."

Brock clapped me on the shoulder. "It'll be fine, Luce. Believe in it."

"I'm trying."

"You know, Claire's been seeing a therapist lately? Just kind of working through some of her old shit and whatever. The therapist she's seeing is kinda... out there, if you ask me, but Claire loves her. She rings one of those bowl things before every session and does a lot of guided meditation or regression meditation and stuff."

I eyed him. "What's this got to do with me, Brock?"

He waved a hand. "One thing Claire has been talking about a lot lately is how the energy you put out into the world determines the energy you receive back."

I snorted. "The fuck's that mean?"

"It means Claire will always be Claire, and you know how she is. It's part of what I love about her, how fierce and fiery and brash and everything she is. But she's been working on being softer, putting out more positive energy, expecting good things out of her day rather than anticipating the negative."

I stared at him. "It's weird as fuck to hear you talk like this, Brock, I'm not gonna lie."

He laughed. "It struck me as mystical hoodoo

mumbo jumbo nonsense too, but..." He rubbed the back of his neck. "Claire has been different since she got into it. It's making a difference. She puts this positivity out there, and it just...it gets to me, and makes me feel the same way, and I just..." He shrugged. "I'm just saying, Luce, try to expect good things, okay?"

I sighed. "Okay, I hear you."

He clapped me on the shoulder again. "Hey. It'll be great, okay? She came back with you. That's gotta count for something, right?"

I nodded. "It does." I shifted, uncomfortably. "Brock...thanks. For taking me to pick her up."

"It's what I do, man."

I shook my head. "You didn't have to. So... thanks."

He laughed as if I'd told a joke. "Luce, dude— you're my brother. You need something, I'm there, man. No question. All right?"

I nodded. Dropped my voice to a whisper. "I think I'm falling in love with her, man. She was gone for...not even a full twenty-four hours and I just..." I shrugged, unsure how to finish it.

Brock laughed again. "You *think* you're in love with her?" He grinned at me. "Lucian, if you only *think* you're in love, you need to work on being more in touch with yourself or something, bro, because that shit is obvious to all of us. You were a cranky, miserable bastard for three months, man. You were pining! Every time you two were in the same room, sparks flew. But you're so damn aloof all the time none of us could get you to talk about it. You'd just be like, nah, I don't wanna talk about it, and go be all 'elven' and mysterious and shit."

"It's that obvious?"

Brock leaned back against the wall. "You've been a different person from the moment she showed up in Ketchikan. You actually show emotion. You speak in more than monosyllables, at least when she's around." He faked a dramatically shocked expression. "You're turning into—*gasp*—a real person!" He actually said the word "gasp" too, which made me laugh.

"As opposed to, say, a chocolate lion?" I quoted. Brock just quirked an eyebrow at me. "It's from *Madagascar 2*. Anyway. What do you mean by a real person?"

"You've just always been…there, but not really present. You'd pop up during a conversation, say something insightful, and then go back to being aloof and almost invisible. Like…there but not there, you know?" He gestured at the still, sleeping form of Joss, visible through the crack in the door. "She brings you to life, Luce. So yeah, she makes you act like a real person instead of the weird, invisible half person you've been ever since you were a kid."

I glanced back through the doorway at the curvy profile of Joss, sleeping on her side, facing away from the door, and felt my heart expand and soften and twist all at once.

"It's scary, Brock." I tugged my hair out of the ponytail and ran my fingers through it. "How much I feel for her, how it's all happened so fast."

"That's how it goes, man. Claire was supposed to be a one-night stand, except by the time it was morning I realized I wasn't ready to stop being around her. Every moment afterwards, that feeling only increased, until I realized I was fucked. I was done. I wanted her, all the time. It's scary. It hits hard and it hits fast and you just have no way of fighting it." He slugged me on the shoulder. "That's why they call it *falling* in love, bro—because there's no stopping that shit."

"Yeah, I think I'm starting to see that."

Brock shoved me toward the door. "Go be with her, Luce." He walked toward the door, and then stopped and stabbed a finger at me. "Word of advice? Grow a pair of balls and tell her how you feel."

I nodded, but couldn't find the words to respond. When Brock was gone, I went into my room, closed my door behind me, and leaned back against it, staring at Joss.

In my bed.

In Ketchikan.

I thought I'd lost her. I thought she was gone. It hadn't really sunk in until I was finally alone that night, after she left. And then I'd panicked. I'd lain in bed awake most of the night, realizing that now she was gone how deeply I really felt for her, how badly I wanted her around, how desperately I wanted there to be an *us*.

Now she was here and my feelings were stronger than ever, especially seeing her here in my bed.

She twisted on the mattress, tugged the blanket up around her shoulder, and lay facing me now. One hand was curled under her chin, and her lips were pursed into a little moue.

God, she was beautiful. Had I ever told her that?

The camera Eva had given me was in the bag sitting on the floor at the end of the bed. I dug the camera out, acting on some kind of instinct, and flipped it on. I focused on Joss's face, tilting to get the perfect angle. Her face filled the viewfinder, in profile, perfectly lit by a ray of sunshine peeking through a break in the clouds. The golden light illuminated her to perfection, making her glow. I pressed the shutter, adjusted the angle slightly, and snapped another. In seconds, I was lost in the process, capturing her beauty in the moment with as many photographs as I could.

Her lips, especially, caught my interest. I closed in on them until they became the sole focus, the curves of them an echo of the curves of her body, evocative in some way. *Snap snap snap snap.*

"Luce?" I heard her voice, mumbling sleepily. "What're you doing?"

She'd never called me that before, never used my nickname before. "I...um." I held up the camera. "Taking photos."

She rolled onto her back, rubbing at her eyes. "Of my mouth?" A small smirk appeared on those lips. "From six inches away?"

I shrugged. "Yeah."

"Why?"

I shrugged, unsure how to answer. Instead of trying to explain it, I brought up the last photo on the display, sat on the edge of the bed, and showed it to her.

She stared at it for a moment, silent, and then her eyes shot to me. "Lucian, that's...that's amazing." She shrugged, and I suspected she was blushing. "It kind of looks like...if you look at it the right way, it kind of looks like a body. Like a woman's body."

"That's what caught my interest," I said.

"I had no idea you were a photographer," she said.

I laughed. "Neither did I, till yesterday."

Silence. I let the camera hang from my neck by the strap, and held Joss's gaze.

"How long have I been asleep?"

"All the way home, and maybe twenty or thirty minutes since we got back."

Her eyes searched mine. "Lucian, about how I left—"

I interrupted. "Joss, I apologize. I should have realized. Once you told me, it all made sense, why you were...the way you were. I should have realized and not pushed you so hard. I should have been more careful. Gone slower. You said you wanted to take it slow, and I let it get out of hand anyway."

She shook her head and put her fingers on my lips. "No, Lucian. That's not what I was saying." She sat up, faced me, sitting cross-legged. "I shouldn't have left like I did. I was scared. I still *am* scared, if I'm being honest, but I shouldn't have run. I should have...I don't know. Given you a chance, I guess."

Her fingers were still on my lips, and my hand caught hers, holding her fingers in place, and I kissed them.

"It's just..." She blinked hard. "I've carried that secret for so long. It hasn't mattered until now, but still. I mean, I was a virgin in high school, as a senior, when all my friends and classmates had been having sex since like sophomore year, if not earlier. But then Mom and Dad died, and I just—and then I met you, and—" She stopped with a bark of laughter. "I'm not making sense."

"Weirdly enough, I understand what you're saying."

"You do?"

I nodded. "When do you tell someone something like that? How do you broach the subject? Especially if you feel…weird about it, or whatever."

She exhaled shakily. "Exactly." Her eyes met mine. "Lucian, you're not—you're not a virgin, are you?"

I shook my head. "No."

A silence.

"Can I ask you—" She stopped, shaking her head. "No, that's none of my business."

"How many?" I suggested, and she nodded. "Two."

"Only two?"

I nodded. "A local girl in Thailand, and another American ex-pat in a hostel I stayed at in the Philippines." I ducked my head. "Both were sort of but not really…things. Not just a one and one thing, if you know what I mean."

She sighed. "I get the sense your older brothers are…or were…um, fairly active. Before they got married."

I laughed at that. "That's an understatement. My older brothers, the oldest four especially, were all major players." I shrugged. "I'm not like that. Never have been. Another thing that sort of made me feel like an outsider, because I didn't have 'game' or whatever, like they did."

She offered a hesitant smile. "Is it okay if I'm glad you're not like that?" She shifted a little closer to me. "It would make me feel weird if you'd been with, like, dozens of girls and I've never even been to third base."

"Is it okay that I think it's kinda cute you still refer to the bases system?"

"How else are you supposed to say it?" she asked.

I frowned. "Honestly, I don't know. I'm no expert. But that's a good point. That system does allow for easy distinction between levels of sexual engagement." I shot her a look. "And, actually, if that's the system you're using, then you have been to third base."

"I have?" She seemed confused.

"Yeah. With me." I cut my eyes away, and then back to hers. "I...we touched each other. You know... direct manual stimulation, or something like that, which I think counts as third base."

"Oh. Right." She let out a breath. "I'm sorry about that. How that ended, I mean. Breaking your nose."

I gestured to my face—the areas under my eyes still showed hints of the injury, but my nose was as good as new. "I'm fine." I hesitated, and then asked the question on my mind. "If you hadn't—if I hadn't accidentally triggered you...how far would that have gone?"

She shrugged. "I don't know. I really don't. I'm still…" Joss toyed with a dread, and then looked up at me. "I've wondered the same thing."

"You have?" I swallowed hard, shifting over on the bed, closer to her.

She moved aside to make room for me, so we were sitting side by side with our backs to the head-board. "I…I want to get past the triggers." She said this so quietly I almost couldn't hear her. "I don't want *him*—that horrible experience—to have a hold on me anymore. I want to be able to move past it."

"How do you do that?"

She met my gaze, reached down and took my hand. "With you, is what I was hoping." The hope in her voice, painted on her face…it resonated in me, mirroring the tumult of my own emotions. "That is, if you still—"

I twisted, leaned in, and kissed her, cutting her off before she could finish. It was just a kiss, at first. Slow. Hesitant. Careful.

"More than anything," I murmured.

"You don't care that I'm a virgin?" she asked, one hand on my face, her golden-brown eyes hunting back and forth, fear and doubt and hope and desire mingled on her features. "It doesn't…weird you out, or scare you?"

"I just want you to…I don't want to push you."

"But you…you…*want*—me?" Her voice broke on the word "want" and lifted with doubt and hope on the last word.

"Of course I do. So much." I kissed her again, once, carefully. "I want to show you how much, but only if you—"

She leaned into me, and now she was the one to initiate the kiss. This time, there was no hesitancy. Just hunger. Desire. She pushed against me, tasted my lips with her tongue and then our tongues danced together and we were sliding downward together, and she was rolling to her back and I was levered over her.

And then I remembered what had happened, and I started to move away.

Joss caught at me. "Wait." She pulled me back down. "Just…just wait."

"Joss, I don't want to—"

She pulled me closer, gazing up at me. "Kiss me like this. Erase that memory. Show me it can be different."

I palmed her cheek and pressed one fist into the mattress beside her shoulder, not quite on top of her, but almost. Slowly, I moved in until our lips touched, and then I gave her a brush of a kiss, and she moved to deepen it, but I danced away. She laughed, a breathy giggle, and I teased her with another kiss. And another, until we were playing a game of it, her trying to kiss me, and me dodging. And then, tired of the game and eager for my kiss, Joss wrapped my hair around her hand and tugged me down to her and demanded my mouth, kissing me fiercely, moaning as our lips met, whimpering when our tongues tangled.

Her fingers knotted in my T-shirt, pulling me closer, and so I gave her more of my weight; I hooked my arm under her neck and wedged my body against hers, so I was almost completely on top of her. I cupped her hip in my hand. Her fingers danced up my back, and then down, edging under the hem of my shirt to seek skin. Her hands smoothed up my spine under the cotton, and then she was tearing at the shirt, ripping it off of me and tossing it aside so she could roam my back and shoulders freely.

We lost ourselves in the kiss, then, and it intensified with every moment, our natural chemistry igniting. I was still trying to keep my need at bay, reminding myself that this was about her, not me, but as the kiss became hotter and hotter, that became a more and more difficult task. Her body beneath me was so soft, so lush, and so tempting, and the more we kissed the more desperate I was to get her out of those layers of clothes so I could see her, feel her…taste her.

Joss's hands explored my torso, everywhere she could reach, pulling me closer as we kissed so our bodies were lined up perfectly…except for the layers of clothes between us.

She broke the kiss. "I'm hot," she muttered.

She pushed me away and sat up, unzipping her hoodie and tossing it aside. She had a sweater on under that, which she also took off. Unlacing her boots, she toed them off, along with a pair of thick wool socks. Then, with a shy glance at me, she lay back on the bed, unzipped her jeans and lifted her hips to work the denim off, revealing a pair of leggings. Barefoot now, and dressed in a long-sleeve T-shirt and the leggings, she remained on the bed, staring up at me. Her gaze was inquisitive, open, and full of desire.

"Lucian…is…are we…" She sighed, searching for the right word. "What are we? What is this?"

I kicked off my boots and socks too, and thought about how to answer. "A thing."

"We're a thing?"

I nodded. "It's what I want, at least. And I've been hoping you do, too."

"But…what's a thing? What does that mean?"

I shrugged. "It's you and me, together."

"Together?"

I nodded. "Meaning, I want you. I want *us*."

"Us," Joss echoed. "I want us, too."

My relief was so palpable and visceral I sagged, exhaling shakily. "You do?"

She nodded, tearfully. "I do. I really do."

"Here? With my whole crazy family?"

"I love them. They're…you're so lucky to have them, Lucian. I've never felt so accepted, so welcomed." She stared up at me, tears in her eyes. "You changed my life the day you rescued me, Lucian."

"You changed me that day, too," I said. "I was talking to Brock while you were sleeping, and he said you bring me to life. And I think I agree."

She smiled tentatively. "You make me feel like… like life can be more. More than what it has been, and more than what I've ever allowed myself to dream it could be."

"I don't know if photography is going to be my thing, but you made me realize that I have to…I have to *live*. I have to find what makes me excited."

"Is photography that, do you think?"

I nodded. "I really think it could be."

Joss's smile was happy, but the flickering spark of need was dancing in her eyes. "Did we just agree that we're together, Lucian?"

"I think we did, Joss."

She lay on the bed, thick black dreadlocks draped on the pillow around her face, staring up at me. "Kiss me, Lucian." She ran her hands across my shoulders. "And this time…don't stop."

FOURTEEN

Joss

He didn't stop. He kissed me, and this time I threw myself into it. I opened myself to it. I knew there was...*more*...coming after the kissing, and I welcomed it with an admittedly not-small amount of trepidation, but I knew Lucian wouldn't rush me through it. I wanted this. I wanted to kiss him and let the kiss morph into the next thing, and the next, and let Lucian guide me where I knew I wanted to go, but was afraid of getting to.

He kissed me, and he began letting his hands wander. I lay beneath him, welcoming the hard heavy weight of his strong body above me, and the touch of darkness was gone, the shreds of reminders that had assailed me last time were gone. The memory was there, I knew what had happened and would never forget it, but I also knew Lucian wasn't him. This wasn't that. This was new, and beautiful, and I deeply, desperately wanted it.

I shook with want for it.

I trembled with desire. His hands skated under my T-shirt over my belly, and I lost my breath for the ache of anticipation of his touch on my flesh. When his palm skated over my bra, I murmured with appreciation. And when he traced beneath the underwire and around to the edges of the cups, I bit down on his lip and sighed. He laughed, and tugged the straps down. I arched my back, pushing my breast into his hand as he cupped me over the bra, and then, while my spine was arched, he reached up under me and freed the clasps.

I pushed him away, sat up, my eyes hot on his, and ripped off my shirt and threw the bra away, breathing hard with the ache of desire, shaking all over. I was topless in front of him, and my breasts swayed and lifted with my ragged breathing. My nipples puckered into hard thick points under his hungry gaze.

"Joss...Jesus—you are so fucking perfect." His voice was ragged, breaking. "So beautiful."

He reached out a hand, his fingers trembling. I bit my lip and held my breath as his palm made contact with my breast, and then I arched into his touch, moaning as his calluses scraped rough against my sensitive nipples.

"Your tits, Joss—they're…"

I sagged back to the mattress, his touch following, his hand caressing my breast. "What, Luce? What are they? Tell me."

"Your tits are so perfect they make me crazy."

"My tits make you crazy?" I wasn't sure who was in control of my mouth, but I liked her; this was the free, unburdened, unafraid Joss who could and would do and say anything, everything. "Crazy how?"

"Crazy like I want to…" He pressed his lips to my stomach. "I want to kiss them, and lick them, and worship them."

I arched my back and brought his face between my tits. "Please, Luce. Show me."

He fastened his lips around my nipple, and his tongue flicked the hard nub until I gasped, and then he moved to the other one and did the same, and his thumb caressed the damp, erect flesh his mouth had just left. I moaned as he worshipped my breasts with his mouth, and his hands. I cupped his head and arched into his touch and gloried in how wanted and beautiful and safe I felt under his attention.

He lifted up, gazing at me. "Joss…god. You're so responsive."

"You make me feel things I didn't know were possible." I feathered my fingers through his hair, possessive, and affectionate. "I love your long hair. Don't cut it, okay?"

"I don't plan on it." He reached up and toyed with the end of one of my dreadlocks. "I love these."

"Oh, don't worry, those aren't going anywhere." I stroked one. "They remind me of my dad. He had dreads, too. Longer than mine, and thicker. I was thirteen when he took me to get these done."

Lucian smiled, and then his gaze went serious. "Joss, I—I love a lot more about you than just your dreadlocks."

My breath caught. "You do?"

He nodded. "I'm falling in love with you." He breathed a sharp sigh after the words emerged, head hanging momentarily, as if saying them had been a terrifying act of bravery. "I have been, since...since the moment you looked up at me as I was carrying you up here."

I felt myself melting. "Lucian...I'm—me too." I owed him more than that; I swallowed hard, sucked in a deep breath, understanding for myself now why it had appeared so difficult for Lucian to say this. "I'm falling in love with you, too."

"Would you...think less of me," Lucian said, each word hesitant, "if I admitted that falling in love with you is fucking scary?"

I reached up and wrapped my arm around his neck and pulled him down to me into a fierce embrace, burying my nose in the side of his throat. "*No*, Lucian. It's scary for me too. I don't think less of you. More, if anything."

We were skin to skin from the waist up, bare together, pressed together. I clung to him, and we breathed together, and I felt his heart hammering in his chest, like mine was. I pulled my face away, and he lifted up. Our eyes met, and the desire I saw in his gaze, all for me, melted me and set me on fire all at once.

A hunger for him ignited. I wanted to feel his skin under my hands. I wanted to hear him moan. I wanted to feel him touch me, and I wanted to know what his release looked like.

I brushed the pad of my thumb across his lips. "Luce…can I…can we take this a step at a time?"

"Of course, Joss. I don't want to rush you. I don't want to rush this. I want it to be perfect."

I smiled up at him. "It is perfect." I rubbed my palm over his chest. "I just, I want you to know that I want this, that I want more, but I just…I want to go slow. I want to remember it. I want to savor it. I'm not going to stop us this time, I just…"

He touched my lips. "You don't have to explain,

Joss. I'm all in, however you want, whatever you want. It's all for you."

I smiled at him. "No, Luce, it's all for *us*."

"The pace we take is all about you, is what I mean."

I just breathed and gazed up at him, desire pooling inside me, courage building. I knew what I wanted, but convincing myself to just *ask* for it was almost as difficult as convincing myself to call Dru had been. I caressed his shoulders, his back, my heartbeat quickening as I traced my fingertips around the waist of his jeans from the small of his back to the fly, where I paused.

"I was hoping we could start over where we left off?" I whispered.

He smirked. "I'm hoping you don't mean me with a broken nose and you crying."

"Don't make fun of me," I murmured, frowning even as I fought a smile. "It's really hard for me to ask for things."

He lost all levity instantly. "I wasn't making fun, Joss, just teasing. We can do whatever you want."

I closed my eyes and breathed. "Sorry, I just—I guess my sense of humor might need work, huh?"

He laughed. "Yeah, mine too. That probably wasn't very funny."

"Don't stop teasing me, okay? Your whole family

makes fun of each other all the time, and you all have so much fun with it. Even when…even before Mom and Dad died, we weren't like that. Dad was always very serious, and Mom was quiet as a mouse, and they always treated me, even as a little girl, like a miniature adult. They spoke to me like they would one of their friends. They didn't tease, not each other, or me."

Luce frowned. "Damn, babe, that sounds… miserable."

I laughed. "It wasn't, though. It was what I knew. We were serious and quiet. It was just the three of us, and we were just comfortable with each other in long silences."

Luce nodded. "I can definitely see how we might be somewhat overwhelming to someone with your background."

"It's like living in a circus," I said, laughing. "Or in a sitcom."

Lucian flopped to his back on the mattress, laughing. "Or a sitcom about a circus." He snickered. "Does that make Bast the ringleader? The twins would definitely be the clowns."

I rolled toward Lucian, my breasts draping against his chest, my fingers trailing down his torso from diaphragm to navel. "Can we go back to my original statement?"

Humor drained out of him, replaced by molten

desire. "About picking up where we left off?"

"Before I panicked and ran away like a coward."

He reached up and palmed my cheek. "Don't, Joss. You ran because you were scared and overwhelmed and upset. And I didn't handle the situation right. I should have been more understanding, should have understood better why you were so hesitant." His eyes didn't leave mine, and the sincerity I saw there was breathtaking, putting a hot lump of throbbing emotion in my throat. "That situation is past, Joss. It's over. You're here, now."

"*We're* here, now," I whispered.

"Exactly." He ran a hand down the outside of my arm, and then to my bare waist; I leaned away from his body to allow him access to my breasts. "Where was it, precisely, you wanted to pick up?"

"Well…" I breathed out shakily, and reached for the fly of his jeans, unsnapping the button and then slowly lowering the zipper. "I would have to start here."

His nostrils flared and he sucked in a sharp breath. "I see."

I paused, after I had his fly open, took his hand in mine and pressed his palm against my breast. "Don't stop touching me, Lucian. Please. Your touch gives me courage."

"You need courage?"

I nodded. "I'm terrified right now."

"You don't have to be scared, Joss. This all about what you want."

I exhaled tremulously as he rubbed a gentle thumb over my hardening nipple. "I am scared, but I want this. I want to touch you, but I'm still…just nervous."

"And me touching you like this," he said, caressing my breast, lifting its significant weight in his palm, "gives you courage to touch me the way you want to but are nervous about?"

I nodded. "Exactly."

He pressed a kiss to my shoulder, and then to my throat, and the valley where my breasts sloped away. "Then I shall give you all the courage you need."

"How noble of you, kind sir."

"I live but to please, fair maiden."

I laughed. "Well, funny enough, I *am* a maiden, in the historical sense." I stopped laughing as his mouth found my nipple. "Oh…oh god…I love the way your mouth feels on my breasts. Don't stop." I held his head in place against me, as his mouth worked my nipple to a throbbing, aching point. "But I won't be a maiden for much longer, will I?"

"That's up to you, Joss," he murmured, the words huffing against my skin. "This all happens on your timetable."

"And if my timetable for today is just…touching…you'd be okay with that?" I asked, watching his reaction carefully.

He glanced up at me, sensing the weight in the words. "Absolutely, Joss. No rush. Whatever you want."

I watched as his hands toyed with my tits, caressing and palming, pinching my nipples, exploring them, hefting their weight. "How can you be so patient? You've touched me, made me orgasm. I—I haven't done anything for you at all. And I always thought that would give you…like, blue balls or something."

Lucian met my eyes. "Joss…" he sighed. "In a sense, yes. I want everything with you. And there is a part of me that's desperate to get there with you. And yes, I want you to touch me. I want to feel that with you. Your touch, it's…it's amazing. It's perfect. It makes me a little dizzy, to be honest, because it feels better than anything I could have imagined was possible."

"Lucian, don't flatter me or try to make me feel better about things. Just tell the truth."

He stared at me levelly for a moment. "The truth?"

I nodded. "The truth, Luce. Don't be tactful, don't be all understanding. Am I irritating you with my up and down and back and forth and all that?

Because even now, we're still talking because I'm scared and nervous."

"Okay, real talk—just plain honesty? Yeah. I get worked up and then things cool off. I'm horny as hell, and I want you. I'm dying to rip your leggings off and bury my face in your pussy." He kept his eyes on mine as he said this, his voice a low growl. "I'm dying to feel your hand on my cock again."

I swallowed hard. "Luce—I—"

"I'm not done. You wanted the truth, here it is." He tugged on one of my dreadlocks, his eyes burning into mine, his voice a lupine snarl. "I'm dying to bury my cock inside you, Joss. I need to feel you come apart around me. Watch you come as I fuck you senseless. Watch you take such pleasure from me as you could never have even imagined was possible."

"Oh…oh my…"I shook all over. "That sounds… nice."

He smirked at me. "I want all that. I *need* that."

"I want to give it to you. I want it *with* you."

"Then take it, Joss." He threaded our fingers together and brought our hands to his stomach. "Take what you want. I'm here for you. I'm here *with* you. And yeah, I want all that, but more than anything, I want this to be right, for *you*. You only get one first time, Joss, and I want yours to be perfect. If you're choosing me out of everyone in the whole world to share this with, I'm willing to wait and be as patient as I have to be, to give you a perfect experience. So if that means a mild case of blue balls as you summon the courage to take what you want, it's a small price to pay."

He cupped my tits, both of them at once.

"And besides," he said. "Just getting to put my hands on these incredible, perfect tits of yours is a gift all in itself."

I gasped as he brushed a thumb against my nipple. "They're so sensitive. I feel like I could almost reach orgasm just from that."

"Then let's see if that's possible."

I shook my head. "No, wait."

His hands fell away immediately, and I levered over him, pressed our palms together, leaned in, and kissed him until we were both breathless.

"First, a kiss," I whispered, "For courage."

"And then?" he whispered back.

I slid down so I was kneeling beside his hips. His fly was open, revealing an expanse of black cotton, stretched around a thick ridge. "And then..." I swallowed hard. "Just be patient with me."

He tucked his hands behind his head. "We have all the time in the world, Joss."

I smiled, and then caught my lower lip in my teeth as I turned my attention to him. To the open fly of his jeans, and the hard column behind the black cotton. I traced a fingertip down it, from where the top bulged against the elastic waistband of his underwear down to where it vanished behind denim and the teeth of the open zipper. I watched him as I did this, watched the way his jaw clenched and his eyes narrowed. I hooked my fingers in the back pockets of his jeans and tugged them down—Lucian lifted up, allowing me to draw them off and toss them off the bed. His thick, muscular thighs bunched as he flexed every muscle in his body and then forced himself to relax. His underwear were boxer-briefs, plain black. His erection was a massive tentpole against the stretchy cotton, now that he wasn't constricted by the denim. I ran my palms up his thighs, past his hips, to his stomach, exploring his washboard abs, and then hesitating at his navel. I swallowed hard, bit my lip, and felt an eager, nervous, silly grin spreading across my face.

He met my grin with one of his own, hands folded behind his head, lying there waiting, patient, but clearly anticipating what I was about to do.

My grin spread until my cheeks ached, my heart hammering. I had a mental flashback to when I'd last touched him—I'd been too caught up in the moment to memorize what he looked like, too caught up in the wonder and fervor of the moment.

This time…this time would be different.

I held my breath, and then curled my fingers inside the elastic. Lucian's belly sucked in and tightened as my knuckles brushed against the very top of him. I slowly pulled the elastic away from his body and tugged the undergarment downward. He flexed his hips to lift his butt off the mattress, and I ran my fingers around to his butt, scraping my nails against the hard bulge of muscle as I removed his underwear, tugging it down and down until the elastic waistband was cinched around his thighs. A swift tug, one of his legs lifting free, and then the black cotton was dropping off of his toes to the floor at the foot of his bed, and he was bare, completely naked, exposed to my gaze. I raked my eyes over his body eagerly, greedily, soaking up the masculine hardness of his physique, the broad shoulders and thick pecs, the washboard abs, the way his torso tapered to a narrow waist. Those sharp V-shaped lines angling from his abdomen to his groin.

I swallowed hard, my eyes widening, teeth catching at my lip, breathing going shallow. His… his cock—I formed the word in my mind, tasting it, liking it—was…well, beautiful. Thick, straight, pink, and beautiful. Veins stood out, the skin stretched taut. The head was bulbous. He had a thatch of hair around the base, which I suspected he trimmed.

My gaze caught and held there, at his cock. How could I look away? It was where all my attention was focused, where all my desires were attenuated. He was just breathing, just waiting, but he was tensed in anticipation.

I glanced at him, met his gaze.

He smiled at me reassuringly. "It's all about you, Joss."

I rested a palm on his thigh, my eyes on his as I dragged my hand upward, to his hip. He licked his lips, sucked in a deep breath and let it out slowly, as if deliberately focusing, slowing himself, restraining his impulses and instincts.

I lifted my palm from his hipbone, desire pooling between my thighs, and wrapped my fingers around his erection. He sucked in a sharp breath and held it, teeth biting down on his lower lip, brows furrowed in concentration. He swallowed hard.

I smiled, another silly, eager grin of excitement. I slid my hand downward, to the base of him, and then upward, my heartbeat ratcheting to an impossible speed. I watched my hand glide over him, enjoying the contrast of his pink, pale flesh to my darker caramel and mocha skin. He exhaled shakily, releasing the breath he'd been holding. I squeezed, and then released, using my fingers, now, to examine and play with the feel of him. Tracing the rim of his circumcision, following the veins, testing the hardness of the shaft and the springiness of the head. Rubbing the slit at the tip with my thumb. He alternately held his breath, abs tensed rock hard, and then let out shaky, focused sighs.

I met his eyes. "Are you okay? Is this difficult for you?"

He shook his head. "I'm…I'm amazing. I'm just trying to control myself. Holding back, so you have time to explore, or whatever."

I smiled. "You feel…I really, *really* like touching you like this."

"Yeah, I don't mind this myself."

I stroked him slowly from root to tip. "You don't mind this?" I grinned as I said it. "It's okay, huh?"

He growled. "Joss, the feel of your hand on my cock is actual heaven. I died and went to heaven."

"That good?" I asked.

He closed his eyes as my hand made another slow glide, this time downward, from tip to base. "You don't even know."

"Well, I'm enjoying this quite a lot myself, I'll have you know."

His eyes flicked open and pierced me. "Say the word and I'll make you come so hard you won't be able to see straight."

My heart fluttered and my thighs clenched.

"What's the word I'd have to say to get you to do that?"

His grin was feral and hungry. "Please."

"That's it? All I have to say is please, and you'll give me an orgasm? Like you did last time?"

He searched me. "Joss, the last time I only used my fingers. This time, I plan on using my tongue."

I whimpered at the thought. "Your...*tongue*? You'd—you'd do that? Really?"

His wolfish grin only widened. "Joss, baby—you have *no* idea."

I squeezed him. "Oh...oh god."

The idea of Lucian's mouth between my thighs had me shaking and quivering—his fingers had felt amazing...what would it feel like to have him kissing me, down there? Heat pooled, desire making itself known as a flood of dampness between my thighs, as an ache and a tremble.

I decided to take my own advice—go one step at a time. He was clearly enjoying my touch, and had said as much. I was a virgin, but I was familiar enough with how things worked to know, mentally, at least, what would happen when Lucian reached the end of his control. He would come; he would orgasm. I knew it would happen, and that it was the goal of all this, but I was only vaguely aware of what it would look like. I wanted to know. Wanted to see. Wanted to feel it happen, watch it happen, and know I'd given him that.

Lucian was just lying there, hands behind his head, breathing slowly, evenly, deeply, watching me as I clutched his erection in one hand, thinking this through.

"You okay, Joss?" he asked.

I smiled. "Yeah…yeah. I'm just…" I shook my head, and resumed stroking his length with one hand. "I was thinking."

"About what? You mind sharing?"

"I will," I said, "just not yet. If I start talking, I won't be as focused on this." I squeezed him.

He closed his eyes briefly. "Well, I certainly wouldn't want you to lose focus."

I added my other hand, then. One hand atop the other, wrapped loosely around his thick cock, sliding slowly up and down. I watched him, watched his reactions and expressions as I explored him with both hands.

"Will you warn me when you're…" I hesitated, flicking my gaze from his cock to his eyes. "When you're almost there?"

"Of course."

I held his gaze. "Is this okay—is it all right? I don't know how things usually go, but I just—"

He cut in. "Joss, this is more than okay. There's

no right or wrong, there's only you, and me, and us, and what we want to do, and how we want to do it."

"And you're okay if I—if I just do this—" I stroked him, my eyes going to the motion to indicate what I meant, and then back to him, "until you...you know?"

"This about you, Joss. Take as long as you want. And if you want to stop before I get there, that's fine too. I can handle it, if that's what you want."

I held him in both hands and leaned over him to kiss him. "No, that's not what I want," I murmured, my lips moving against his. "I want to take you there. I want to feel you come. I want to give you that."

He let out a sigh of relief. "And trust me when I say I *really* want that too. But however you want it, whenever. Okay? Don't worry about me."

I kissed him again, and let myself explore his cock with one hand, and then the other, and then both again, feeling the hardness in my hands, the contrast of the iron-hard shaft wrapped in silk-soft skin. I went a little faster, feeling his cock slide between my fists, feeling his breathing quicken and his stomach tense.

"Keep going like that, and it won't take long to get me there," Lucian murmured.

"So the slower I go, the longer it takes?" I asked.

"Yeah...pretty much." He groaned as I slowed again. "And if you alternate, go fast and then slow, it's kind of like teasing me. Getting me close and then slowing down."

"Is that bad or good?"

"Both, in a good way."

"That's confusing," I said.

He laughed. "Yeah, I suppose so." He flicked open his eyes and looked at me. "Maybe you'll let me show you how it works, after...this."

"Maybe I will."

I didn't want this to end, though. I loved the feel of his cock in my hands, the restraint on his face, the tension in his body, the fact that he was so clearly enjoying how I was making him feel with just my hands. How would he react if I wanted to see what he tasted like, what he felt like in my mouth, between my lips? I was feeling daring. His patience and restraint made me feel in control, and safe at the same time.

"I'm gonna try something," I warned him. "Just...hold still."

"I won't move," he assured me.

I stroked him once more with both hands, glanced at him, offered him a shaky, nervous smile, and then shifted forward, leaning over his body.

He understood what I intended moments before I did it. "Oh shit, Joss, you don't have to—oh *fuck*... fucking hell, Joss—Jesus!"

His outburst of shocked profanity sent a thrill of

pride through me.

I touched my lips to the tip of him, feeling the broad bulb of flesh against my mouth, and then I parted my lips until my jaw was stretched wide, and my mouth was filled with him. He was soft and thick against my tongue, and even with my jaw opened as wide as it could go, it was still a tight fit. And he tasted…god…amazing. Salty skin, and a musky tang of… him, of his arousal. There was wetness against my tongue, the source of the flavor, something seeping out of him. I gripped his shaft low around the base in one hand, holding him away from his body as I filled my mouth with his cock.

"Ohhhh fuck, Joss. Jesus. Fuck." He was arched off the bed, spine arced, hips flexing, and his hands shot out from under his head to grip the comforter in knotted bunches of fabric in white-knuckled fists.

I backed away, working my jaw, watching him. "Was that okay?"

He barked a laugh. "Was it okay? Joss, did you see how I reacted?"

"You looked like…" I considered my phrasing carefully. "Like it felt so good it almost hurt."

"Exactly." He brushed my cheek with his palm. "You do that, Joss, I won't last long at all."

Daring, eager, and full of erotic zeal and pulsing arousal, I let a leering smile cross my lips. "Then I might just do it again."

"Fuck, fuck, fuck," he hissed, knotting his fingers in the comforter again, as I took him into my mouth.

I felt him throb between my lips, and then I felt veins against my tongue as I took more of him, fist sliding up from the root until my fingers touched my lips. The taste was unlike anything I'd experienced, and the feel of him in my mouth, knowing his most sensitive organ was at my mercy, knowing it felt so good that he couldn't even control the words that came out of his mouth—it empowered me.

I backed away until the damp crown of his cock was at my lips again, and then, without thinking, flicked my tongue out to taste him, lapping the flat of my tongue over the slit. He jerked at the touch of my tongue, hissing another curse. His cock was wet with my saliva from tip to midway down the shaft, which was as far as I'd dared take him. He was breathing hard, now, gasping raggedly.

"Joss, god—you do that again and I'm done, honey."

"Really?" I stroked him with both hands, smearing my saliva on his skin. "I do...*this*...again, and you're done?"

I took him into my mouth once more, and this time slid my lips around him and went farther and farther until I felt him brush the back of my throat, as far as I was willing to go. He was groaning, and his hands, trembling, went to my back, sliding up my spine to my shoulders, and then, shaking, framed my head as I slid my mouth back up his cock until the softness of his crown was between my lips.

"Joss—" he groaned, his voice a hoarse rasp. "You have to stop—I'm close, Joss. I'm right there."

I backed away, glancing up at him. "You want me to stop?"

"No! No. But—" He had to stop, breathing hard, teeth gritted, clearly focusing every ounce of control on holding back. "But if you don't stop, you're gonna get a mouthful, babe."

"Oh." I licked the tip again, tasting his essence as it leaked out of him, clear, viscous. "Yeah, I don't know if I'm ready for that yet."

"That's why I'm warning you."

I clutched him in both hands, shifting away so I could watch what was about to happen. I stroked him, then, slowly, root to tip, with both hands, and this time, I didn't stop, or hesitate. He was arched off the bed, gasping, groaning, and his hips were flexing uncontrollably.

"Joss—god, I'm—oh god, oh god."

I paused to rub the tip of him with my thumb. "You're going to come, now, Lucian?"

"Yeah, god yeah." His eyes were closed, head

thrown back, jaw clenched, abs taut. "So hard."

I ached. My thighs were clenched, my core seeping—watching him edge closer and closer, and knowing I was making him feel this way...it was a rush, sending lightning bolts of need through me. Watching him reach the verge of orgasm was...it was sending arousal through me, turning me into a shaking, needy mess of wetness between my thighs.

One touch is all it would take, I realized, to make me come—just from the intensity of giving him this.

I held it back, clung to the edge as I stroked his cock with both hands, faster now.

Lucian was thrusting into my fists, groaning wordlessly.

"I'm—fuck, Joss—I'm gonna come!"

"Now?" I asked, caressing him even more swiftly, fists sliding in a blur up and down his thick, tensed, throbbing cock.

"Oh fuck—fuck, now, Joss!" He arched, pulsing his erection through my fists, his shout morphing into a wordless snarl.

I felt him spasm, felt his cock throb, and then a stream of thick white come shot out of him to splash against his stomach, and I kept stroking, slowing down so I could soak up every arousing moment of this, watching his face tense into a rictus of release, watching his abs flex as he thrust into my fists. I clutched the crown of him with one hand and gently pulsed my fist around him in short shallow gentle movements, and he cried out again as another spurt of come burst up his torso, over his navel nearly to his diaphragm. He thrust and I caressed and stroked, and yet more thick white viscous hot semen left him, dripping over my fingers and into the curly thatch of hair around his base, and then again and again, until the backs of my fingers were coated in his come, a pool of it on his stomach and navel.

He was gasping raggedly, his body sagging as if he was suddenly boneless, his cock still throbbing hard and thick in my fists. "Holy shit, Joss."

I grinned in pleased pride at the stunned stupid sound of his voice, at the raw ecstasy obvious in every line of his body. "That was…" I bit my lip, holding up my hand to look at his come on my fingers. "That was incredible."

He opened his eyes. "You have no idea." He glanced down at himself. "I'm a mess, now."

I showed him my fingers. "So am I."

"Sorry, I should have warned you it'd be messy."

I shook my head. "I like it. No—I *love* it. Watching that, watch you come? It was…amazing." I shuddered. "It was…hot. Arousing."

He fixed me with a piercing stare. "You get off on watching me come, huh?"

"*God*, yes." I didn't shy away from the truth, from how he made me feel; I embraced it. "One touch, and I could explode."

"One touch?" He reached up to tweak my nipple, sending an electric thrill through me. "Like that?"

I squeaked in surprise, and then shuddered as the thrill sizzled down to my core, igniting the pool of desire flooding me. "Yeah—a lot like that."

He palmed my breast, and then pinched my nipple, suddenly and hard. "How about that?"

I jumped, whimpering as the pinch, as the pain and the pleasure of it left me quaking. "Yes…god yes."

"Remember what I said?"

I blinked at him. "What you—what you said?" The pulsing hammer of my arousal was making me dizzy, clouding my mind, need replacing everything.

I needed him. I needed his touch. I needed to come.

"One word. That's all it takes."

I remembered, then. "But…you're all messy."

He tilted halfway off the bed and snagged a towel left on the floor after a shower. Dizzy, thoughts slowed as if I'd been drugged, I took the towel from him and wiped him clean, and then glanced at my hand, still wet with his drying essence. A thought struck me, and I gave into it before I chickened out—I touched my tongue to the wetness on my knuckles, and the flavor of him burst through me: salty, musky, tangy, almost-but-not-quite sweet.

"Mmmm," I murmured. "That's not so bad."

"No?"

I shook my head. "Not what I was expecting."

He pinned me with a look. "Joss, don't ever think I expect you to—"

"If I do—*when* I do," I told him, "it'll be because I *want* to." I grinned at him, biting my lip. "And believe me, I'll want to."

He reached for me, hooking a finger in the waist of my leggings. "Can we get back to that word you were gonna say?"

I squirmed. "The word that gives you permission to make me come so hard I won't be able to see straight?" I asked. "That word?"

"Yes, Joss. That word."

I stopped breathing for a moment, as we sat side by side on the bed, his eyes fierce and wild and eager, one finger curled into the elastic waistband of my leggings. One word, and he would show me things I'd never even dared dream of or fantasized about. He was waiting, and I knew he wouldn't go any further until and unless I gave him permission.

He kept one finger hooked into the hem, leaned close to me, pressing our bodies together, caressing my breast with his palm and brushing his lips against mine. "Let me taste you, Joss," he whispered. "Let me make you scream."

"I'm..." Embarrassment flooded through me, making my cheeks burn. "I'm really, um...down there—"

He pulled back to meet my gaze, rolling one of my nipples under his thumb. "You're what, down there?"

"All worked up."

"I sure as fuck hope you're worked up."

I swallowed hard. "No, I mean—I'm turned on like crazy, from wanting you, and—I...um—it's..."

He teased kisses across my cheek, down the side of my neck, to my shoulder, and then to the upper slope of my breast. "Don't be shy, Joss. Just say it."

"I'm wet," I whispered. "So messy...so wet."

He groaned, forehead resting against the swell of my chest. "Ohhh fuck, Joss—don't tease me like this."

I frowned at the top of his head. "Tease you? I'm warning you. You said you wanted to taste me, and I'm saying...you may not, because I'm—"

He lifted his head to look at me, and his grin was equal parts amused and aroused. "Joss, honey, please trust me when I say that's *exactly* why I want to go down on you so bad right now. I can smell how turned on you are."

He leaned into me, touched his lips to my ear.

"Lay down. Trust me."

I slid to my back, and Lucian leaned against me, teasing kisses as I squirmed to a comfortable position. "I trust you," I whispered.

"Say it," he murmured.

I met his gaze. "Please, Lucian." I smirked at him. "You just wanted to hear me beg, as payback for all the back and forth from before."

He nibbled my throat, kissed my clavicle, and then slid his tongue between my breasts. "Joss, honey, that wasn't begging. That was just giving me permission to make you feel good." He nipped my nipple, and I felt it throb into an aching, diamond-hard point. "I'll show you what it's like to beg."

I breathed a whimpering sigh as he flicked my erect nipple with his tongue, and then slid his mouth across the valley to the other one, lips stuttering across my flesh. I arched my spine and trailed my fingers along his shoulders and through his hair, giving in to the bliss of his mouth on me, anticipating the downward slide.

He shifted down my body, cupping my tits in his hand, and kissed my ribs, and my navel, and then paused to glance up at me, dragging his fingers down my front to the waist of my leggings. I bit my lip and flexed my hips in silent permission, and he tugged the stretchy cotton downward, stripping them off in a single smooth jerk, tossing them aside, leaving me in nothing but a pair of plain white cotton underwear. He didn't remove them immediately, like I expected him to. Instead, he nudged my hipbone with his nose and then used one finger to inch aside the gusset of my underwear, baring a slice of skin between the crease of hip and core, and his tongue slid along that exposed flesh, causing me to gasp, and tense. He ran his palms up my thighs, shifting his weight over my legs so he was kneeling between my calves, hovering over me. I stared down at him, having trouble breathing as I anticipated him stripping me naked, leaving my damp core bare to his eyes...and his mouth.

He continued to defy my expectations and anticipation, however. He kissed my stomach, again and again and again, from the curve of one side to the other, and then lower, across the elastic band of my panties, and then his mouth moved over my core without making contact with the fabric covering me. I was so wet with need, now, that I could feel the cloth sticking to my skin, and I knew how that must look— the white cotton would be nearly see-through, plastered against the plump lips of my core. I knew the word he would use, but I couldn't quite bring myself to use it, even in my own mind.

Lucian's gaze raked over me, from my face and my eyes to my breasts, to my core, and I saw the moment he saw how wet I was. "Shit, Joss—you're fucking *soaked*," he groaned.

"I told you."

His thumb brushed the soaked cotton, and I jerked at the contact. "It's sexy, Joss. You don't even know what it does to me to see you this turned on, this wet."

"Really?"

"Abso-fucking-lutely," he growled.

His fingers tugged the sides of my underwear down, exposing my hipbones, and he kissed each of them. And then, instead of pulling them the rest of the way down, he kept kissing, moving his lips down my thigh and around inside, pushing my thighs apart as he did so, until his lips were dancing across the tender flesh of my innermost thigh, his cheek brushing against my core over the cotton. I felt his breath on me, cooling dampness, making me gasp sharply, and then his lips were sliding over my other thigh and his teeth were grazing and nipping. His hovered his mouth over my core, and I tensed all over, aching, breathless—he hooked his index finger in the leg of my panties and tugged the gusset aside to bare my core. Momentarily bare, I quit breathing entirely, waiting, waiting, waiting, watching for the moment he put his mouth on me.

He extended his tongue…and I flinched and my

lungs squeezed and my heart stuttered as he touched his tongue to me, sliding up the seam where my nether lips met.

I whimpered at the wet warmth, the teasing slide.

And then it was gone and he was letting the underwear cover me again, and I was wild with need, aching, desire pooling through me, making me wetter than I already was. I wanted that. I wanted him to do that again. To strip me naked and put his mouth on me, his tongue.

God, I wanted it.

"Luce...*please*."

"See, if I wanted to hear you beg, that's how I'd do it. Tease you, really tease you. You'd go crazy if I held out long enough."

"Don't, Lucian. Please don't."

"No?"

I brushed a lock of hair away from his face, tucked it behind his ear, and shook my head. "Don't tease me. Not this time." I flexed my hips, biting my lip. "I'm already begging. Please, Lucian. Do that again."

He repeated the action, pulling aside my underwear and licking me, once. "Like that?"

I groaned. "More, Luce. You know what I want. Please."

He grinned at me. "You want me to lick your pussy."

I laughed in aroused embarrassment at his filthy words. "Yes, god, yes."

"It'd be really hot to hear you ask me to do that."

"Haven't I, already?"

He kissed the insides of my thighs again, and I let my legs fall apart, wanting more. "I want the words, Joss. I want to hear that beautiful, innocent mouth of yours talking dirty to me."

"My mouth wasn't so innocent a few minutes ago," I reminded him.

He shifted up, to my navel again, and kissed along the hem of my underwear. "True."

"I don't like that word," I lied, to cover my embarrassment.

He just grinned at me. "You're lying, Joss."

"God, how do you know?"

"I can just tell when you're lying." He tugged the elastic down so the upper swell of my core was exposed. "You're just embarrassed to say it."

"Damn you."

He laughed. "Try it, Joss. Ask me to lick your pussy."

I stared down at him, his fingers in the waistband of my panties, preparing to draw them off me. "Lick me, Lucian. Put your mouth on me..." I got the words out, then, finally. "Lick my pussy. Make me come so hard I can't see straight."

He groaned and slid my underwear down to my thighs, exposing my core—my pussy. I lifted my butt off the mattress, and he tugged them all the way off of me, and now, once again, I was naked with Lucian. This time, I wasn't afraid. I was eager. I was beyond ready, shaking with arousal as he stared with obvious and greedy appreciation at my core.

"So beautiful," he murmured. "Just as beautiful and perfect as the rest of you."

I ached, god, I ached. Arousal was a throbbing drum inside me, a volcanic pressure consuming me. I felt like if Lucian didn't make me come soon, I would lose my mind.

He was still teasing me, kissing my hipbone, my thigh, my navel.

"Lucian—" I breathed, my voice nearly a snarl. *"Please."*

He pressed his palms to the insides of my thighs, caressing, and I let my eyes close at the sudden tenderness in that caress, and then, while my eyes were closed, head thrown back, he pushed them farther apart and his mouth slid along the crease where thigh, hip, and core all met, and I whimpered. I opened my eyes and lifted my head to watch, not wanting to miss a single moment.

I didn't wait long, after that. A moment of hesitation, his eyes meeting mine, and then he covered my seam with his mouth, and I lost my mind. The heat of his mouth, the pressure of his lips, his tongue sliding wet and strong into my opening—I threw my head back and moaned, a wild, wanton sound. He groaned, and I felt his tongue slither between the lips of my core, and then glide upward—my breath caught, lightning searing through me as his tongue circled around my clit. My groan was ragged then, and I couldn't help clutching in desperation at his head.

"Don't stop—oh god, Luce, god, please...don't stop!"

He grunted a negative, and then his lips suctioned around my clit, and his tongue flicked against it, and I whimpered, trying to contain a rising need to scream as the pleasure built inside me. I felt him drag his palms down my stomach to my hips, and then I felt a finger gliding through my damp lips inside me, penetrating me, and just that finger felt like *so* much, so thick, such an intrusion, that I felt a moment of panic trying to imagine actual sex. But that worry was blasted away as he drew that finger out and then slid it back in, curling it just so, massaging inside me, careful, gentle, even as his mouth and tongue worked in alternation, licking, suckling, circling around my clit, building the pressure of ecstasy inside me to frenzy.

I moaned, and whimpered, and my hips began to

flex, and my thighs started to quake. "Lucian!" I heard myself breathe his name, a raw, desperate exhalation.

It only prompted him to drive the wild pressure of need to a crescendo; he slid a second finger inside me, stretching me, and I cried out at the burning ache, and then his tongue flicked and fluttered against my clit and the burning pain of being stretched by his fingers vanished into an inferno of pleasure. I felt myself teetering on the edge, clutching at him, and my hips were flexing, my ass lifting off the bed, breasts swaying.

"Oh god, oh my god, Luce, please, yes—" I heard myself say.

I was outside myself, hearing and feeling my reactions, but in no kind of control.

Lucian worked his fingers in and out of me, mimicking sex, stretching me, and his tongue flicked against my aching, throbbing clit, and everything inside me built and built and built into a mountainous weight of pressure and heat and need and exquisite, agonizing ecstasy. I was going to explode, detonate like never before. I would come apart, and it was going to be such a furiously intense explosion I would have been afraid of it, if I only didn't need it so fucking badly.

There was nothing else in that moment, nothing in the entire universe except the wild, desperate need to reach orgasm.

"Oh—oh god—oh my fucking *god!*" I heard myself say, the words a whimper, and then a wail.

I was gone, utterly lost. He was driving me to it, now, thrashing my clit with his tongue, two fingers slicking noisily between the spasming walls of my pussy.

And then...

I came apart.

And I screamed. This time, my scream was one of release, of helpless, violent orgasm. I writhed against him, weeping, screaming in choking, gasping wails as I was seized by wave after wave of raw intensity, through which his tongue and lips and fingers worked constantly, pushing me higher and higher, until the crescendo broke and I was sobbing, hips thrusting madly, grinding my pussy against his face with crazed abandon.

The waves only slowly and gradually subsided, and the intensity became too much—I couldn't take any more. I caught at his face. "Luce, I—I—stop, you need to stop—I can't handle any more."

He lifted up, and I saw the wet evidence of my orgasm smeared on his face.

I pulled him toward me, and he lay on the bed beside me as I gasped, whimpering occasionally as aftershocks shot through me. When I was capable of coherent movement, I reached over and wiped at his face with my palm.

"You're messy again," I said.

He licked his lips. "Best kind of messy."

I shrugged a shoulder. "I dunno…I kind of liked the mess we made of you earlier."

He smirked, and then gently, carefully swiped a finger through my opening, making me flinch and gasp. He brought the finger to my lips. "Taste yourself, Joss."

I touched a finger to his mouth, to his lips, still glistening, and leaned in. "I'd rather taste it on you."

I kissed him, licking at his lips, and tasted myself on his mouth, the smoky musk of my essence. The kiss shifted, then, morphing from a teasing taste of my juices on his lips into something more.

Something heated, something deep.

Something wild.

Our bodies pressed together, and I felt his thigh between mine, his hands on my ass, cupping and kneading possessively, and I felt his cock hardening against my hip, driving against my belly. His hands were everywhere, and so were mine, carving at his muscular bicep, trailing down his waist, clawing at his ass. We were lost to the kiss, groaning as we exchanged control, him taking the kiss deeper, and then letting me claim his mouth, his tongue.

God, I was crazy, aching again already.

The feel of his cock against my hip was maddening.

I clutched at him, then, needing to feel him in my hands again, needing the evidence of his desire.

I was going to be addicted to this—to the wonder and glory of his cock, the pulse of it in my hands, the way he lost control as I brought him to the edge—I could even see myself needing to taste him, to feel him in my mouth, to feel him so desperate, so needy for what only I could give him.

But…there was more.

His fingers inside me had introduced a new element to all this. The intrusion of them, the stretch, even the slight burn, the ache of it. I needed that again…

I needed more.

I needed to be closer to Lucian, to feel him all around me, inside me, above me.

I broke the kiss, my palm on his jaw, our bodies tangled together. "Lucian…I need you."

"I'm here, Joss," he breathed. "You've got me."

I met his eyes, clutching his cock in one hand, and rolled to my back. "No. Luce…I *need* you."

"Joss…" He searched my eyes with his.

I ran my fingertips down his spine, to his ass, cupping the bubble of hard muscle. "Luce, I want this. I *want* it. I want you, I want us."

"Now?"

"Yes, now."

He leaned in and touched my lips with his, and then groaned when I squeezed his cock. "I need to get a condom."

"You have some?"

He rolled away from me to the bedside table, opened the drawer, and pulled out a new, unopened box. "Perhaps somewhat anticipatory, but I went and got some before Brock and I left to get you. It was the desperate act of a very hopeful man."

I laughed. "I'm glad you did."

He opened the box, withdrew a string of square packets, and ripped one free. I watched as he tore the foil open and took out a ring of latex.

I sat up, reached out and took it from him, toying with it, figuring it out. "Let me do it?"

He knelt in front of me, setting the string and the box on the table, and he waited as I gently pressed the ring to the crown of his cock, rolling it down gently with both hands until it was snugged at the base.

I smiled at him, pleased with myself. "That was fun."

"Never had anyone else do it for me before," he said.

I didn't like the way that phrase sat inside

me—more accurately, at the insinuation of having done this before. I knew he had, but I didn't want to think of it. I was jealous, I realized. Somehow, Lucian had become *mine*.

He saw something in my expression. "What?" he asked.

I shrugged, smiling at him. "I just…I got all jealous, when you said that."

He frowned. "Oh. Sorry, I didn't think—"

I shook my head. "It's fine. I just want you to know, I'm jealous of you." I reached for him, wrapping a hand around his waist, resting my fingers on the small of his back. "You're mine now. That's what I was thinking."

He leaned close, kissing the corner of my mouth. "That goes both ways, Joss." He kissed my lips, shifting so we were facing each other, sitting up, and his hands brushed my dreadlocks behind my shoulders so they didn't obscure my breasts. "I'm yours—and you're mine."

I smiled into the kiss. "I like the sound of that."

"Yeah?" He backed away, our eyes locking.

"There's nothing I want more than to belong to you, Lucian. To belong *with* you."

He smirked at me. "There's *nothing* you want more?"

"I want you to make love to me." I wrinkled

my nose at him. "Is that phrase cheesy, or passé, or whatever?"

He cupped my face in both of his hands, eyes searching me. "I just want you to be absolutely sure it's what you want."

I withdrew from his touch, lying on my back, catching at his hand. "I've never been more sure of anything in my life, Lucian."

FIFTEEN

Lucian

THERE'S NEVER BEEN ANYTHING MORE BEAUTIFUL IN MY life than Joss in that moment—reaching up to hold my hand, pulling me toward her. On her back beneath me, eyes shining, eager with passion and love and need. Heavy breasts swaying, dark nipples rigid points.

She pulled at my hand, reaching for me. I knelt between her thighs, on my hands and knees above her. I wanted this so bad it hurt, but I knew I needed to be careful, no matter how much she wanted it.

I trailed my fingers along her thigh, toward the juncture, never taking my eyes off of hers as I slid my middle finger up the damp, slick seam.

She shivered, biting her lip. "Luce, I want *you*."

I bent to flick at her nipple with my tongue. "I want you back, more than you know." I fluttered my tongue against her other nipple, then, and teased her clit with my finger. "Can you trust me?"

She gasped at the touch of my finger. "I trust you, I just…oh, oh…"

I slid my finger inside, and then withdrew it, smearing her essence against her. "I want this to be perfect."

"It already is."

I spoke in between flicks of my tongue against the erect buttons of her nipples. "If you're on the verge of coming…it won't hurt as much…or so I've… heard."

"I'm all about it not hurting."

I took my time building her up, plying her with my fingers, circling her clit, flicking her nipples, kissing her mouth, until she was whimpering and her hips were flexing. When she reached that point, I slid a finger inside her, and then a second, and she whimpered again, this time at the stretch of it, and I moved down her body again, sucking her clit into my mouth until her whimpers turned to wails of pleasure and her hips were driving against me and she was moments from her orgasm.

She pushed me away with her hands, pulled my

face up her body. "No, no—not like that," she panted. "I want—I don't want to come again unless it's
with you…unless it's together." Her eyes met mine,
fraught with emotion and racked with bliss. "I want
to come with you."

I settled between her thighs, and her hands
reached for me, palming my shoulders and drifting
down my back to cup my ass, a smile on her face as
her fingertips dug into the muscle.

"I love your butt," she said.

I laughed. "I'm glad. I work hard on that ass."

The humor faded from her eyes as I pressed my
fists in the pillows beside her face, levered over her.
"Luce…" She pulled me closer, wrapping a hand
around my condom-sheathed cock. "I'm ready."

"No doubts, no hesitation?"

She leaned up to kiss me. "None. I'm nervous,
and a little scared, but I want it. I want this, *so bad*."

I slid my fingers against her opening, touching
myself against her seam, and then she took over, guiding me. Our eyes met, and I felt a whirlwind of emotion flood through me—a raging maelstrom of need,
a fear of how intense this was and how badly I wanted
her, how intensely I was beginning to care for her.

This was love.

I'd told her I loved her, because I'd realized it and
admitted it to myself while she was gone, but it wasn't

until then, until I felt her fingers wrapped around my cock, guiding me into her opening, how deep the love really went. It was more than this—more than this act. But this act in and of itself, that Joss was giving me— *me*, Lucian Badd—this amazing, beautiful, priceless gift of her virginity...it was so enormous in its meaningfulness. It made me breathless, made me ache with the preciousness of it. It made everything inside me melt and expand at once, made me say a vow to never take this woman for granted, to spend every moment she would give me making her happy, taking care of her, being there for her. Love was...it wasn't just this one emotion, I finally understood. It was so, *so* much more. It was the act of trusting each other, of each of us mutually falling, trusting the other to have arms open, ready to catch.

I was falling, and I knew Joss would catch me.

Just as I would catch her.

All this flew through me in the instant she pressed the crown of my cock to the tight lips of her pussy.

She was trusting me. She was giving herself to me. Something she'd never given to anyone, she was giving to me.

I was her first, and, maybe, her only.

The weight of it, the enormity of it crushed me, shattered me.

Joss saw this in me, saw the emotion in me.

"I know," she whispered, choking on a sob. "Me, too."

"Yeah?" It was all I could manage.

"Yeah." She palmed my cheek, and I bent down, kissed her.

She whimpered as I feathered two fingers between us and touched her again as she gasped and writhed into my touch.

"Now, Luce," she breathed. "Now. Please."

I held off until she was mewling, whimpering, and then I nudged against her, a gentle flex of my hips.

She groaned, her fingers clawing into the flesh and muscle of my ass. "More," she breathed.

I braced my weight with one hand and pushed a little deeper, until she whimpered, a noise clearly of pain. "Joss, you okay?"

She nodded, her forehead against my shoulder. "Yeah, yeah. I just...just give me a second."

I reached between us, but she caught my hand and pressed my palm against her breast.

"No...I'm already so close I could come, and I don't want to, not yet."

"I don't want to hurt you."

She smiled up at me. "Kiss me, Luce."

And so I kissed her, playing with one of her perfect tits, forcing myself to stillness as her impossibly tight channel pulsed around me. She was so tight it nearly hurt, and I wasn't even halfway in, yet.

Joss kissed me, then, as if that kiss was a lifeline, the only thing keeping her sane; and for me, that's exactly what it was—the need to move was maddening, the effort to wait, to keep still almost more than I could take.

She palmed my ass again, pulling at me. "More," she murmured, breaking the kiss to meet my gaze. "Give it all to me, Luce."

I held my breath, reaching up to press my palm to hers, fingers tangled; she clutched my hand, squeezing my fingers in anticipation, her other hand clawed into my ass.

"Look at me, Luce," she breathed.

I kept my eyes on hers, heart hammering wildly... and pushed into her the rest of the way all at once. She cried out, her hand crushing mine in a sudden vise grip, and I held myself utterly immobile, our hips locked together, all of me inside her. She was breathing shakily between pursed lips.

"Touch me now, Luce," she gasped.

I used our joined hands as a brace to keep my weight off her, sliding two fingers between us to her clit. She cried out again as I touched her, and this time the sound was less of pain and more of pleasure. I held still, aching, throbbing, needing desperately to move, and guided her to the edge of orgasm, and then slowed, and brought her back, until she was whimpering and gasping.

"How do you feel?" I asked. "Are you okay?"

Her eyes flew open, and she blinked up at me. "God, Luce. You feel so...so *huge*. I'm so *full*." She tested a movement, flexing her hips against me, and her eyes flew wide. "Oh...ohhhh!"

I groaned at the feel of her moving. "God, Joss. I need—"

She nipped at my earlobe, her death grip on my ass cheeks loosening. "What, Luce? What do you need? Tell me, so I can give it to you."

"I need to move," I growled, forcing myself to be still until I was sure she was ready.

She surprised me, as she always did. "Like this?" And she gave a thrust, pulling away, and then filling herself with me.

I could have wept with relief. "Yes! God, Joss... you feel..." I rested my forehead against her chest, between her breasts. "You feel like you were made for me."

"I feel the same way," she said, cradling my head against her. "More, Luce. I need more."

"More?" I lifted up to meet her fiery, golden-brown eyes.

"Move with me, Luce."

Gradually, hesitantly, I pulled out of her, paused,

and then thrust in, and Joss's eyes, already wide, widened further, and her mouth fell open, and I knew the pain was gone, now, replaced by perfection. Again, we met, thrust for thrust, and now Joss whimpered, and the whimper became a shriek as our pace increased, her need making itself known. She found herself, then, and gave over to it. Her feet drifted up my calves and hooked around the backs of my thighs, and her fingers scratched and scraped down my spine. She gasped with each movement, and now the shrieks became wails of ecstasy, and my voice was joined with hers, growls and moans tangled with her cries.

"Oh god, Luce!" She was gone, flying over the edge, screaming as she came. "YES! Oh fuck, YES!"

I watched her come apart beneath me, not daring to miss a single second of this, of the tightness as she pulsed around me, each minute movement and shift sending throbs of pleasure through me.

She gasped as her climax surged, and her eyes were hooded and wild on mine when she realized I hadn't come yet. "Luce, I want you to come."

"I don't want it to end."

"Me either." She pulled at me. "Give it to me, Lucian. Let me see it. Let me watch you come while you're inside me."

I let go, then. I let myself thrust harder, let the climax build. Faster, harder, and the sight of her tits bouncing as I thrust into her drove me wild, and I had to bend to kiss them, take those thick, dark, delicious nipples into my mouth, hips working, cock sliding through her tight pussy. She moaned, and I felt it in my chest, in my soul.

"Can you come again?" I asked.

"Just the feel of you like this is almost enough to get me there," she admitted.

"Touch yourself."

"While you're inside me?" The idea seemed to shock her.

"Yeah—I'm close, Joss, I'm so close. I want you to come at the same time as me."

I felt her wedge a hand between us, and then felt her fingers moving against her clit, and her channel tightened around me immediately, and her cry of ecstasy was loud in my ear. She moaned, writhed, and I thrust in time with her moans and the desperate flex of her hips, an orgasm surging through me.

I tried to hold it off, but I couldn't. "Joss! Oh shit, Joss, I'm—god, I...oh god!"

She bit my shoulder and yanked her hand away as I lost all control, driving into her. "Luce! Now, god, come with me, *now!*"

She screamed, then, and I roared, and the blast of my climax shattered me. I felt her walls clamping down on me, and she was so tight around me I could barely move through the spastic clamping tightness, each wave of her orgasm milking more of mine out of me. An eternity passed, in that moment, her beautiful golden eyes fixed on mine as we came apart together. She was weeping from the intensity of it, and I was gasping, sweating, panting, chest heaving, buried deep inside her.

"Luce—oh my god…oh my *god*—" She palmed my cheek, laughing breathlessly. "I had no idea it could be like that—I didn't know."

"Me either, Joss…me either."

"That was—god, it was…" She clung to me, kissing me wherever her lips could reach. "That was the most intense experience of my life."

"Mine too, I swear to god." I rolled to my back, bringing her with me so she was resting on my chest. I had to pull out of her, but didn't move otherwise.

She panted for a moment, her head pillowed on my chest, and then she lifted up on one elbow. "Lucian?"

I smiled up at her. "Yeah, babe?"

"I love you. It's crazy, but I do."

I leaned up and kissed her, pulling her back down to me. "I love you, Joss. It's just as crazy for me, but it's just as true."

"I didn't know you could fall in love this fast," she said.

"Me either." I laughed. "Although I should have, since I watched it happen to six of my brothers in quick succession."

Resting her head on my chest again, she sighed, a sound of utter happiness. "Can we…can we just stay like this for a while?"

I breathed a sigh of relief. "That sounds perfect."

She squirmed against me. "Although, if you could get rid of the condom first, I wouldn't mind. It's…wet and squishy."

I laughed and rolled out of the bed. She watched with interest as I stripped it off, tied a knot in the end, and dropped it into the wastebasket in the corner of my room, and then used the same towel from earlier to clean off a little. When I was done, I lay back down on the bed and held out my arm. Joss eagerly nestled into the crook of my arm, and I draped the blanket over us. She nuzzled her face in the side of my neck, sighing again.

"I really, *really* like this part," she whispered.

"Me too," I murmured.

Her fingers trailed down my cheek, came to rest on my shoulder. "Is it okay if I fall asleep?"

"I won't be far behind you."

———✳———

When I gradually floated up to wakefulness, it was gray outside, and my clock said we'd slept through until after six in the morning. Neither Joss nor I had moved at all in our sleep; her cheek was still pillowed in the nook of my shoulder and arm, one hand on my chest, her thigh thrown over my mine. My arm was asleep, and my bladder was screaming. I didn't want to move, though. I ignored the minor discomforts in exchange for the feeling of Joss in my arms. I cupped her waist, her skin softer than any silk under my hand, closing my eyes and sighing at how amazing it felt to have this woman here in my arms, our bodies tangled together.

I felt her wake up, shifting, murmuring. She rolled, tensed, stretching against me like a cat, and I felt the round bulge of her breasts against my chest. She shoved the covers away in the process, craning her head to look at me.

"Hi." Her smile was sleepy and sweet and shy.

"Hi," I said back. "You're beautiful."

She buried her face in my shoulder. "You're silly."

"No, you are. You're more than beautiful."

Joss looked at me again. "You make me feel that way." She rubbed my chest. "You're pretty damn gorgeous yourself."

A silence between us, comfortable and easy.

Joss shifted. "I...um...I have to pee." She

squirmed, consternation on her face. "Like…really bad."

I laughed. "God, me too. So bad." I reached down and snagged my T-shirt off the floor. "Here. Put this on. You go first."

She tugged the shirt on, pausing to sniff it as she shoved her arms through the holes, smiling and giggling to herself as she climbed out of bed.

"What's so funny?" I asked.

She shook her head, pausing at the door. "Nothing." Her smile was wide, and bright, and made me delirious with love. "It's just my first time wearing my boyfriend's shirt. It makes me kind of stupidly happy, that's all."

"Oh." I grinned at that. "My girlfriend is wearing my T-shirt." I laughed. "I see what you mean."

She made an uh-oh face. "And on that note, I'll be right back."

She left the bedroom door open in her hurry to get across the hall to the bathroom, tiptoeing carefully yet swiftly. The shirt didn't quite cover her butt all the way, a fact I appreciated as she vanished into the bathroom and locked the door. The moment the door was locked, I heard another door open and footsteps on the floor. I tugged my blankets up over my waist just in time, as Corin and Tate both entered my room. Tate had her hands over her mouth, laughing silently, while Corin just grinned at me.

"So *that* happened," Corin said.

"Yeah." I rubbed my hand through my hair, fingering through the tangles. "That happened."

Tate leaned close. "Did you tell her you love her?"

I held her gaze, tugging the blankets higher up my torso. "Yeah. I did."

Corin held out his fist, and I tapped my knuckles against his. He jerked his head at Tate. "You know she's pregnant with twins, right?"

I nodded. "Yeah."

"She's got a scheduled induction tomorrow. Just wanted to give you a heads-up. We mentioned it a while ago, but in all the chaos lately, I'm guessing you may have forgotten."

"A what?"

Tate smiled at me. "Having twins is complicated, so they don't usually let you go into labor on your own. It just means they're having me go in so they can bring me into labor in a secure environment."

"Oh." I cleared my throat. "And you had to tell me *now?*" I gestured at the bathroom. "Like, *right* now?"

Corin just laughed. "Well, we also wanted to get the dirt on how things went." He made a face, and I knew what was coming next. "Although, we kinda heard how things went, na'mean?"

Tate whacked him. "Corin!" She shoved him toward the door. "Don't embarrass them!"

"He's my brother, it's what I'm here for." Corin pointed at me. "Kidding. Sort of. I'm glad you got your shit figured out so you could get that girl back here where she belongs, brother."

"Me too," I said. "Now get out of here."

"We are," Corin said, gesturing to a pair of duffel bags. "We're staying at Zane and Mara's tonight."

I sighed. "Scared you off, did we?"

Corin shrugged. "I mean...no?" Tate laughed and smacked him again. "Kidding, kidding. It's closer to the hospital, and they want us there first thing in the morning."

"And also," Tate said, "we wanted to give you privacy. To finish...um...working things out." She winked at me.

Corin gaped at Tate. "You go around whacking me left and right for that shit!"

She shrugged primly, exiting the room. "Yeah, but I'm a woman, and I'm pregnant with your babies." She laughed, a tinkling little sound. "Deal with it!"

They left then, and a moment later I heard the front door open and close. After a pause, the bathroom door opened and Joss peered out. "Are they gone?" she asked, glancing me from across the hall.

I nodded. "Yeah, they are."

She bolted across the hallway and into my room. "Your family has no sense of boundaries, do they?"

I laughed. "No, they really don't."

She frowned at me. "They heard us?"

"We're not a shy family, Joss. Don't worry about it."

She quirked an eyebrow at me. "I hid in the bathroom until they left so they wouldn't see me wearing just your T-shirt."

I laughed again. "Stick around, babe, you'll see a lot more than that."

Joss smirked as she leaned in the doorway. "I kind of already did. When I was getting onto Brock's plane, he was looking at his phone. I didn't look intentionally, but just kind of happened to catch a glimpse."

I shot her a wry, knowing look. "Let me guess, Claire sent him a nude?"

She nodded, covering her mouth with a hand, laughing. "Oh my god! I couldn't believe it! It was like something out of a porn magazine! She was all spread out and…" Joss shook her head. "I mean, wow."

"And Brock just laughed it off, I'm assuming?"

"Yeah, pretty much."

I got up, still naked. "We just go with it, usually," I said. "You'll learn."

Joss's eyes raked over me. "I don't know. I'm a

pretty private person."

"That's okay." Knowing we were alone in the apartment, I didn't bother with clothes on the way to the bathroom.

When I was done, I washed up and went back to my room. Joss was sitting on the bed, still in my shirt, just waiting for me. Her eyes lit up at the sight of me, and then heated as she looked me over.

"Hi," she murmured.

Now that I'd used the bathroom, things were more in a ready state, so to speak, and her gaze, openly and hungrily fastening on my cock, started the blood flowing.

"Hi there." I moved toward her, kicking the door closed behind me.

Gnawing on her lower lip, Joss stood up, her eyes on mine; I could see nerves warring with desire as she stood facing me. "I just wanted to say thank you."

I wrinkled my brow. "For what?"

"For last night." Her smile was sweet and tender and loving and sultry all at once. "For making me feel so special. For making my first time…perfect."

"Joss…" I had no idea how to respond to that; I huffed a laugh of helplessness. "I don't even know what to say."

"Just say you're welcome." She gripped the lower hem of the T-shirt in her fingers, eyes flicking up to mine and then away. "I also wouldn't mind if you told me last night wasn't...a heat of the moment fluke."

"Joss, honey...last night was—" I touched her chin with my fingers, and her eyes lifted to mine. "It was just the beginning."

She shifted her weight from one foot to the other. "So what you said—what we said to each other..."

Ah—I understood, then, the source of her nerves and trepidation. "Joss, I wouldn't have told you I loved you if I didn't really, truly, and deeply mean it."

Joss's laugh was one meant to disguise a half-sob of relief. "I was so scared you'd feel differently, afterward."

"Once I got what I wanted, you mean."

She nodded, not looking at me. "I wanted desperately to believe you're different, but I'm just still so—I don't know. Just scared it's all going to vanish on me."

"You have no reason to trust me, Joss. I have to earn that, and I know it." I slid an arm around her waist and pulled her up against me. "So I'll start earning it by telling you again, outside the context of a heat-of-the-moment kind of situation, that I am without a doubt deeply and irrevocably in love with you."

She sobbed a laugh, resting her face against my bare chest. "You are? You really are? You're not just saying it?"

"Let me let you in on a little secret about the Badd family—we tease each other and make fun and say offensive things because that's how we demonstrate that we love each other. We don't say the words. Not to each other. My dad didn't tell us he loved us—up until Mom died, at least, he found ways of showing us. Mom said it, but then she died and we stopped hearing it. So…my point is, the phrase 'I love you' is a really, really, *really* big fucking deal for me."

"Oh." She smiled hesitantly, still not quite looking at me directly. "I get that, though. Dad wasn't big on saying it either. Mom was, almost to an obsessive point, as if making up for how seldom Dad said it. So I heard it, but almost never from Dad."

"Would it help if I tried to make up for that?" I brushed a thumb over her cheekbone, and sought her eyes. "If I told you I love you as often as possible?"

Her smile was hopeful, tentative, and sweet. "I would like that."

"Then look at me." I waited until her golden brown eyes fixed on mine. "I love you, Joss Mackenzie."

She breathed out shakily. "I love you, Lucian Badd." She giggled. "I like that. Hearing it, saying it. Meaning it."

She was still off, somehow, still holding something back. "Joss, can I ask you something?"

She nodded. "Sure. Of course."

"What else aren't you saying?"

She frowned at me, eyes darting to mine and then away again. "What do you mean?"

I shrugged. "I don't know. I just feel like there's something else bothering you, but you're not saying it."

"It's not something bothering me, like I'm upset, it's just…" She traced a vein in my bicep with a fingertip, one shoulder rolling in a half-shrug. "It's more something I don't really know how to…how to say, or how to express."

"Just try, then. Do your best."

"I can't."

"Why not? Start there, then. Why is it hard for you to express whatever it is?"

She sat on the edge of the bed, and I sat beside her. "Um. Well…it's partly just how I am, how I've always been, and partly a habit forced on me from being on my own for so long." A pause, as Joss gathered her thoughts. "I was always independent. I got my own breakfast as a little girl as soon as I was capable of doing it. Everything, I just learned to do myself. I never asked my parents for anything if I could help it. And then being on my own, I refused to beg. I refused to become a panhandler. I had three things I wouldn't do, even if I was starving—I would never become a stripper, and I would never sell myself, and I would never beg. I would do literally anything else for change or cash. Wash dishes, shovel shit, clean bathrooms, anything. I never asked for handouts. I never accepted charity."

"I get that. You had to know you were surviving on your own merit."

She nodded. "Yeah. I'm not a beggar. That's why, last night, your whole thing about making me beg was a big deal. I totally knew you didn't mean it like that, but that kind of thing is hard for me. I don't beg." She glanced at me, and I realized we were getting to the real root of the issue. "But when it comes down to it, I'm just…it's almost impossible for me to ask for anything. It's hard for me to admit I want something, hard for me to accept something even if someone is willingly offering it."

"So you may want something, but find it hard to say so?"

"Not just hard, Luce—like, literally impossible. I just *can't*."

"So last night—when you said you were ready, that you wanted more…"

She laughed, somewhat bitterly. "I'm scared that was a fluke. Like, I'll never be able to be that bold about wanting anything ever again."

"I think I'm starting to see what you're getting at."

Her gaze flicked to mine, hesitantly hopeful. "I just don't know any other way of being."

"What if instead of trying to jump right into saying what you want, you found ways of making it obvious?" I twisted to face her. "I get why coming out with 'hey, I want this,' or 'can I have that' would be hard. But with some things—like, for instance, between you and me, if you were to…be in a certain mood, but you didn't know how to communicate that in so many words…"

She smiled at me. "I could just show you."

"Right."

Joss sat staring at me, and I could see the wheels in her head turning. Deciding, perhaps, how to show me what she wanted. With a shaky, nervous breath, she stood up. Turned around to face me, a foot or so of space between us. For a moment, she just stood there, hands at her sides, breathing nervously. She shook her hands as if to fling away the trembles, clenched her fists, and then grasped the hem of the T-shirt. For a moment, she just held it, arms crossed over her stomach to grasp the hem at opposite hips, eyes on me, searching me. And then, in a single, lithe, smooth movement, she peeled the shirt off. She held it in her hands, knotted in front of her body, and then she forced herself to drop it, and to let her arms hang at her sides.

I could see the war in her. Her shoulders hunched, her head ducked, eyes downcast; and then, with obvious effort, she drew up straight, lifted her chin, and met my eyes. Talking herself into confidence. Into standing in front of me, naked and bold.

"God…" I breathed. "You're fucking gorgeous, Joss."

Her smile was hesitant. "Does this communicate clearly enough what I want, Lucian?"

I grinned up at her. "I think I might have an idea where you're going with this, yes."

I reached for her, grasping the backs of her thighs to draw her toward me. She stood between us, gazing down at me. Her hands rested on my shoulders. She pressed her thighs together, breathing slowly and deeply, and I couldn't help watching the way her breathing lifted the heavy teardrops of her breasts, sending them swaying gently side to side with each breath.

"Be bold, Joss," I whispered. "You're safe with me. Anything you could possibly want, I want just as much."

"I'm scared of how…how strong all this is inside me," she admitted.

"Me too."

She shook her head. "No, like, ever since we woke up, I've been…" She ducked her head, and I knew if she was fairer of skin, her cheeks would be red from blushing. "I can only think of one thing."

"What's that?" I asked, knowing full well, but hoping to get her to talk about it more openly.

She ran her hands over my shoulders, slid them through my hair, petting me, caressing me, affectionate and loving and possessive. "Luce, I'm serious. I'm worried I'm going to scare you with how crazy I feel."

"You can't scare me."

"You don't know how I'm feeling."

"Try me."

She drew several deep breaths, thinking hard, and then dropped her eyes to mine. "I feel like you... god, I know this is going to sound stupid or cheesy, but I feel like you woke something up inside me." Her laugh was self-deprecating. "Maybe that's normal, I don't know. I just know this feeling, this wanting you, it's scary intense."

"That doesn't scare me, Joss, that excites me."

A ray of hope bloomed on her face. "Really?"

I nodded. "And trust me, I'm sitting here feeling just as crazy, but I'm scared to show you how much I want you. I don't want to scare you off or overwhelm you, or make you think sex is all I mean when I say I love you—"

She breathed a sharp sigh of relief. "Thank god you said that," she breathed. "I was scared if I even said it I'd sound shallow or something."

"I'm not sure I'm going to say this right, but…"
I swallowed hard, letting out a breath. "Being in love
with you feels like this whole big puzzle. It's emotion, it's a feeling of wanting to take care of you and
protect you and show you that you're safe and that
you belong, but it's also got this physical component.
Being attracted to you, wanting you, it's part of it. It's
not the *only* part of it, but it's an important aspect."

"It's all I can think about right now," she whispered. "The physical aspect, I mean."

I laughed, resting my forehead against her belly.
"God, me too."

"Is that normal?"

I shrugged. "I don't know. This is new for me,
too." I glanced up at her. "But honestly, I don't care
what's normal. All that matters is what works for us."

Her fingers scratched into my scalp, massaging,
caressing. "So—god, this is hard to say…I know last
night you were being careful and gentle, and I appreciate that. But, I—I don't think I would mind if—if
going forward you were less…careful."

"Then let's be open with one another, Joss. You
be bold, too. Show me what you want. Take what you
want. And you can be damn sure I'll do the same. We
do that, we'll both be sure we're getting exactly what
we want."

She breathed a sigh. "I like the sound of that."

I let my hands drift upward to cup her ass, staring up at her as I did so.

She smiled, biting her lip—a gesture I was beginning to recognize as one of pleasure and desire, a gesture of sensual delight. "That feels nice."

"Your ass feels nice," I said, caressing the globes, playing with their juicy bounce. "It's a beautiful piece of anatomy, I must say."

She giggled. "I'm glad you think so. Even with all the walking I did, it never got any smaller. I've always been a bit self-conscious about how big my butt is." She wiggled her hips, sending her butt into motion. "It's so jiggly."

I growled as her ass cheeks shook in my hands. "Jesus, Joss…you have no idea, do you?"

She frowned at me. "No idea of what?"

"How much I love your ass…and how crazy it makes me when you do that."

She bit her lip again. "When I do what?" she asked, coy, now. "This?" She shook her hips again, and this time added a little dip of the knees to it, making a dance of it.

My cock responded accordingly, dancing and throbbing to life, something I made no effort to hide. "You see what it does to me?"

She groaned in her throat. "Yeah, I see."

Joss was at the perfect height, standing in front of me, and I was done trying to suppress the desire to do one thing—now that I knew she was as crazy eager as I was, I felt like it was safe to give in to my need for her without holding back.

I clutched her ass and hauled her up against me. She gasped as I jerked her forward, and I watched her thighs press together. "Are you wet, Joss?" I asked in a snarl.

"Luce…" she breathed.

"Are you?"

She threaded her fingers into my hair, gnawing on her lower lip, brows furrowed, and she pulled my face toward her core. "You should…you should check and see for yourself."

"Check how?" I asked, and nudged my knee between hers, and she shifted her feet apart, gradually at first and then more eagerly as I leaned in to nip and kiss the velvet and silk of her inner thighs. "Like this?"

She dug her fingernails into my scalp at the back of my head. "Please, Luce…"

I couldn't help a laugh. "Please what, Joss?"

She moaned in frustration. "Don't make me say it again."

"But it's so hot hearing you say it."

I took mercy on her, more because I was as eager to devour her as she was to be devoured. In reality, I couldn't wait. I need her. I needed to taste her again. I'd been sitting here with her sweet pussy inches from my face, smelling her desire, and wanting to taste her all over again, and denying myself. And now...I was done waiting.

So was she, it seemed—she tilted her hips toward me and dipped at the knees and pulled my face against her pussy, a breathy whine escaping her throat as I buried my mouth against her desire-damp slit. I plunged my tongue inside her and lapped at the seeping essence, and then flicked my tongue against her erect little clit, and her breathy whine became a loud moan. It was mere moments before she was grinding against my mouth. I clutched her ass and devoured her with all the eagerness I possessed, thrashing her to climax as fast as possible.

She screamed as she fell over the edge, head thrown back, shrieking as her orgasm racked her.

She collapsed against me, and I caught her, letting her weight carry us to the mattress. She gasped for breath, shaking all over, limp against me. And then she lifted up, staring down at me, and the heat in her eyes seared into me. She looked as if she was about to say something, but then, instead, she stretched out over me and across the bed to the nightstand, snagging the string of condom packets. We were on the edge of the bed still, my feet on the floor with her weight on me, my throbbing cock wedged between us. When she had the string of condoms, she sat back down, ripped a packet free, and tore it open. After withdrawing the condom, she hesitated, sitting on my thighs, staring down at me.

I just smiled at her. Waited, my hands on her hips.

She reached for me, tilted my cock away from my body, and rolled the condom on with a hand-over-hand motion that drove me wild. I shifted backward on the bed, and Joss moved to get off me, as if to go to her back again, but I stopped her, holding her in place with my hands on her hips.

"Stay like this," I said.

She settled back down astride my thighs. "Are you sure?"

I ground against her, sliding my palms up to her breasts. "Absolutely."

After another moment of hesitation, Joss leaned forward to lift her ass off my thighs. Her eyes fixed on mine, she planted one hand on the mattress—I moved her hand to my chest, so I was supporting all of her weight. She reached between us, grasped me, guiding me to her opening. I watched her blossom, then. She hesitated again, my crown just barely splitting her open. Her other hand came to rest on my chest beside the other, her weight pitched forward.

I brushed my thumbs across her nipples, and she

shivered; I dragged my palms down her sides to grasp her by the hip creases, and then touched her clit with my thumb, rubbing in circles, just barely making contact. Her shiver turned to a shudder, eyes shuttering closed, and she moaned, still leaned forward, keeping me not quite inside her, just the very tip splitting apart the lips of her pussy.

"Joss," I whispered.

Her eyes flicked open.

"Take me, baby."

She sucked in a long, sharp breath, held it, fingers clawing into my chest. And then, slowly, she sank down around me, groaning as I filled her and stretched her wide.

"Ohhhh—fuck!" she groaned, as her ass settled against my thighs, eyes sliding closed again. "Jesus, Lucian…"

I pushed up against her, deeper, and she whimpered, hunching over me.

"Joss…" I growled, my voice hoarse and ragged. "So…fucking…tight."

She wrenched her eyes open. "Oh fuck, oh fuck, Lucian—you feel even bigger like this."

"Because I can go deeper from this angle."

She lifted up, a long whimper dragging out of her with each inch of me that slid between her pulsing walls. "I feel like I'm stretched apart so far I could break."

"Are you okay?"

Pausing when I was nearly falling out of her opening, Joss stared down at me with wide, fraught eyes. "So much more than okay."

"Well, I don't want to break you," I said.

She sank down on me again, impaling me into her. "Luce, please—*please*—"

"What, baby? Say it. Anything."

Her voice was a ragged whisper. "Break me."

"Oh...thank fuck," I groaned. "I want to let you have this, but I need..."

Joss's fingers pressed against my lips, silencing me. I bit playfully down on her fingertips, and she hooked her fingers against my teeth, leaning back to balance on me, sitting upright. She lifted up again, and this time I met her on the down stroke, our bodies crashing together with a loud slap. She cried out, throwing her head back, spine arching, tits bouncing, ass slapping against my thighs. My snarl was loud, feral, and her cry was raw and ragged. She lifted up, hands going to her breasts, lifting them, clutching, and letting them fall with a lush, swaying bounce that made me crazy. I lost all control, then, driving up against her—which only served to ignite her even more, setting her on fire. She whimpered as I filled her and gasped as we drew apart, and screamed when we slammed together.

"Luce, god, Lucian—the way you feel, like this—fuck, Lucian…it's too good—so amazing…" The words seemed ripped out of her. "Like you hit me just right, and I can't—oh god, I'm gonna come again, but I don't want this to ever end."

"Come for me, Joss," I snarled. "Don't hold it back. Just let go, baby."

She gave up all pretense of control, then. She fell forward, hands clawing into my chest, dreadlocks dangling and dancing around my face, breasts swaying and flying back and forth as she rode me. She rolled her hips on me, driving me deeper, and then pulled forward and began slapping her ass against me with crazed abandon, riding me and screaming as she came apart. I was helpless against the vision of her like that, an erotic goddess taking her pleasure, dusky skin flushed golden and limned by the sunrise shining through my window, thick black dreadlocks dancing, big heavy breasts swaying forward and clapping back against her chest, her ass crushing against my thighs, her eyes closed in ecstasy, mouth open as she screamed her release, crying my name over and over again.

I came when she did, her orgasm forcing her pussy to clamp around me, bringing me to orgasm instantly. I felt it rip through me like an earthquake, hot and furious and concussive, my bellowing roar of release loud in my own ears, mingling with her breathless screams and shrieks.

She rode me through her orgasm until neither of us could move or breathe, and then she collapsed forward onto me, arms wrapping around my neck, her tits crushed between us, her face in my neck.

After we regained our breath, she lifted up, bracing her elbows on my chest. "I really, *really* fucking liked being on top, Luce."

I couldn't help laughing. "I could tell."

She laughed with me. "I kind of lost control for a minute, huh?"

I caressed her flesh wherever I could reach, shoulders, back, butt, thighs. "I love it when you lose control."

She nuzzled my throat. "I felt sexy."

"You looked like a goddess."

"I felt like one." She lifted up again to fix me with a hot look. "Next time, I want to find out what it's like when *you* lose control. How can we do that?"

"You're becoming rather voracious, aren't you?" I asked, grinning.

She ducked her head, and I knew she was blushing, even if her skin was too dark to show it. "That's what I meant, earlier. I feel like you brought something to life inside me, something so...so wild and hungry for sex that I'll never be able to satisfy it."

"Joss, baby?"

She looked up, embarrassed. "Yeah?"

"That's actually the exact opposite of a problem."

"Oh. Really?"

I nodded. "That's every man's dream—a woman who can't ever get enough sex."

She buried her nose in the hollow of my throat. "Oh. Well...good, then. I want to be your dream woman."

I laughed softly. "You already are, Joss."

I rolled to my back and she moved to curl into me, finding a comfortable position immediately, tangled up with me, cradling my head in one hand and my ass in the other, her lips against my chest.

More minutes passed like that, and we may have dozed for a few minutes, I don't know.

Eventually, she spoke without looking up at me. "That...was...*incredible*."

I touched her cheek with my palm. "I didn't—I didn't hurt you, did I?"

She looked at me, then, smiling sweetly. "No, Luce." She shifted, wincing. "I *am* a little sore down there, though. Can we take a little break?"

"I need one myself," I admitted. "Need to recharge, if you know what I mean."

She giggled. "If I wasn't sore, I'd want you again

right now."

"How about I make us something some breakfast?"

She gripped my arm excitedly. "Eggs? And bacon? And some of those waffles?" She lifted up to meet my eyes, hers dancing, manic and alive and full of joy. "And coffee?"

I laughed. "Someone worked up an appetite, I see."

She bit my chest. "All that fucking made me hungry—what can I say?" Joss glanced up at me in sudden consternation. "Should I not call it that?"

"It was lovemaking, and it was fucking. It can be both. It can be whatever we want to call it." I chuckled and squeezed her butt playfully. "I like hearing you curse, though. It turns me on."

I stood up, snagged my T-shirt off the floor, and tugged it on over Joss's head. "My shirt, for my beautiful, sexy-as-fuck girlfriend."

She shoved her arms through the holes, eyes shining up at me. "You talk to me all sweet like that, Luce, and I can't be held responsible for what it'll make me do, sore or not."

I tugged on a pair of gym shorts, grabbed her hand, and hauled her to her feet. "Come on, babe. Let's eat. And then I have something I wanna show you."

SIXTEEN

Joss

AN HOUR AND A HALF LATER WE'D EATEN A HUGE breakfast, and had taken a shower—together, a first for me, oddly scary in its vulnerability. Being naked with him in bed, having sex was one thing, but being naked with him in the shower, just naked? I was nervous, at first. But then, as I realized he couldn't keep his eyes off me any more than I could him, that we were both curious about and attracted to each other, I relaxed. We washed each other, taking our time exploring each other's bodies in a way that was at once sexual and merely affectionate, exploratory and arousing.

I really was sore—more so than I was letting on

to Lucian, but he seemed aware of this, and the shower remained merely a shower. I was sore enough that I was even walking funny, which I wore as a badge of pride—at least around Lucian…if I saw any of his family I might feel differently.

He'd said he had something to show me, but wouldn't say what. When I pressed for more information, he just shook his head and said it was something he had to show me. So, finally, bellies full, bodies clean and dressed, I tugged on Lucian's hand.

"What do you want to show me?" I asked. "The curiosity is killing me."

He sighed, eyes searching mine, and then stood up. I followed him into the bedroom, confused; he dug in the pocket of his jeans, but I couldn't see what it was. He tangled our fingers together and led me to the stairs.

"Come on," he said. "It's outside…sort of."

Baffled, I followed him through the studio and outside into the cool early spring dawn. He led me toward the bar, but stopped before he got there, and stood in front of an empty storefront.

I frowned. "Didn't there used to be a little business here? A travel guy or something."

Lucian nodded. "Yeah. He, uh, he moved to Florida."

I eyed Lucian—he was acting truly odd. "Luce,

what's going on? What did you want to show me?"

He cleared his throat, jingling whatever it was in his hand. "Um. I'm gonna show you." He gestured at the storefront. "This is it. This is what I want to show you."

Puzzled, I turned to face him, taking his hands. "It's an empty retail space."

He flipped our hands, so my palm was facing up, and placed something in my hands. "It seems crazy, now that I'm telling you." He closed my hand around what felt like a set of keys. "I, uh—I put a deposit on it."

I blinked. "You—what?"

He pointed at the storefront. "This, Joss. I put a deposit on it."

I breathed out shakily. "You're kidding."

He rubbed his face with both hands—I used the opportunity to look at the keys he'd given me, two sets containing three different keys. "I'm making a mess of this."

I laughed. "Well, just a little bit. And maybe I'm a little clueless right now." I leaned up and kissed him, a brief touching of lips. "Why don't you start over?"

He led me to the front door of the storefront. "Let's go in. It'll make more sense if we're inside." He indicated the keys. "That's two sets of keys, the original and a duplicate set Dave made for me. There are three keys—one for this door—the front door—one for the back door, and one that unlocks the door to the stairs between the retail space and the living area."

"Wait, what? A living area?"

He nodded. "Yeah. Let's go inside and I'll explain as we go." He tapped a key. "This one is for the front door. Why don't you unlock it?"

"But Lucian, if you put the deposit on it, why are you giving me the keys? You're buying it, not me." An inkling of an idea flitted through me. "Lucian, you're not giving this to me, are you?"

"Not exactly, no. Not like you're thinking." He darted a nervous glance at me. "I was…I was hoping we'd buy it together."

"But I—I have no money. Like, a couple grand saved up, but that's it." I frowned even harder. "And I know nothing about setting up a purchase like this.

"Dru is in real estate," he said. "She'll arrange things. You'll have to sign in a few places, but that's it. Your name will be on the deed."

"Just mine?"

He held my gaze. "Next to mine."

I let out a shaky breath, unlocked the front door and went in. "What does this mean, Luce? I mean, I think I have an idea of what you are proposing, but I need you to explain it to me."

As we entered, Lucian pushed past me, tugging me by the hand into the interior. The front half of the space was all open, with built-in shelves lining the walls, and then, about halfway toward the rear of the space, there was a flimsy, hastily built wall with a doorway in it. On the other side was a kitchen area, which seemed mostly neglected, as if it needed a good cleaning. The back wall was all windows—with a view of the alley and the building behind, and a ton of natural light filtered in. Tucked into a corner was a closed door; Lucian unlocked the door, but let me go up the stairway first. The stairway ended at another door, which opened directly into a living room area, opening into a small but cozy kitchen and a hallway, where I saw three doors—two bedrooms and a bathroom.

There was a small, round table in the open area of the kitchen.

I sat at one of the two chairs that went with the table, glancing up at Lucian. "Can you please explain what's going on?"

He took the other chair, and spent a moment in silence, thinking. "So, when my dad died, his will stipulated that we all had to come back to Ketchikan and live here and work at the bar together for a full calendar year. After that year, the terms of his will would be completed, and his estate would be distributed equally amongst all eight of us. Our inheritance came to about thirty grand each."

"Luce, so—what's that got to do with this place?"

He held up a hand. "I'm getting to that. I worked a lot of hours and saved my money for years. When I traveled, I traveled cheap. Stayed cheap, walked a lot, took buses and trains. Point is, I have a lot of money saved up. Or…I did." He let out a shaky breath. "I worked out a deal with Dave, the previous owner of this place. I used most of my savings and inheritance to put a hefty deposit down."

"But what is your plan? What are you going to do with this place?"

"Dave and his wife used it as a travel agency, but it wasn't always a retail space. Think about the kitchen in the back. This place was originally built as a cafe or something. I'm not sure. It has all those built-in shelves, with plenty of space for more shelves around front. Zane and the guys and I can knock down that wall in about ten seconds, update the kitchen, put in some tables and couches…" he trailed off meaningfully. "I…my thinking was, this is The Garden."

My throat closed. "Luce."

"I know it's your dream, and I'm not trying to hijack it, but…I thought—if you and I were together, we could create The Garden together. I'm good at numbers, and I've been doing a lot of the inventory and ordering for Bast lately. I grew up watching my dad and Bast run the bar, so I know how to run a business, the back end, nuts and bolts of the process, I mean. Which would leave you free to be out front, doing what you do."

Tears pricked at my eyes. "Oh my god. I don't even know what to say. Why would you do this?"

He let out a shaky breath. "It was a bit of an impulse. I mean, I thought about it for a couple of days, and it just made sense. I knew I loved you, and I knew I wanted us to be together, and I was banking on the hope that you felt the same." He stood up, pacing away. "Dave wanted to sell, badly. He just wanted out of Ketchikan, so he's giving me—giving *us*—a hell of a good deal. I mean, I almost feel bad, basically stealing this place from the old guy, but it's what he wanted. He didn't care about money, and told me as much."

I shook my head. "This is crazy."

He stared at me. "It felt right at the time. Crazy, yeah, but right. It's between the studio and the bar, and we could put doors in between them, or even connect all three apartments." When I still didn't say anything, he rubbed his face in his hands. "Shit. Shit. I've fucked this up."

I stood up, crossing over to him. "No, Luce, no. You haven't fucked up anything. But answer me this—why?"

"Because I love you, Joss. Because—I wanted you to have a reason to stay. I thought—I thought if I could give you somewhere we could build The Garden, you'd...you'd be more likely to stay here." His eyes flitted to mine, and then away. "With me, I mean."

I choked on tears, felt them on my cheeks, tasted the hot salt of them. "Luce..."

He shook his head, pacing away. "It was stupid." He wiped his face with both hands. "It was so stupid of me."

I caught his hand and pulled him back to me. "No—"

He resisted. "It was. I thought it could be our thing. But you're not—you hate the idea."

I stepped into his space. "Lucian—shut up a second, you idiot."

He stared down at me, frowning. "What?"

"I'm speechless. I'm stunned. I'm overwhelmed." I held on to his hands, squeezing hard to override his objections. "But only because, never in my life, ever, has anyone done something like this for me."

"You deserve it...you deserve this and more."

"Luce, I didn't need a reason to stay. I *don't* need a reason, except you." I gazed up at him, letting the tears flow, letting my smile bloom, letting my happiness truly shine. "But this? I couldn't have even dreamed of this."

"I did this before you told me how hard it was to ask for anything, or to accept anything. I was worried it was too much, but I just had to go with my gut."

"What's messing with my mind right now is the way you said we, right? *We* build The Garden. *We* do this together. That little word means *so* much, Luce."

He nodded. "That's…yeah. That's what I was hoping. That you'd let me be involved with it."

"Lucian, can I admit something to you?" I said.

"Sure, of course."

"My dream of opening a place like my parents had? That was a way to motivate myself to keep walking. I never let myself think about it beyond a fantasy of one day doing it. But in reality? I don't have the first fucking clue how to—" I laughed, shrugging. "I *don't* even know where to start. It was probably a silly fantasy of a lost and lonely kid just trying to survive."

"It's not silly or dumb or anything else, Joss. It's a beautiful tribute to your parents."

"When I left Ketchikan—when I ran away, it was because I was so scared of how much I wanted Ketchikan to be my place. How much I wanted to belong here, how much I wanted Ketchikan to be home, but that also meant you, and I was falling in love with you, and—I was doing everything I could to stay away from you." I threw myself into his arms. "But now?"

"But now, what?" His voice was a rumble in his chest, buzzing against my cheek.

"But now I know loving you doesn't have to be scary. I mean, it's still scary, but it's also beautiful and perfect." I craned my neck to gaze up at him. "And now *this*? I mean, is this for real?"

"If you want it, Joss, yeah. It's real."

"You, me, and The Garden?" I kissed him. "Yeah, Luce. I want it. More than I've ever wanted anything."

Luce and I had a future together. I don't know what the future will look like, but I do know I can face anything with this incredible man—and his loud, vulgar, crazy, funny, loyal family—by my side.

He let out a shaky sigh of relief. "Holy shit." He laughed. "When you didn't say anything, I thought you were mad, or...or that you are going to run again."

"I'll never leave you again. I'm here, with you, forever."

He pulled away. "You, me, and The Garden?"

"You, me, and The Garden."

And just like that, The Garden was born.

EPILOGUE

Harlow

"M ISS GRACE, OVER HERE!"

"Miss Grace! How do you feel about being called America's new sex symbol?"

"Have you ever thought about baring it all for the camera, Miss Grace?"

"There are rumors you go topless in your new movie—can you confirm this, Miss Grace?"

"What do your parents think about your status as a sex symbol, Miss Grace?"

"What was it like filming with Dawson Kellor, Miss Grace?"

I ducked my head, as if the barrage of questions was a physical assault, and that's sure how it felt. I ignored the questions and pushed through the jostling crowd, shutters clicking and flashes blazing. My bodyguards held me between their bodies, their thick arms barring anyone from getting too close, but even the imposing statures of Trace and Van couldn't block out the questions. I was less than twenty feet from the door of the hotel to my limo, but it felt like a mile. You'd think that by the hundredth time you'd gone through this you'd get used to it, but you don't.

I talked to Dawson about it on set once. Having been famous for a lot longer than me, he had some wisdom on the topic.

"You don't ever get used to it," he said, his deep voice conveying his own distaste for it. "And if you do, it's time to quit Hollywood."

Dawson's wife, Grey, had smiled at me. "Harlow, honey, you'll be fine. The paparazzi is part of the job, that's all. He hates it, I hate it, and I don't think I've ever met another actor who didn't hate it. But if you love the work, you just...deal with it."

Dawson's loving smile as he gazed at his gorgeous wife had melted my heart. "Yeah, well, you're more pragmatic than I am, honey. That shit makes me cranky."

She'd just giggled. "Good thing I know how to cheer you up, huh?"

How could they still be so sweet, so in love? They

were Hollywood's darling couple, Dawson and Gray Kellor. They had three kids together, and were clearly just as in love as the day they met.

But their advice had been good—the paparazzi were part of the job, one we all had to deal with.

As good as the advice had been, it didn't make it any easier to deal with having invasive questions shouted in my face, having cameras snapping at me from every angle. And then would come the flood of wildly speculative articles in all the gossip rags and rumor blogs—

Which Hollywood hunk had I hooked up with? Had Dawson and I carried out a torrid affair during the filming of *December's Last Light*? Did Grey know? Was he leaving Grey for me? Were the nude photos leaked onto 4Chan really of me? Had I leaked them, or had I been hacked?

It was all bullshit, of course. Dawson was so in love with Grey it was stupid. Our kiss scene had been carefully choreographed, and Dawson had insisted on one take only, with Grey watching—and as soon as the take was done, he'd bolted away from me and gone to her. The sex scenes had been faked using body doubles and CGI—a topic Dawson had been vocal about during the press tour. And yes, there had been a body double for me, too. No, the photos on 4Chan weren't of me. After all the leaked photo scandals of recent years, there was no way in hell I'd ever take a nude selfie, even if I *did* have a boyfriend—which I didn't.

But still, the rumor mills loved to create drama.

And the rumor mills loved me, more than anyone else right now. There were so many rumors circulating about me it was impossible to keep them all straight, and it could be a full-time job keeping on top of them all. My publicity team killed the nasty ones, and the blatant lies right away. I categorically denied the rumors about Dawson and me in a series of carefully scripted interviews. The nude photos were obviously not of me, so those I ignored.

But no matter how much damage control I did, the press seemed determined to turn me into some sort of…well…sex symbol. Regardless of the fact that I'd never appeared topless in a movie, or shown any more skin than what you'd see in a bikini. I'd never done a full-on sex scene myself; I used body doubles exclusively …yet I was a sex symbol. There were posters of me, memes of me, photoshopped nudes… someone had even used an open-source CGI face-re-placement software to put my head on a porn star's body, and had then uploaded the video to all the most popular sites. It had gone viral within days, despite my team getting it taken down as quickly as possible—the internet is forever, and now that stupid "deep fake" video crops up every few months on a different site, under a different name, from a different source, but it's always my face on that woman's body, doing things I'd never done, or ever would do, and would certainly never do on film.

I wanted to be an actress, not a sex symbol. I was careful about the roles I took—I was careful to take roles that were serious, and that would further my career. I had no interest in being tits-and-ass fodder for a boobs and guns and explosions flick. I had an education in film from NYU, had earned my chops on stages and sets from the time I was sixteen years old. I'd acted on Broadway with some of the biggest names in theater, and had filmed my silver screen debut with Steven Soderbergh, to rave reviews. My second film had been my big mistake. The director had insisted on a bikini shot—me on the beach, nothing revealing or sexual. The scene had fit in with the rest of the plot, so I'd done it happily enough—because shit, what was the point of paying nutritionists and trainers to keep me looking this good if I never showed it off?

The roles I was offered after that had all been about the T-and-A.

I'd turned them all down, and instructed my agent to stop sending me anything that wasn't a serious role. Eventually, I'd gotten a decent script, a drama in which I played the love interest and foil to Dawson's character. It was serious, a heavy, intense role, and early buzz was that it was an Oscar contender. I'd gone all in for the role, and had, I felt, turned in my best performance to date.

Yet all the talk in the press was all about me in the sex scene—which, again, I hadn't actually filmed. The rumors were that it really was me, that I was playing coy, or something.

So here I was, leaving a hotel after an exhausting six-hour press junket, being assaulted by the paparazzi, bombarded with the same stupid mindless questions. Denying that I was sex symbol just made it worse, it seemed. How did that make me feel? I wanted to be an actress. I wanted to be taken seriously, and I had no interest in being perceived as a sex symbol.

I wanted to be seen for more than my body.

Yet that's all they saw.

Harlow Grace: five-nine, 32DD, 26-inch waist, and 35-inch hip line. Strawberry blonde hair that grew in perfect, natural spirals. Flawless skin and eyes so blue people often assume I wear contacts. Abs you could wash clothes on, an ass you could bounce a quarter off of, and legs a mile long.

To most people, that's me—a bunch of statistics...a sexy body.

Not the fact that I graduated high school at sixteen, made my professional stage debut at eighteen, received a degree in Fine Arts from NYU at nineteen, made my film debut at twenty, and had three major Hollywood acting credits to my name by twenty-one. No mention of my MENSA IQ, perfect SAT and ACT scores, or the fact that I was valedictorian in high school *and* at NYU.

Trace and Van pushed through the crowd of paparazzi to the limo and Van opened the door for me while Trace blocked anyone from reaching for me while I climbed in; I was wearing a short skirt, which made climbing in and out of a limo without letting the paps get an up-skirt photo difficult, something else Trace's broad physique was useful for.

Once I was in the limo and the door was closed, Trace rounded to climb in on the other side while Van took the front passenger seat next to Enrique, my driver. The interior of the limo was as I liked it— sixty-eight degrees, with a chilled Perrier on hand. Emily, my assistant, was already seated across from me, iPad out, stylus flying.

She launched into her spiel the moment I sat down. "All right, Low—you have a sixty-minute hot stone massage back at the hotel in thirty minutes. You'll have a little over an hour to take a shower and get dressed before the glam squad arrives to prep you for your Vanity Fair interview. Then dinner with Martin—I think he has a few new scripts to discuss with you. After dinner, you're scheduled to make an appearance at a party downtown, hosted by…Damon and Yolanda, I think it is—yes. You've already RSVP'd so you really should show up for at least a few minutes, especially since it's going to be attended by quite a few important producers."

I sighed, twisting off the top of my Perrier. "At what point do I get to stop and take a breath, Em?"

Emily blinked at me, trying to formulate a response. "Well…now that the press tour is over with, we might be able to schedule you a few days vacation time, but remember you've already agreed to guest star in those episodes of *Westworld* next week. Ummm…" She consulted her iPad, where she kept my master schedule. "You have the Dior perfume commercial after that, followed immediately by a *Vogue* shoot in Prague, and you're hosting SNL after that. If you don't take any new scripts, I can get you two weeks off in…August."

I stared at her. "Two weeks…in *August*? It's *April*, Em."

She shrugged one thin shoulder, her neat blonde bob swinging as she tilted her head in an attempt at sympathy. "We really need to ride the wave of publicity this film is generating, Low. We talked about this, and you agreed. I have Prada in talks with Martin for a whole series of shoots—they want you to be their spokeswoman. If the Dior commercial goes over well, they want you for some fashion shoots. There's a team at Netflix developing a period drama mini-series set during the French Revolution, and Martin is hearing talk of you as the star—no script offers yet, but it's still early."

I groaned, head thumping back against the leather headrest. "I'm tired, Em. I'm just...tired."

"It's another fifteen minutes with good traffic back to the hotel, and you have that massage. You'll be relaxed and refreshed in no time." She tried a bright but fake smile of encouragement.

Emily was a fantastic assistant—she was hard-charging, whip-smart, efficient, organized, had a sixth sense for what I needed and when I would need it...but she was cold as ice and brittle as porcelain, and absolutely terrible at anything like sympathy or empathy.

I took another sip of Perrier, wishing it were something stronger. "I don't mean I'm sleepy, or under the weather, I mean I'm fucking *tired*. Like, bone-tired. I haven't slowed down or taken a single day off since...ever! It's been nonstop, every day, all day for years, and I'm just *tired*."

Emily stared at me, her mouth working. "I...um. I can see if Dior is willing to reschedule—if they can, I could get you a week."

I shook my head. "I need more than a week or

two, Em. I need a real break."

She flipped the stylus around her index finger repeatedly; it was a nervous tic that showed up when I messed with her carefully choreographed scheduling of my time. "I'm...I don't know what to say, honestly, Low. If we canceled *everything,* you could take the summer off, but your visibility and relevance would suffer immensely."

"My visibility? Let's worry about my sanity!" I resisted the urge to scream at her for not understanding my stress level. "Between the latest round of rumors about Dawson and me, and the fake nude scandal, and the million, billion questions about whether or not I'm topless in this movie, I'm just done with everything, Em. I can't handle any more bullshit right now. Okay? I just can't. I'm at the point where yeah, I'm about to cancel everything and just vanish."

"You—you *can't* cancel *Westworld,* Harlow," Emily stammered. "You've signed the contract. You've gotten half the money. You *have* to do *Westworld,* at the very least."

God, I knew Emily was panicking if she called by my full first name—she only ever called me by my nickname, Low.

I groaned. "Fine! Okay. I'll do the stupid show."

"You love that show, Low."

I threw the Perrier bottle cap at her. "I KNOW I

love that show, goddammit! But I don't want to do it!"

Emily was silent, toying with the cap that had beaned her in the Botoxed forehead. "I'm sorry, Low. I'm just trying to—"

I cut in over her. "No, I'm sorry. It's not your fault. You're just doing your job, and you're amazing at it." I smiled at her. "Let's get through today, and we'll figure the rest out tomorrow, okay? What do I have tomorrow?"

Back on more familiar ground, Emily perked back up. "Tomorrow is light. Brunch with the publicity team, a blowout and manicure, that tour at the children's hospital…and that's it." She shrugged. "Oh, and you have a training session with Marcus at six."

"In the *morning*?"

"Um, yes? It's your first session with him, and he's *the* personal trainer everyone is talking about. You wanted to make a good impression on him, remember?"

I groaned again. "Next time I have a genius idea like that, smack me."

"Um, yes ma'am."

I laughed. "Don't actually smack me, though. You're a twig, I'd break you in half."

Emily smirked at me. "I have a brown belt in Aikido, actually."

My eyebrows shot up. "You do?"

She nodded. "My brother is an instructor at a dojo in San Bernardino. I take lessons once a week."

"Wow. I had no idea."

———— * ————

Even during the massage, I couldn't quite relax. I was too stressed, my mind flitting from one thing to another like a manic housefly. Interviews, photo shoots, commercials, hosting SNL, guest starring in *Westworld*—it was all evidence that I'd made it. I was an A-list celebrity, almost a household name, and the press tour for *December's Last Light* was pushing me into a whole new stratosphere. I was certain my agent, Martin, would be giddy with excitement at dinner, and would bombard me with his ideas as to which scripts I should look at.

I loved the work. I honestly did. Being on set, creating characters, working with my idols…it was a dream come true, it's what I'd been fantasizing about since the first time Dad took me to a movie theater. I'd watched Julia Roberts on the huge movie theater screen, and I'd just *known* that would be me someday…and my first role had been in a film with Julia, which had been surreal. Everything was golden.

So why was I so…

Unhappy?

It wasn't unhappiness, though. It was something else.

Loneliness?

I was surrounded by people: Emily, Trace—who was sitting beside me in the limo, burly arms crossed—Martin, Lindsey my publicist, the glam squad that went pretty much everywhere with me.

But they weren't friends.

I'd had plenty of offers for dates, of course, and from some pretty eye-wateringly famous and gorgeous men. But I was too busy, and I didn't trust anyone. Especially not anyone in the industry—I'd watched too many costars go through breakup after breakup, and I'd only been in the Hollywood a few years. You just never knew if the notion of a celebrity hunk wanting to date me was genuine, or if it was a publicity move. No thanks.

So yeah, I was lonely.

———— * ————

I was up the next morning by five and at the gym by six, and Marco ran me through a grueling, brutal workout. Back to the hotel to clean up, carefully coordinate my outfit, get made up by the team, brunch with Lindsey and her crew, during which she ran a million different ideas past me for how to leverage various pieces of press and which to squash and which to ignore.

The brunch was winding down, but I could tell Lindsey had something else on her mind. On the far side of forty and looking barely twenty-five, Lindsey was the type to talk a mile a minute and say whatever was on her mind, so for her to shift and squirm in her chair, glancing uncomfortably at me…

Whatever she was sitting on wasn't good.

Picking at the last of my salmon Caesar, I fixed her with a hard stare. "Out with it, Linz."

Brushing a lock of artfully dyed black hair away with a long, French-manicured fingernail, she smiled at me and sighed. "You can tell, huh?"

"You don't wear bad news well, babe," I said. "Just hit me with it."

"Remember that girl's night you had with Grey and Jen last month?" she asked.

I eyed her warily. "Yes?"

"There are…pictures."

I chewed on my lip, trying to remember. "Pictures of what? We had dinner, drank some wine, and sat in private booth in a nightclub."

"You also danced."

I sighed. "Yeah, well, it was a nightclub. And it was dark, and I danced with Grey."

Lindsey brought out her iPad, and flipped it

around to show me the photo. It was of me, wearing a little silver dress, hair in my face and sticking to my forehead. I looked drunk—because I had been. Grey was behind me but her head was turned so it wasn't immediately obvious it was her. In front of me was a guy—big, thick arms and a five o'clock shadow, a bit of a belly, too much product in his hair. The photo made it look like we were dancing together. In reality, he'd been dancing with his *boyfriend*, and hadn't even looked at me, but the angle, and the fact that I looked visibly intoxicated…

"Several blogs have it."

"It's just a stupid photo. I don't know him, I wasn't dancing with him, and he's fucking *gay*! I watched him make out with his boyfriend on the dance floor! Did they get shots of *that*?"

"No, and it wouldn't be any better if they had. The articles are all saying you and Grey had a three-some with him. You and this guy and Grey were also photographed getting on an elevator together."

I groaned. "Coincidence, Linz. Jesus."

"I know. It's just one more stupid story." She fixed a concerned look on her face, but I knew this was the kind of thing she lived for. "But combined with the fake nudes and the rumors about Dawson that won't go away, your image is taking a hit."

I groaned out a sigh. "Linz—I really don't care.

I just don't. Let them think I had a threesome. Grey and I know the truth, and so does Dawson—he picked us up from the club himself that night. I'm just past caring."

"You want the serious roles? You want to be taken seriously as an actress? You have to manage this stuff. You have to care."

"Yeah, well...I don't."

Lindsey sighed, tapping a nail on the counter. "You should do that charity gala next week. I'm sure Emily could fit it in while you do *Westworld*. They have plates available still, and it would be a great photo op."

Emily, beside me, was already working. "Yeah, absolutely. They have you shooting all day Monday and Tuesday and then on Thursday, and the gala is on Wednesday. It would totally work."

I sank low in my chair, biting hard on my lip. "No, no, no." I sat back up, hands flat on the tabletop. "Em, I told you yesterday I wanted to *cut back* commitments, not add to them!"

"But your image, Low," Lindsey said. "Managing your image has been a priority since day one."

"There's one day between tapings," Emily said. "We can get you a private flight from the Utah shooting location back to LA for the gala, keep the jet on standby, and fly back that night."

I shook my head. "Fine. Whatever. But nothing else."

———※———

It was the last day of filming. I was sweaty, exhausted, and ready to go home. Makeup dabbed the sweat off my forehead, cheeks, and upper lip, touched up my makeup while a stylist fixed my hair and tugged the bodice of my western-era gown—complete with hoops—back into place.

The director called for places, and I took my mark. On the snap of the clapperboard and the call of "action," I started my walk down the boardwalk, across the dusty street, and to the opposite board-walk. I was supposed to flaunt the walk, twirling a parasol, making the hoops of my skirt jostle and bounce. Don't cover up my cleavage with my arms, keep my chin up—glance provocatively at the other guest star...move my eyes away just so. My fingers had to be in just the right positions on the handle of the parasol. Don't trip as I stepped down from the boardwalk. Ignore the dust crunching in my molars and coating the inside my nostrils. Ignore the droplet of sweat trickling down my spine. Ignore the fact that I've done this walk eighteen times already, and it's never quite right—my hands aren't right; my arm covers my *décolletage*, ruining the allure of the shot; my hair gets blown out of place by an errant gust of wind; I turn my ankle when my heel catches on a stone the crew missed when they raked the street. It's always something.

This is meant to be my introduction, this scene, even though it's the last one I'm filming. Finally, after the twentieth take, I got the walk across the street perfect, and the director called cut, and a wrap for the day. Once I was out of costume and makeup, I sat for a moment in my trailer, just breathing. I had a car waiting to take me to the airfield where the private jet would take me back to LA. A masseuse was waiting at home, along with a bottle of cabernet.

None of it sounded appealing.

I'd done the gala yesterday, but it had been a disaster. My date—a former costar—got drunk, embarrassing me and himself, and there'd been pictures of us. Of me, awkwardly trying to help him stay on his feet as he fell into the limo. Of me, a forced smile in place as he leaned against me during a photo op. He'd whispered filthy insinuations the whole time, lewd suggestions of what he'd like to do to me if I went back to his hotel with him…

Lindsey had apologized for my date's behavior at the gala, but the damage had been done. What had been intended to massage my image had only done worse damage, adding fuel to the roaring inferno that was the Hollywood gossip machine—*Harlow Grace enabling former costar's downward spiral; Harlow checks Tom into rehab; Exclusive photos: Harlow and Tom's drug and alcohol-fueled sexcapades revealed!*

And then I'd twisted my ankle on the sixteenth take of that stupid walk—I'd said it was fine and had acted as if it didn't hurt, when in reality it was throbbing like a bitch, and I wanted to cry.

I reached down, massaging the ankle, wincing and whimpering as the touch sent jolts of pain through me.

And, at that moment, my phone rang. I answered it on the fourth ring. "Hello?"

I should have checked the ID—the last person I wanted to talk to right then was Lindsey. "Low, thank god you answered."

I held back a sigh of irritation. "What's going on, Linz?"

"How'd filming go?"

"I twisted my ankle and had to do the same dumbass scene twenty times before it was good enough. I'm tired, my ankle hurts, and I'm cranky. What do you want?"

Lindsey sighed. "You're going to hate me."

"Fucking *what*, Lindsey? Just say it!"

"A video surfaced."

I groaned. "A video of what? If it's another fake porn, just pay whatever you have to and make it go away."

"No, this one…is definitely you."

"There *aren't* any videos of me."

Lindsey's pause was revealing. "It's a cell phone video of you from a few years ago. From your NYU graduation party."

I sat up, my blood running cold. "That was a private party. I knew literally everyone there."

"Someone took a video of you wearing nothing but a mini skirt and a bra…um…doing a keg stand, and then doing a lewd dance with a young gentleman."

I let out a string of curses. "He was my *boyfriend*. Everyone else was gone. It was just my roommate, Carla, my boyfriend, Harrison, our best friends Frida and Rain, and me."

"Well, someone took a video and sold it."

"Who?"

Another heavy pause. "Carla."

"Can we bury it?"

"No. It's viral already. It's a pretty high-quality video, and the dance you do at the end is…well…"

"It was a lap dance for my fucking boyfriend."

"Low, I know. Okay? I know. I'm doing what I can to suppress it, but—"

"It's already viral." I swallowed tears. "I can't

believe Carla would do that. We were roommates for three years."

"Some people will do just about anything for a payout."

"If she'd asked me for money, I would have given it to her."

Lindsey sighed. "I'm sorry. I really am. I thought you should know."

"Thanks."

I hung up and sent Emily a text asking her to have the car ready. I put on a ball cap, donned my biggest pair of sunglasses, gathered my bags, and exited the trailer. Van and Trace were outside my trailer, waiting, and they took my bags from me. They were impassive as they escorted me away from the set and to my car. Emily was in the back seat of the SUV when I got in, and she handed me a Perrier as soon as I was buckled in.

"Did Lindsey get hold of you?" Emily asked.

"Yeah."

"My contacts at the airport are saying the paparazzi are already waiting."

Panic shot through me. "I can't—" I swallowed hard; Carla's betrayal was weighing heavily on me, sitting in my gut like acid. "I can't handle that right now."

"What do you want to do?" For once, Emily

seemed to realize I was in no shape to be argued with.

"Reroute."

"Where?"

"Anywhere!" I shouted. "I don't care. Anywhere. Not LA, and not New York."

Emily hurried forward to confer with the pilots, and was back within minutes. "Seattle?"

I nodded. "That's fine. Get me a hotel under a fake name, and get me in without being seen. Delivery door, cargo elevator, the works." I fixed her with my *do not fuck with me* glare. "Not one picture, not one question. I am on a hair trigger right now, Em. I *will* have a fucking meltdown."

A few hours later, I was in a hotel room in Seattle under the name Sandy Olsen. Emily answered the door when room service brought me dinner and a bottle of cab, and poured us both a glass.

"So." Emily took a sip, glancing me over the rim of her glass. "Now what do you want to do?"

I'd been thinking about that question all the way here, and I'd arrived at the answer. "No one is going to like my answer to that. Just fair warning."

Emily set her wine down and picked at the cheeseboard. "Seeing as you're supposed to be heading to Paris for the Dior commercial in two days and we haven't packed you yet, I'm guessing we won't."

"Get Martin and Lindsey on the phone," I told

her. "I'm not going to repeat myself when I say this."

When the conference call was going, I took the phone from Emily and paced with it. "Martin, Linz, you're not going to like this, but after Carla selling that video of me, I'm just done."

"Done how, babe?" Martin asked.

"We can spin this," Lindsey said. "You were young, it was a private party, he was your boyfriend at the time. It doesn't have to be a big deal."

"I've seen the video," I said. "It is a big deal. I'm all but topless in it. That bra—I still have it. It's basically sheer. I wore it for Harry—" I paused, anger and disappointment and sickness billowing through me. "Anyway. It's fuel for the whole sex symbol thing. Everyone is going to think I put it out there myself. It's already everywhere, and it's only going to get worse."

Lindsey sighed. "You're right there, unfortunately. The buzz is...not good. I mean, you're trending all over Twitter, but you're spot-on in terms of the speculation."

"We've already gotten at least fifty offers for you to do what amounts to soft-core porn," Martin added. "*Hustler*, *Playboy*, and *Maxim* all want exclusives. More serious offers all include significant sex scenes."

"See?" I suppressed a sob. "I'm not that actress. I'll quit before I do any of that."

"So what do you want to do?" Lindsey asked.

"I'm taking a break," I said. "Indefinitely. Once the hype dies down, we can see about some serious scripts, but for now, I'm out."

Martin groaned. "I can get you serious scripts, Low. You vanish now? You'll have to take bit parts again just to build your credibility back up. Demand is high for you, right now. And I know you hate the nature of the attention, but it's adding zeros to what you can ask for in a contract. I know you don't want to hear this, but if you did *one* scene, not even frontal, just a butt shot or something with a strategically placed towel—Jesus, Low, I could put you in the top tier of earners within months."

"Fuck you for even suggesting it, Marty. I said no the first, second, fiftieth, and hundredth time you suggested that and I'm saying it again now. I'm *not* doing it. I won't." My sigh was shaky. "I didn't even want to do the bikini scene."

"I'm just saying," Marty simpered. "It's my job to get you work, and to get you the most amount of money for that work. I'm just informing you what I could do for you, under the right circumstances."

"Enough," I snapped. "I'm leaving Hollywood for a while. The city, and the industry. End of story."

"How long?" they both asked in unison.

"I don't know. Until I can handle the idea of

going back."

"Where will you go?" Emily asked. "Finding privacy is going to be tough, especially now."

I collapsed backward onto the bed, sighing. "That's the part I don't know."

There was a silence, then.

Marty was the one to break it. "I, um, have a suggestion."

"If it involves me doing a nude scene, you're fired," I said.

"No, I meant about where you could go." I heard him tapping on a keyboard. "My second wife and I took a cruise for our third anniversary. One of those Alaskan cruises, you know? It was great. Beautiful scenery all around you, day hikes and things like that, whale watching, kayaking."

I snorted. "I'm not doing a fucking *cruise*, Martin."

"Well, not on a public cruise line, no."

I sat up, starting to understand what he was saying. "Go on."

"My buddy is a yacht salesman. I just sent him an email, should hear back by tomorrow. We get you a boat, and I don't mean, like, a little harbor jumper, I mean the real deal. Oceangoing, you can live on it indefinitely, that kind of thing. You head up the coast and get lost in all those little passages and inlets. It's deserted up there, Low, and I mean it's *remote*. But there are lots of little towns and fishing villages and stuff. Life is different up there, I'm telling you. Even if someone did recognize you—which they may not, way up there—they'll leave you alone. Maybe take a selfie to show their grandkids, but you don't have to even leave the boat if you don't want to."

"So I live on a boat?" I asked, not sure how I felt about that prospect.

"One of the stops on the cruise was a place called Ketchikan. Cute, quaint, remote—and accessible by boat or air only, and you have to take a ferry to the airport." I heard the glug of booze pouring into a glass, and he took a sip. "There's always yachts at the dock and cruise ships and stuff, since it's got deep water and it's on the main part of the Inside Passage, so one more boat shouldn't attract too much attention. If you keep your head down, literally, you should be able to hang out up there for a while and catch your breath."

I thought about it, and the more I thought, the more I liked it. "Martin, you just earned your commission, my friend."

"That one's on the house, baby. I'll email Emily some yacht options when Nicky gets back to me with some ideas."

"Thanks, Martin."

I heard him take a drink. "Low, baby, you're golden, okay? You get yourself some R-and-R, and when you come back, I'll get you a script you'll fall in love with, okay? That's a Martin Fitzpatrick promise."

"Sounds good. Bye, Martin." I heard him disconnect. "Linz?" I prompted.

"We'll ignore the video, and Emily can cancel all your slots—it'll hurt you, but we'll make it work, if you're absolutely sure you need this."

"Linz, Carla selling the video put me over the edge. The straw that broke the camel's back. I need a break. Okay?"

"Okay, honey. I hear you loud and clear. Consider it handled."

"Thanks."

I ended the call, and lay on the bed, trying to imagine several months alone on a boat, sailing along the Alaskan coast—no Wi-Fi, no blowouts, no manicures...but no paparazzi, no interviews, no rumors, no six in the morning personal trainer appointments, or nutritionists telling me to cut back on the carbs and eat more fucking celery. Just me, and the ocean, and whatever the hell I wanted to do.

And just like that, I could almost breathe again.

A few minutes later, Emily interrupted my daydreaming. "Okay, I have emails out to everyone, canceling all appearances, shoots, and interviews indefinitely."

"Have all my phone calls ping over to you," I told her. "If it's someone I really want to talk to, you can have me call them back. I'm going off the grid, Em."

"Can I come with you?" she asked. "It sounds nice, honestly."

I laughed. "Hell no. The point of a vacation is to not need an assistant. Duh." I smiled at her. "But don't get too excited. I'll still need you when I come back."

She let out a breath, and, for the first time since I'd hired her, closed her iPad and put it aside. "What will I do in the meantime?"

I shrugged. "I'll pay you for the rest of the year in advance, plus a little bonus for putting up with me." I waved a hand. "Go lay on a beach and drink rum and flirt with the pretty cabana boys."

"Now you're talking." She waggled her eyebrows. "There's a bartender in this little dive bar I know in the Turks and Caicos, and...oohhh honey. He...is...*fine*."

I laughed. "Go get 'em, tiger." I frowned. "*After* you work out the yacht and the crew and stocking it and getting me clothes and all that."

Emily blew a raspberry. "That's already half done. I have a caterer ready to stock the boat, a hiring agency vetting potential staff—you'll need a chef and a butler, at least, along with the boat crew—and, oh what else? Oh yes, I have Iris gathering your wardrobe and shipping it to us."

I lay back on the bed with another laugh. "And *that's* why you're getting a bonus, Em."

———✳———

Two weeks later, I was the owner of the newly re-christened *Lola*—a reference to my nickname, and my favorite childhood dog, a yellow lab named Lolly. The *Lola* was a thirty-meter cruising yacht with two full cabins and four smaller ones. It wasn't the new-est, or the fastest, or the most expensive, but it had seemed the homiest and most comfortable, to me. Unassuming but lovely from the outside, the interior had recently been totally refitted in a sleek, comfort-able, airy modern look, with every amenity you could imagine.

It came with an experienced captain and crew, each of who had been thoroughly vetted and had signed ironclad, draconian NDAs. I paid cash for it— my financial gurus had balked, but I'd told them in no uncertain terms that I'd earned the money and would use it as I saw fit; sell the New York condo, if they wanted extra moveable cash. Five million dollars later, she was mine, rechristened, fully stocked with months' worth of food—healthy food as well as comfort food, thank you very much—and a large selection from my wardrobe. My phone was off, my email and calls rerouted to Emily, who could contact the captain if I was truly needed—e.g., a medical emergency with my parents, for example—and we were motoring up the coast. I was sitting on the deck, reading a book, and drinking a glass of wine at…well, before noon, possibly. I wasn't sure of the time, and I didn't care.

We would reach Ketchikan in another few days, the captain had informed me. We could hold there, or keep going up the coast if I wanted, and circle back. Or go wherever. Now that I owned the *Lola*, I could go literally anywhere.

I don't know why I hadn't thought of this before.

———— * ————

Ketchikan was not what I expected. At once cute and charming and rustic, it was larger than I expected. I decided to put in for awhile, give the crew some time off and just be totally alone on the boat. After all, the chef had prepared several weeks' worth of meals, so all I had to do was heat them up.

Thus, I found myself on the *Lola*, tied up to a slip at the end of a long series of docks. There were several other ships near mine, smaller sailboats, a few larger fishing vessels, a couple pleasure crafts, and another cruising yacht like mine—my *Lola* didn't stand out at all, which was exactly how I liked it. I could sit on the deck, sip coffee in the mornings, watch the locals and tourists come and go, and enjoy the peace and quiet.

I'd been in Ketchikan about a week when trouble finally caught up to me.

I was on the front deck, nearest the shore and the docks, doing yoga. I had some nice peaceful piano music going, and I was halfway through the first series of poses when I heard footsteps on the docks. Running feet, a quick, light, powerful tread. My slip was on the very end, so the only place to go was to turn back around, which made me wonder why anyone would jog this way—there were plenty of other, more scenic places for a morning jog than the far end of the Ketchikan docks.

I shifted poses, which allowed me to get a look at the runner.

Name a Hollywood hunk, and I've met him. Nice guys, most of them. All gorgeous, obviously. Rich. Suave. Cultured.

None of them did a damn thing for me.

This guy? Heart palpitations.

I don't know why, either. It was just…something

about him. I mean, duh, he was damned beautiful—over six feet tall, lean and shredded, with perfect abs and nice arms. Tattoos on his forearms, and dark, almost black hair held out of his eyes by a running headband, earbuds hanging from his ears. Sweat all over his body, pouring off his face, running in rivulets down his chest. Even from twenty feet away, I could see his eyes were a shocking, intense shade of green… and they were locked on me.

Did he recognize me? I wasn't sure yet. I wasn't going to give myself away by bolting inside, but nerves hammered through me. The last thing I wanted was for my nice peaceful morning yoga session to be interrupted by an awkward, sweaty fan thinking he had a shot with me.

Keep running, I chanted to myself, continuing to the next pose. *Just keep running.*

But holy hot damn, the boy was beautiful. How old was he? A little younger than me, maybe? Twenty? And so pretty. I mean…I'd be lying if I said I didn't feel butterflies in my stomach—and lower—when he ran closer to my boat. God, those abs. That chest? Those arms. Ugh. Distracting, is what he was.

I started a complicated variation of the Warrior Three sequence as he approached—a bit of a show-off, but hey, he was looking, so why not be at least a little impressive, even if I didn't want him to know who I was, or stop to talk? Looking was free, right? And if he didn't take a picture or bother me, what was the harm?

Only, I was distracted by him.

My foot slipped on the mat, and then my ankle rolled out from underneath me mid transition, and…

I fell.

My head cracked against the deck, and I saw stars, dizziness keeping me flat on my back as pain blasted through my skull in waves.

I heard the runner curse, and caught a dizzy image of him making a running leap from dock to deck, a lithe, impressive move, I noticed, even in pain and dizzy.

He knelt beside me, breathing hard. "Are you all right, miss?" There was an odd formality to his manner of speech. "Are you injured?"

I groaned. "My head."

"Do not move, please." He tugged a cell phone from the pocket of his running shorts, pressing a button that silenced the tinny music from the earbuds now dangling from his neck, and then turned on the flashlight on his phone. "Look into the light, please, miss. Look to the side…the other direction, now, if you please…"

With just his fingertips, he lifted my head up off the deck, and then probed where I'd hit my head—at his touch, as gentle as it was, I moaned. "You are bleeding, and I believe you have a mild concussion."

"Are you a doctor?" I asked, my voice tight with pain.

"No. I have received concussions before, however, and I am familiar with their symptoms." He stood up, flexing his hands into fists and then shaking them out. "Can you stand up on your own?"

I tried, but dizziness washed over me, and I only made it to one knee before I nearly fell over. His hands were strong and warm on my bare arms as he caught me, and then he helped me to my feet, but let go of me immediately, wiping his palms on his shorts. Strange, but okay. Germaphobe, maybe? I'd certainly met plenty of those in LA, but it seemed odd in Alaska, unless he was a tourist.

I wasn't making sense, even to myself.

I tried to keep on my feet, and even managed a few steps, but a wave of pain washed through me, nearly knocking me to my feet. "Jesus. I hit my head harder than I thought."

"May I help you inside?" He wrapped an arm around my shoulders, carefully holding me upright.

Which was weird. Anyone else would have used the opportunity to put his arm around my waist, probably as low as possible. I was only wearing a pair of tight capri yoga pants and a sports bra, so there was plenty of skin, yet his arm went to my shoulders, holding me up but taking no liberties at all.

I pointed the way to the saloon—the living room—and he helped me to the couch.

"Thank you. I'll be fine, now," I said.

His smile was tight and uncomfortable. "You should ice that bump before the swelling becomes too bad." He glanced around. "I could get you ice, if you wanted."

I gestured. "The...god, it hurts... the galley is over there. Through the door."

I heard him go past, and then heard him rattling around in the kitchen. In a moment, he was back beside me, kneeling on the floor and touching a make-shift ice pack to my head. He smelled good—like sweat, but not body odor. His eyes were truly shocking in their green intensity and, up close, his features were even more beautiful than I'd first thought.

"My name is Xavier Badd," he said. "I apologize if I distracted you. I did not mean to stare, but you are very beautiful—that is...I mean—" He blinked rapidly. "I should not be so forward."

God, he was an unusual one, wasn't he? I didn't see any sign that he knew who I was—just that I was a beautiful woman, it seemed.

"I'm..." I hesitated. "My name is Low."

He frowned. "Low? As in, the antonym of high?"

I nodded, and then winced, regretting the movement. "Yeah. Exactly."

"Low." He smiled, another of those tight, uncomfortable, practiced smiles. "I am sorry we met under such circumstances."

I grinned. "Well, I'm not. If I'm going to fall and embarrass myself trying to show off, it may as well be in front of a hot guy, right?" I groaned. "God, I'm still embarrassing myself."

"Hot guy?" he asked, seeming confused. "Whom?"

I snorted. "Funny. Like a guy as sexy as you doesn't know what he looks like."

He blinked at me again. "Oh. You were referring to me?"

He was serious? "Um, yeah. Me, Low. You, hot guy. Xander, you said your name was?"

"Xavier."

"Xavier, sorry." I winced again. "I'm usually better with names."

"Difficulty with short-term memory is a common side effect of a concussion."

"And you're not a doctor?" I asked.

He shook his head. "No, I am not a medical professional."

"So…what *do* you do, Xavier?" God, I was flirting with him? The concussion must have knocked my better sense out of my head.

He shrugged. "I, um. I build robots and sell them on my website. I also work at a bar I own with my seven brothers."

"You build robots, work at a bar, and you have seven brothers?" I let my head rest against the back of the couch.

"Yes."

"And you look like...that?"

He frowned. "I—ah. Well...I do not see the relevance of my appearance to this conversation." He winced, closing his eyes hard, and then opening them again and fixing them on me. "Sorry. My social skills tend to suffer when I am nervous."

I smiled up at him as he stood up. "Why are you nervous, Xavier?"

He shrugged uncomfortably. "You make me nervous. Beautiful women make me nervous, and you are...very, very beautiful."

"Thank you, Xavier." I patted the couch. "Why don't you sit down? I'm not sure I should be alone just yet."

He sat on the edge of the couch. "With a concussion, I believe you are correct in not wishing to be alone just yet."

He stayed.

And I was intrigued.

Jasinda Wilder

Visit me at my website: **www.jasindawilder.com**
Email me: **jasindawilder@gmail.com**

If you enjoyed this book, you can help others enjoy
it as well by recommending it to friends and family,
or by mentioning it in reading and discussion groups
and online forums. You can also review it on the
site from which you purchased it. But, whether
you recommend it to anyone else or not, thank you
so much for taking the time to read my book! Your
support means the world to me!

My other titles:

The Preacher's Son:
Unbound
Unleashed
Unbroken

Biker Billionaire:
Wild Ride

The Ever Trilogy:
Forever & Always
After Forever
Saving Forever

The world of *Alpha*:
Alpha
Beta
Omega
Harris: Alpha One Security Book 1
Thresh: Alpha One Security Book 2
Duke: Alpha One Security Book 3
Puck: Alpha One Security Book 4

The world of Stripped:
Stripped
Trashed

The world of *Wounded*:
Wounded
Captured

**The Black Room
(With Jade London):**
Door One
Door Two
Door Three
Door Four
Door Five
Door Six
Door Seven
Door Eight
Deleted Door

Standalone titles:
Yours

Non-Fiction titles:
You Can Do It
You Can Do It: Strength
You Can Do It: Fasting

Jack Wilder Titles:
The Missionary

To be informed of new releases and special offers,
sign up for
Jasinda's email newsletter.

82235394R00242

Made in the USA
Lexington, KY
27 February 2018